The warrior guards a dangerous secret . . .

To the ladies of the *ton* he is the "Irish Wolf," an unobtainable object of their most hidden desires. But centuries ago, O'Banyon fell victim to an enchanting witch. Once ruthless in battle—and in the bedchamber—he is now cursed . . . and the wolf is set free.

The lady has a dark gift . . .

Antoinette Desbonnet knows there is much to fear from this dashing, magnificent stranger who stirs heated longings deep within her. And, in turn, O'Banyon's aroused senses warn him to beware this alluring young countess in shimmering white—for he knows he can never conquer her . . . yet cannot resist her. Something mysterious and powerful in her is calling to him. And he *must* have the bewitching beauty—even if it costs him his twice-damned soul.

By Lois Greiman

If You've Enjoyed This Book,
Be Sure to Read These Other
AVON ROMANTIC TREASURES

Coming Soon

Lois Greiman

Tempting the Wolf

An Avon Romantic Treasure

AVON BOOKS
An Imprint of HarperCollinsPublishers

AVON BOOKS
An Imprint of HarperCollins*Publishers*
10 East 53rd Street
New York, New York 10022-5299

Copyright © 2006 by Lois Greiman
ISBN-13: 978-0-06-078398-3
ISBN-10: 0-06-078398-2
www.avonromance.com

First Avon Books paperback printing: August 2006

Avon Trademark Reg. U.S. Pat. Off. and in Other Countries, Marca Registrada, Hecho en U.S.A.
HarperCollins® is a registered trademark of HarperCollins Publishers Inc.

Printed in the U.S.A.

10 9 8 7 6 5 4 3 2 1

To Karen Kay,
road warrior and friend.
I'll remember our book tours
with trepidation and laughter
for years to come.

Prologue

"**T**hey call you the Irish Hound," she said. Her face was illumined and shadowed, cast gold by the dancing flames and etched to stunning perfection.

O'Banyon shrugged as he watched her. She was the enemy, but the enemy was comely, and as darkly alluring as sweet sin. "Meant as an endearment, I am certain," he said.

"Are you?" She raised one fair brow. Her face was magic sung aloud, a light in a dark place. "Perhaps whilst you yet lie in their beds, my handsome hound, but after . . . when your eyes have roved to another?" She paced away from the fire, but the

1

light seemed to follow her, playing across her silken gown like music, glimmering like jewels in her loosened hair.

"I've taken naught but what they've willingly offered, me lady."

"Willingly." She tilted her head slightly, watching him. "Aye, I would imagine there have been more than a few maids willing indeed. But perhaps they thought you might remain in their arms for more than a scant hour's time. I am told, in fact, that there have been a few who hoped to bind you to their sides forever."

He spread his hands. "As ye have already said, me lady, I am called the hound. They knew thus when first they met me. I made no pretense to be a house dog, content to lie upon their laps forevermore."

She laughed. The sound was enchanting. There was a reason her men followed her like sheep to battle, a reason her holdings grew larger by the year. "Have you not heard that women love a challenge, Sir O'Banyon?"

"Aye, I have that," he said and did not attempt to stifle his grin, though it too had been called enchanting by more than a few. "And I have na desire to condemn any woman to unhappy tedium."

"Thus you supply the challenge."

"Just so, lass."

She nodded. "Very well, then, my good knight, if you are eager for a contest, I shall suggest one." She moved again. One could not quite call it walking, for she seemed to glide across the floor, her simple ivory gown caressing her barely hidden curves.

He held himself steady, waiting, though his body felt tight and hard with anticipation. Rarely had he been called a patient man, but he would not rush a woman, adversary or no, regardless of the rumors that washed about her like potent wine. "A contest, me lady?"

"Aye," she said and took the few short steps that separated them.

Her fingertips were soft against his face. His skin seemed to catch fire beneath them. His body galvanized instantly, but he managed to hold steady, to speak with a modicum of normalcy that belied his aching need. "Surely any match between meself and such renowned beauty as yours is a welcome one indeed," he said, but he wondered if perhaps the gossipmongers spoke truth this time. Perhaps she truly was a sorceress. And perhaps he should turn tail and run like the cur some thought him to be, but indeed, he too loved a challenge—and women. God's truth, he loved women.

3

The golden lady was silent, slipping her fingers down his throat and lower. It took all his dubious self-control to stop the tremble, to hold himself still, to await her pleasure.

She arched a slanted brow. "Might the rumors be true, I wonder?"

He forced another shrug, but even that simple movement was difficult, as though his body was turning by slow degrees to polished marble. "Are they rumors of me skills as a lover?" he asked.

"Aye, they are."

The smile came easier, though flame danced in concert with her fingertips against his chest. "Then I fear ye musts be the one to decide."

"You wish to lie with me?"

He laughed. The sound was low, rumbling quietly in her cavernous bed chamber. "I am quite certain ye ken the answer to that, me lady. In truth, 'tis said ye can read a man's thoughts."

"Indeed?" she asked. The corners of her mouth curled up, but her gaze lowered, skimming his body to settle beneath his belt, where his desire reared, hard and steady against his straining plaid. "Foolish rumor, of course," she murmured and reaching up, brushed her knuckles absently across his nipple.

He jerked against the impact and curled his

4

hands into fists, holding himself steady. She watched with a tilted smile.

"But in any case, the gift of sight is hardly necessary where you are concerned, my good knight." Her hand drifted lower, down his abdomen and across the throbbing head of his straining member. The force of her was a physical blow, and in that moment he would have fled if he could. But he was transfixed, planted firm and eager before her, breathing like a winded destrier, flushed like a lovesick lad.

"I would ask a favor of you," she murmured.

He felt himself nod, though he had no intention of doing so.

Her gaze held him steady. "You shall rid me of Hiltsglen," she said.

Her words barely made a ripple in O'Banyon's consciousness. For at that moment, she was everything, all consuming. "Rid?" he asked, his own voice barely audible in the melee of his desires.

She shrugged. "He has proven difficult."

O'Banyon frowned. Reality seemed hazy, a fragile vessel on a misty sea. "Ye wish for me to slay him?"

Her lips curled up the merest degree. Her hand moved knowingly against his plaid. "You are a mercenary, sir, and he is no friend of yours. Indeed,

5

I am told you have oft been opponents on the field of battle."

"But for now, we stand together." Forcing out the words was near more than he could manage. Indeed, the strain made his mind weary and his limbs as heavy as molten iron.

"You cannot best me," she said. "Not with all your dark master's might behind you. You know that in your heart."

He did—felt it suddenly in his soul.

She smiled and stepped back a pace. "Do as I ask," she said and reaching up, tugged loose the silken cord that held her gown in place. It floated to the floor, a gossamer dragonfly, leaving her naked at its departure.

Her gilded ivory skin gleamed, every curve as precious as gold, and he wanted nothing but to reach for her, to take her, to lose himself in her magical beauty.

"Me lady." It hurt to speak, ached to do aught but touch her, but he kept his hands welded at his sides. "Killian of Hiltsglen, while terrible irritating, be a friend of sorts."

She smiled and stepped closer. "With me as your friend, you will not need another."

He felt hot yet chilled, frozen and molten, but managed just barely to shake his head. "Me regrets," he began, "but I canna—"

"I am the golden lady," she said, and suddenly the world seemed bathed in white light, blinding him. "You are my hound of war. Kill him, or you shall surely wish you had."

Chapter 1

London, 1818

Women. Nairn O'Banyon loved them with every inch of his being.

He loved the look and feel and sound and taste of them. Loved the way they thought and laughed and glanced at him from the corners of their long-lashed eyes.

Two were watching him even now. He could feel them peruse him from behind. Could sense their interest and so much more. One was young. One was middle-aged. They were both lovely, regardless how they looked.

"Sir O'Banyon, isn't it?" called the older of the two.

He turned at the sound of his name and was not disappointed. The sweet, heady scent of them tickled his nostrils.

"Aye, me lady," he said and bowed. The tail of his brown cutaway coat brushed his boot tops, and the ivory buttons on his fawn-colored waistcoat gleamed. 'Twas a silly costume. 'Twould be no good a'tall in the heat of battle, yet the snug buff breeches accentuated the muscles of his thighs to full advantage, and did no small favor to some of his other attributes. And though the hilt of his ancient blade caused a slight rumple in the fabric at the small of his back, he was forever loath to set it aside, for in his experience, there was no friend so trusted as the dagger he called MacGill.

The women approached, pastel gowns rustling against the cobbled walk, frilled parasols tilted just so.

He filled his senses with them. Through the dark years behind him, ladies' costumes had changed, but the essence of a woman had not. 'Twas one of several things for which he would be eternally grateful.

"Mrs. Murray," he said, and reaching for the older woman's hand, kissed her knuckles. The titillation of skin against skin caused a prickle of sensation to quiver across the back of his neck.

Cecilia Murray gave him a flirting smile. "We missed you at Lord Bayberry's ball yesterday eve, sir."

Her gown was mint green, made of a kindly fabric that seemed to show every swell from toe to bosom, where it gathered lovingly to display a wealth of dove-white breast.

Feelings sharpened, scraping like fingernails down his spine. O'Banyon drew his hand cautiously away. "Then I must surely be absent more oft," he said, "if I be missed by such a bonny lass as yerself."

"Lass?" she said and laughed huskily but her cheeks flushed and her eyes shone. "You, sir, are a terrible tease."

"Na a'tall," he said and held her gaze, "I am but an Irishman. And we take lovely lassies verra serious, indeed."

Her hand fluttered to her bosom. His gaze followed it. His senses sharpened, his nostrils flared, and for a moment he feared he had gone a bit far, but in that instant the younger woman stepped forward, distracting him.

"Sir," she said, extending her hand, " 'tis such a pleasure to meet you. I am Rosanna Rutledge. Aunt Cece has mentioned you on more than one occasion."

There was little he could do but take her hand. Anything less would have been considered rude. And he was never rude . . . not where women were involved.

Her fingers felt soft against his palm. Her scent was sweet and heady. His body tightened another notch. "Then ye have me at a disadvantage, lass," he said and kissed her knuckles. Sensations crowded in, feelings as sharp as knives. Images of pale skin, succulent bosoms, long limbs tangled, hot and sweaty, about his.

The bed in his rented townhouse was surely large enough for three. But there were problems . . .

Releasing her hand, he stepped back a pace and put the thoughts behind him—where they tingled along his backside like a wanton caress.

"A disadvantage?" she asked.

"Aye. For I dunna ken if I should deny yer aunt's words aboot me or swear they be true."

The girl gave her head an inquisitive tilt. "She said you were the most alluring man in all of London."

"Did she now?"

She held his gaze with bold tenacity. "She did indeed."

"Aye well," he said and turned toward the aunt. "It seems the truth will out then, little matter how I try to hide it."

The widow laughed low in her throat.

O'Banyon tightened his defenses against the rousing effects.

"She also informed me that you were quite vain," said the girl. Her tone was cool, as if impatient at his lack of attention.

He turned slowly back toward her with feral slowness. Their gazes met. Her eyes widened the slightest degree, and her breath seemed to stop in her fragile, white throat.

"I can but apologize for me shortcomings, lass," he said.

"Have you many then?" she murmured.

"Counted with the stars," he assured her.

"Truly." She stepped forward. "Then we must surely spend some time together, sir, so that ye might confess—"

"Rosanna," said Mrs. Murray, her tone just a tad sharper than it had been only moments before. "I believe a breeze is picking up. Will you be a dear and fetch my shawl from the curricle?"

The girl hesitated just a moment, then pulled her gaze from O'Banyon's and crafted a careful smile. "But auntie, the carriage is halfway across town."

The women's gazes met steadily. "I know, my dearest, and I do so apologize, but if I catch a chill

I fear your visit may very well be cut short and you'll be forced to return prematurely to your mother in Worcester."

Temper darkened the girl's eyes, which were met by her aunt's knowing stare.

Then Rosanna nodded sharply and turned toward O'Banyon. "Another time, sir," she said.

He bowed and watched her go.

"My niece will be visiting her cousins this afternoon," said Mrs. Murray, pulling his attention back to her. "Perhaps you could come round for tea."

O'Banyon grinned, well flattered. "I fear I dunna drink tea, lass."

"In truth, sir, neither do I."

He gripped his hands behind his back. "Did I na hear ye are betrothed to another?"

She lifted her chin slightly. "Sir Banyon," she said, her voice low and steady, "I have been wed twice before. My first husband kept a mistress at Brighton. My second was more fond of hazard than he was of me. I have no intention of being—"

"Then both yer husbands were fools," O'Banyon said and bowing, caught her eye again. "But as I can see ye are na, I will tell ye straight and true— I've na the restraint to be at me gentlemanly best if we be closeted together alone, lass. Nor have I a wish to damage yer reputation and ruin your future with a wealthy lord, thus . . . I fear I must say adieu."

She opened her mouth as if to argue, but he knew better than to delay, for he had already waited too long. There was a tingling in his thighs and a sharp honing of his senses, as if the world held a thousand secrets he could not quite yet fathom. Giving her a quick nod, he turned on his heel and strode away.

He would walk it off, he told himself. Let his mind wander until all was well.

Evening was settling across London, but the darkness could no longer dim the wealthy burgs of the city, for they were lit by stately iron lamps that held neither tallow nor wick. Their workings were a mystery to him, but what was not these days?

Striding down a cobbled boulevard, O'Banyon passed a young couple just exiting a silversmith's shop. Their arms were entwined, their faces wreathed in smiles, but the woman turned her sultry gaze to his momentarily and that alone was nearly his undoing. He strode resolutely on.

His rented townhouse was nestled snugly in Hans Town, a shabby but comfortable annex. It was not a particularly safe section of town, but that hardly mattered. It afforded him some privacy and suited his modest budget.

But a short distance from the elegance of shops and coffeehouses of London, the city began to deteriorate toward the slums. An old man slumped against a wattle and daub inn, a bottle in hand. Across the street, a portly woman stood on her broken steps and smoked a pipe rough-crafted from a stag's ivory antlers.

The smell of aged leaf and red deer melded harmoniously in O'Banyon's twitching nostrils. Some things had not changed with time.

Removing the pipe from her lips, the matron cast a narrow glance up and down the Irishman's still tingling form.

"Come hither," she called, "and I'll 'elp ya with that problem of yours."

"Me thanks," he answered. Cutaway coats and skin-tight breeches may well flatter the wearer, but, as he had learned to his pride and chagrin, they left little to a bawdy imagination. There was naught like five yards of sodden wool and an ancient horsehide sporran to hide a man's appreciation of the fairer sex. "But I've na troubles, lass."

She laughed, her brown face wrinkling like a winter apple. "And I'm a sweet-faced virgin. Come over, lad. I've got girls. Young girls."

O'Banyon smiled, but it was becoming more

taxing. His skin felt hot beneath the snug confines of his fashionable costume. "I would like to accommodate ye," he said, "but I fear I canna."

She eyed him up with worldly knowledge. "I believe you're wrong there, love," she yelled. "But another time, then. 'Ell, I wouldn't mind 'avin' a go at ya meself."

He sighed and moved quickly on. The night slipped around him, allowing him to relax marginally, forcing himself to put the scents and sounds of women behind him, allowing him to breathe.

What he needed was a hobby. Some little thing to occupy his mind, to tire his body. A battle mayhap. But nay, battle seemed to be frowned upon amidst these posh Londoners, unless one took their silly pistol duels into account. Which he did not.

He could try his hand at badminton, he thought, and forced his mind down other paths just as idiotic. Cricket mayhap. Or lawn bowling, which was favored by the fashionable crowd referred to as the *ton.* But bowling on the green had never held his interest, not even when it had been banned to commoners.

Making love, on the other hand . . .

Desire grated at him. But he forced his mind away once again, for he dare not chance the changes passion wrought in him. Dared not loose his other self. If he could not burn away his frustrates in the arms of a willing lass, he would prefer to spend his time with a claymore in his hands and a shield slung across his back, but battle in jolly ol' England was now fought with weapons that spewed flame whilst standing a good furlong from one's opponent.

'Twas terrible impersonal. Not the same a'tall. And even if he should succeed in getting himself a commission to fight for the regent's royal army, the lust of battle might well prove to be more than his human skin could—

A whimper of noise snared his attention. O'Banyon jerked his head to the right. The dank taste of fear snaked out from a dusky alley that yawned off to the side.

"What's your rush, girly?" crooned a quiet voice. " 'Aven't ya learned no respect at all for your elders?"

Another whimper was heard amidst a rustling of feet.

"There now. 'Old still so's we can gets a good look at ya. Ahh, yer rather a pretty thing, don't ya think Joles?"

Senses as old as time prickled along O'Banyon's spine. He could feel a young girl's terror, could taste the bite of her captor's menace on the tip of his tongue.

"A bit skinny for my taste," said Joles. "But ya knows what they says about beggars."

The two men chuckled in unison.

O'Banyon curled his fingers against his thighs and shifted quiet as midnight toward the maw of the alley.

"Come along with your ol' uncles now, girly. We got a little surprise for yah, don't we, Joles?"

"Indeed we—" began Joles, but suddenly there was a yowl of pain. Someone gasped, and then there were footsteps thundering madly in the deepening darkness.

"It's a chase she wants," rasped a voice, and in less than a heartbeat a ragged girl burst onto the street.

Eyes wide as twin moons, she turned her cobalt gaze on O'Banyon and froze, mouth round in speechless terror.

God's teeth! Had he changed already, he wondered, but his musing was interrupted by a noise from behind. He spun about, legs splayed, a snarl ready on his lips.

But 'twas naught more terrifying than a woman behind him. Dressed all in white, she shone with an unnatural brightness.

Their gazes met and fused. O'Banyon stood transfixed, for she was an element out of place, a blinding shaft of light in the darkness.

But in an instant, she pulled her gaze away. "Sibylla," she said, her voice calm in the maelstrom. "Come."

The child broke from her trance and dashed toward the lady just as the two men burst from the mouth of the alley.

O'Banyon turned toward them. They skidded to a halt, breathing hard, searching the area. They were a skinny pair, stretched hard and mean by life in London's dark underbelly.

"Well," said Joles, still panting, "it seems as if we 'ave us a dandy amongst us. Ho then, fancy pants . . ." They parted, Joles tall and bent, his companion as straight as a crusader's lance. They eased out on either side of him. O'Banyon remained perfectly still, senses flaring. "Kinda far from your purdy home ain't ya, m' lord?"

The Irishman said nothing. If he had learned aught in the past mind-spinning months, he had learned to avoid causing a spectacle.

"Want to challenge us for the pair of 'em?" asked the shorter of the two.

O'Banyon tilted his head. "I've na wish for trouble, lads," he said. For the most part it was a true enough statement.

But the two laughed in unison, a rasping sound that grated against O'Banyon's vibrating senses. "Ye hear that, Joles? 'E don't want no trouble."

"Then 'e should have stayed put in his parlor, drinkin' 'is fancy teas and—"

"I dunna drink tea," O'Banyon said. His voice sounded ever so reasonable to his own ears, yet did naught to soothe the brigands.

Indeed, he knew the moment Joles drew the knife, knew the instant the villain sprang forward, though the shadows were as deep as the lochans of his homeland.

As for O'Banyon, he left MacGill hidden beneath his coat, but struck just as quickly, and suddenly the knife took flight, springing through the air and clattering with staccato clarity against a mortared wall. The would-be attacker fell backward, nursing his hand and staring.

O'Banyon growled and took a step forward. The brigands stood for a moment in indecision, then turned as one and galloped back into the alley from which they'd come.

O'Banyon let them go, exhaled carefully and glanced down, assessing himself, but nothing seemed amiss. Though his fingers were spread like reaching talons, all was well. He curled them carefully into his palms and took a steadying breath. The lassies were safe and no one was injured. He rolled his shoulders and turned about.

"Me apologies," he began.

But the street was empty.

He glanced right and left, but he knew there was none hidden in the shadows. He was suddenly and inexplicably alone. So the white lady had not been foolish enough nor stunned enough to remain in harm's way, but had fled at the first possible opportunity.

Still, he would not have thought her so fleet.

Striding forward, O'Banyon eased into a trot and peered down the next alley. But that too was empty.

It was then that he heard a shuffle behind him, then that he realized the girl's tormentors had returned with friends.

Smiling, he turned slowly, savoring the moment. Five men stood spread in an arc across the muddy street. Five, and each one armed.

He should back away, he knew. Should retreat into the shadows, avoid spectacle, keep well out of sight. But he did so need a hobby.

Chapter 2

❧◦◦◦◦∞◦◦◦◦❧

Dancers whirred and dipped, a swirling kaleidoscope of colors, dark coats pressed intimately to pastel gowns, swallow-quick fans plied before flushed faces and gleaming eyes.

O'Banyon smiled. Women were everywhere—elderly matrons watching their wards like sharp-eyed peregrines. Tender maids, soft-lipped and eager. Young mothers. Content wives. He loved them all.

But he felt another's approach. Someone neither tender nor young.

"O'Banyon," rumbled Hiltsglen.

The Irishman half smiled. In many ways he

liked this new world. Though London was far gone from the windswept hills of his homeland, there was much to appreciate in this raucous city. Women, for instance. Yet there were elements from his past that he missed from time to time.

Sir Killian of Hiltsglen, called the Black Celt by those who knew him well, was surely not one of them.

"Hiltsglen," he said, not glancing sideways as he took a sip of punch. It had neither the bitter earthiness of ale, nor the full richness of spirits, but the fantastically delicate glass that contained it was a marvel to behold.

The Celts stood side by side, eying the blurring colors as they twirled about the ballroom.

"Choosing yer next victim?" Hiltsglen's voice was rarely more than a rumble and oft resembled a feral growl when he spoke to O'Banyon. Their *friendship* had been long and fractious, and one oft punctuated with oozing wounds and bright contusions.

But the Irish Hound still lived. Or perhaps he lived, again. Though the Golden Lady of Inglewaer had wielded terrible power, she had not destroyed him. Oh aye, she had cast a dreadful curse. But neither she nor his own vengeful liege had quite managed to best him. And although some might have found death preferable,

O'Banyon was not amongst them. Nay, he would take life at any price.

"Na need," said the Irishman, and didn't bother to turn from his perusal of the elegant crowd. "As it happens, I've spoke to yer wee bride just hours hence."

"To me Fleur?" O'Banyon could feel the Scotsman turn toward him and had to contain his raucous amusement. It was too simple to raise the old man's ire. Hiltsglen had no subterfuge, no appreciation for a lie well told, and damnably little sense of humor. On the other hand, those who met his fist tended to stay where he put them for long periods of time. Which may be a good detail for a man to remember, if that man weren't spoiling for some sport.

"Have ye another bride?" O'Banyon asked, still skimming the crowd.

The Scotsman was as tense as a battle ax, a condition which was generally followed by men fleeing like doused rats in every possible direction. Also something to keep in mind. "What did ye speak to her aboot?"

O'Banyon nodded to a dark-haired maid who gave him the eye as she was wheeled away by her partner. "Who?" he asked.

Hiltsglen was gritting his teeth now. O'Banyon

could tell without turning toward him. The Scotsman was not a handsome man even when jovial. Anger made him look like a gargoyle with a toothache, but he had been feared from Amman to Luxemborg. A little something to recall.

"What did ye speak to me wife aboot?" he asked again, his voice growing deeper by the moment.

"Ahh," O'Banyon said as if just remembering, though it was damnably difficult to keep his grin at bay. "We were speaking aboot tonight. She said she would dearly love to meet me in—"

"Good sirs." Hiltsglen's wife appeared suddenly beside her oversized husband. O'Banyon should have seen her coming, of course, but the Scotsman oft tended to block the approach of anything smaller than a war horse, which she was.

"Me lady," he said and gave her an easy bow. She looked to be a wee bonny piece of fluff, but circumstances had proven otherwise. In fact, she had once threatened him with dismemberment. He contained his chuckle at the memory.

"I do hope I'm not interrupting anything," she said.

"Certainly not. Indeed—" O'Banyon began, but Hiltsglen broke in.

"Irish here was just aboot to tell me where ye agreed to meet him this eventide."

The lady's eyes widened slightly, then lifted to her husband's. Their gazes met and melded, before she visibly relaxed.

"Ahh," she said and reaching up, rested a small hand on the Scotsman's bulging arm, "and yet the hound still breathes. 'Tis good of you, my love."

"I had na wish to disappoint ye," rumbled Hiltsglen. He was as big as a damned castle, and yet he seemed to blush like a dairy maid as he turned his adoring attention upon his bride. " 'Tis the only reason the cappernoited nidget be still upright."

O'Banyon could contain his laughter no longer. 'Twas a habit that had gained him more than a few scars. "Ye speak as though ye've been spewed from the days of yore, Scotsman."

Hiltsglen turned his darkling gaze toward O'Banyon. "Why the devil be ye here, Irish?"

O'Banyon shrugged. "Well, 'tis a long and winding tale, but if ye've an hour and a good ale close to hand I shall enlighten ye with a story of witches and warlocks and evil curses cast upon innocent—"

Hiltsglen snorted as though the word "innocent" had tickled his dubious sense of humor. "Why are ye here at the Regent's grand ball, ye daft callifudger?"

"Ahh, Lady Evengard had the good graces to

invite me," Banyon said and lifted his glass in a sort of salute to a stodgy dowager who gossiped to a group of her aging peers. Her gown was powder blue, not so vastly different than her hair, which was piled a good ten inches atop her head and sported a miniature ship in full sail—a style reminiscent of bygone days, if tales be true. "She said I have old-world charm and boyish dimples. I believe she may have her eye on me for her goddaughter."

"What you have is a pirate's black heart and a hunting wolf's morals. She would be wise to deny ye access to so much as her dancing slippers."

O'Banyon laughed again. Sparring with Hiltsglen was always lively sport. If they couldn't clash with broadswords and brawn, conversation would have to do. "As it happens I have na interest in her dancing slippers."

Killian was watching him. "What happened to yer bonny face, lad?"

"Me face?" he said, then remembered the particularly close contact he'd had with Joles's weapon. The stringy miscreant had plied a hammer like a Saracen might swing a scimitar. "Oh, aye, 'twas naught but a rousing game of cricket."

"Cricket, ye say?"

"Aye. Played in the back alleys of this fair city."

Something glowed in Killian's eyes, something

27

hard and dangerous and not quite tamed. So the bright baroness had not completely gentled the Celtic beast. 'Twas a good thing to know.

"I wasn't aware you played cricket," Fleurette said.

"Oh, aye," O'Banyon assured her. "A man must have his interests."

Killian was still watching him. To look at the old Celt's face, one could easily underestimate his wit. More than a few had regretted that mistake. "And what of the other players, Irish?" he asked. "How did they fare?"

"Good eventide," he said to a tall matron who twirled past, then, "They may refrain from sport for a short while."

"Until their bones knit?"

O'Banyon shrugged. "If they be weaklings."

"I'm going to pretend we are truly talking about cricket," said the baroness, and turned with aplomb to a richly attired trio that approached from their left.

"Lord and Lady Batterling," she greeted.

Introductions were made all around.

"And this is our lovely daughter," said the matron. A young woman stepped forward. She had a pleasant face, regal bearing, and a good stone of pearls about her neck. "Eleanore. 'Tis her first season."

"Eleanore," Fleurette greeted but the girl didn't seem to hear.

"Sir Banyon is it?" she asked, eyes wide as a doe's in her plump face.

"Aye." O'Banyon bowed and took her hand. "And never has me name sounded so fair as when spoken from yer lovely—"

But suddenly he noticed a flash of white. He raised his head and caught his breath, for it felt suddenly as if he had been grasped by the throat. Across the ballroom, he glimpsed a flowing, ethereal vision in white—the lady from the dark alley. He knew it somehow. Simply knew. She had appeared and then she'd been gone, like a vision, like an angel. Yet here she was again.

"O'Banyon?" Fleurette said.

Hiltsglen rapped him solidly between the shoulder blades, bearing him smartly back to the present. "Irish, what the devil be wrong with ye?"

O'Banyon realized suddenly they were alone, that the elegant Batterlings were gone, which was odd, because he'd been holding the girl's hand just moments before. Holding her hand and flirting, but he found that he failed to care. "Who is that?" he asked, peering through the crowd.

"Who?"

"The an . . ." He caught himself. "The maid in white."

The baroness craned her neck. Hiltsglen scowled across the heads of the crowd.

"I see no one in white."

"Might you mean the countess of Colline?" Fleurette asked.

"I dunna ken," O'Banyon said and not waiting for more information, strode into the crowd.

A flash of white caught his eye again. He moved toward it, drawn in. The lass turned and with her movement, the world seemed to take on a slow richness, a magical cadence. Her face was a pale and perfect cameo against a backdrop of color, her emerald eyes a feline slant as their gazes met.

"Sir O'Banyon. Sir."

He was tugged from the trance. Two women stood at his elbow. But they seemed strangely vague and nondescript, barely visible in the face of such white-hot intensity.

The world settled unevenly around him.

"Are you well, sir?" asked the nearest of the two.

"Aye." He drew a careful breath, trying to catch his balance, to focus.

"Are you certain? You don't look quite yourself."

"Oh?" He managed a smile. "What then, do I resemble?" And what the devil was this girl's name?

"I fear our last conversation was cut rather short by my aunt's untimely chill."

Rosanna Rutledge. The name came to him on a burst of relief. He never forgot a woman, not her scent, nor her voice, nor the feel of her skin against his. Bowing, he reached for her hand. Only the slightest shiver coursed through him, allowing him to maintain contact, to enjoy the feel of her skin against his. "And how fares Mrs. Murray, lassie?"

Her lips had parted, but for a moment no sound came forth. He realized dimly that he was caressing her knuckles.

"Rosie," said her friend. "Rosie, I'd like an introduction, if you please."

"Oh. Oh, yes, of course," said Rosanna. "Good sir, this is Miss Sophie Pilter."

He loosed her hand, but found for an instant that it remained clinging to his.

" 'Tis so good to meet you, sir," said Sophie. Rosanna moved aside, possibly due to the jab of the other's elbow in her ribs.

"Sophie," he said. "A name as comely as yer smile."

She giggled. He felt the tingle of it in his gut.

"Girls." Mrs. Murray approached from behind. "I do hope you're not being wearisome."

"Wearisome?" He straightened and tried for

just an instant to find the lady in white. But she was gone. "Nay indeed. Cold be the day that a rough-haired Irishman be not warmed by a maid's fair beauty."

Murray watched him for a prolonged moment, then, "Rosanna dear, I fear I feel a draft. Would you be a love—"

"I brought your shawl with me, auntie," Rosanna said and dragging it from some unseen source, draped it unceremoniously across the matron's back.

"Oh, well, aren't you a dear?" said the other, but her eyes suggested otherwise.

O'Banyon smiled. There was little as exhilarating as a bit of feminine battle centering around him. Indeed, now that he thought on it, he couldn't think of a single situation that could compare—

A flash of white accompanied a strange spur of sensation in his gut. And for just a moment, for one brief heartbeat, he saw the gleaming apparition again.

He never remembered stepping into the crowd. Never noticed the angry stares of the three women who watched him go, for the light of the white lady blinded him to all else.

Her back was to him, and yet it was as if he could see her face, had already memorized every glowing feature in his mind. He moved toward her as though she were a beacon. She spoke to a tall woman who watched him approach, and yet it seemed almost that he could imagine the white lady's countenance better than he could envision the one facing him. He concentrated, moved closer until he could all but touch her.

"Lady Anglehill, is it na?" he asked.

The stately woman smiled, and the lady in white turned toward him, her lips lifted in a slight bow, her eyes an unblinking, earth-shattering green.

"Sir O'Banyon," greeted the countess of Anglehill.

He focused hard, drawing himself from the vision in white. "Me sincerest apologies regarding yer friend," he said.

She scowled. "And what friend might that be, sir?"

"Hiltsglen's fair bride," he said. "I tried me best to distract your Fleurette from the barbaric Scot afore 'twas too late and she succumbed to his plea of marriage, but alas . . ." He shrugged.

Lady Anglehill laughed. "Well, if you couldn't manage it, I'm certain no one could." She pulled her gaze from his, resting it momentarily on her delicate companion. "I'd like to introduce you to the Right Honorable Countess of Colline. Antoinette, my dear, this is Sir O'Banyon. Some call him the Irish Hound, I believe," she added, but he barely heard her for the lady's name was singing in his veins.

Antoinette. He turned slowly toward her, lest the shock be too much for his strangely fragile heart.

Her skin was ivory smooth, her chin was peaked, and her cheekbones high, but it was her eyes that transfixed him. Tilted like an inquisitive cat's, they were a green so lively, it all but stole his breath.

"Me lady," he said and prepared to reach for her hand, only to realize that hers were gloved and well occupied. One with a punch glass. One with a fan. "I believe we have already met."

He waited for her to agree or disagree or speak in any manner. She did not, but watched him in silence.

"Last eventide," he prompted. "When yer serving girl was set upon by Aldgate brigands."

The world dredged by in slow motion. She blinked once, her heavy lashes a lush fan over her mesmerizing eyes.

"Surely ye dunna disremember," he said.

"I fear you are thinking of another," she said finally.

Her voice, when he first felt it against his quivering senses, titillated him. It was rich and earthy, not at all as he had expected, and drifted through

34

his blood like dark wine, scrambling his thoughts, tilting him off balance.

Pulling her gaze from his, she gave her companion a smooth nod. "If you'll excuse me, Lady Anglehill."

She was leaving. "Do you say yer lass was not troubled by miscreants just this night past?" he asked.

She stared at him, a sleek tigress with secrets that will not be spilled. "I do not have a *lass*, good sir. And if I did I very much doubt she would be *set upon by Aldgate brigands,* as you say. But I fear I must be off as I promised a dance to Mr. Finnegan."

O'Banyon watched her walk away from him. Indeed, it may well have been the first time since boyhood that a woman had done so.

It was Lady Anglehill's laughter that drew him out of his misty quagmire.

"Surprised, Sir O'Banyon?" she asked.

A thousand questions roared through his mind. "Why—" was the best he could come up with.

"I don't believe she likes you," said the countess.

"But how—"

"I don't know actually. I find you rather charming, and I detest everyone."

"Where—"

"Gone, I believe," she said and rising onto her

35

toes, strained to gaze above the heads of the swirling mob.

"I—" he began.

"Should go," she finished.

And he did so, hurrying through the crowd like a smitten pup. But she was gone, vanished. He turned a tight circle, scowling.

"Out the south doors, lad," rasped a voice.

O'Banyon glanced down. An old man squinted up at him, gnarled hands brown as acorns atop a twisted staff.

Misty memories flitted like fireflies through his mind—the heady fragrance of roses, the gaffer's distant voice, the dark drape of days beyond count. "Who—"

"Never mind that, now, or you'll be losin' her. South doors, white carriage."

O'Banyon stared.

"Off ye go, boy," he ordered and O'Banyon went.

Chapter 3

She was being ridiculous, of course. He was only a man. An attractive man, yes. A man with a powerful allure. But a man nevertheless and surely not one from whom to flee like a harried fishwife. But she had done just that. Had left the Regent's ball with all due haste. And why?

She had known many men. Had been desired by more than a few. Had outsmarted all and lived to tell about it. Well, no, not to tell about it. The Countess of Colline, Antoinette Desbonnet, Petite Fayette, was not so foolish, no matter which name she went by. Not any longer, for she could not afford the price.

37

The night was dark and still outside the beveled windows of her carriage. Mists roiled silently up from the lowlands, casting eerie swathes of ragged silver about her conveyance. She rode in a two-wheeled Eddings brougham, not as elegant as the phaeton she'd left at home, but costly and luxurious nevertheless, for she was wealthy. She was titled. She was beautiful. Indeed, maybe she was even liked in a manner of speaking. The way one likes thorned roses and feral cats—from a distance. Always from a distance. Always outside the circle. Outside the light. Secrets well hidden.

Cold memories crowded in. Shivering, her grubby fingers digging hard into dank, rotting wood. She remained hidden, not moving, not making the slightest sound. Barely breathing. They were coming, and they hated her with a passion she could not comprehend.

The carriage lurched violently beneath her. She stifled a scream, but no one leapt forth to drag her from her hidey hole. Beneath her, the brougham slowed to a shuddering halt, and with that motion, her wits returned.

She was neither small, nor hungry, nor alone. She was the white countess, serene and wealthy and aloof.

By the time her driver reached her door, she was composed.

"My lady." Whitford jerked an ungainly bow. "My apologies. I fear there has been a mishap."

She watched him in silence. The shifting light of the lanterns were not kind to him. His mouth was misshapen, pulled tight at the left corner, making his expression look like an evil leer. But she knew evil. Had long since made its acquaintance and found that it did not wear such an obvious façade.

"What has happened?" she asked.

"A log—" His face was pale, his head lopsided. He jerked spasmodically as though struck.

She waited. The spasm would pass.

"There was a log across the road, my lady," he said. "I did not see it. We were going too fast. I fear . . ." Tears. Dammit all. There were tears in his perfect, amber eyes. Antoinette tightened her fists against the seat and raised her chin to lofty uncaring.

"Can you shift the barrier?" she asked.

He nodded. A tear dripped down the battlefield of his face. He swiped it away with the back of his hand. She clenched her teeth, waiting for his next words.

"But Ebony . . ." He paused, broken.

"The gelding," she said. She did not name her beasts. But sometimes others did. Others who could afford that luxury.

"Yes. I am sorry, my lady." Another tear. He straightened his misshapen back and let the tear roll down his face. "The gelding, I fear he may have broken his left fore."

Her stomach cramped. Had she been in a crowd, she may have made a sound of impatient disapproval, but the effect would be wasted on Whitford. He knew things others did not. Sensed things best left undisturbed. 'Twas one of several reasons she had hired him, and the only reason she sometimes wished she had not.

He stepped back as she exited the carriage. It was as black as sin outside, the moonlight shuttered beneath ragged clouds. But she had no quarrel with the darkness. 'Twas her fellow man that worried her. She scanned the woods. They were naught but a vague abyss beyond the range of her senses, a black void where things unseen played at will. A tingle of apprehension crept up her spine.

"My lady," Whitford said, " 'tis no place for you to tarry."

"Nay," she agreed, and turned, feeling the eerie sensations skitter up the length of her back.

Her footfalls sounded unnaturally loud against the muddy road. The gelding stood absolutely still, head high, muscles rigid against the pain.

But it was his fear that arrested her. She could feel it clouding the animal's mind. He was broken, unable to run, and the woods were so near. Predators prowled there, waiting to pull him down. She felt his primitive thoughts as her own. He was an animal of flight, born for the open hillocks, and yet he did not turn his attention toward the dark forest that loomed beside him. Instead, he watched her, unblinking and trusting.

"Release him from the traces," she ordered and pulled off a glove. The horse's neck felt hot beneath her palm, but the pain was hotter, burning, stabbing.

"My lady." Whitford's voice was as broken as the steed when he shambled up behind her. "Perhaps if we press him he could yet get us to—"

"Release him," she said and turning away, quickly pulled the soft leather back over her fingers. The gelding hobbled toward her, pulling the brougham, trying to follow, but Whit stopped him, murmuring soothing words as he tugged the reins from the terrets.

It was her fault. She stood staring into the woods. Her own idiotic fear had made her press too fast in the darkness. She'd made a mistake and others would pay.

A sound whispered in the woods. She turned

41

toward it, breath held, but Whitford hobbled to her side, distracting her.

"You must return to the carriage, my lady. 'Tis not safe . . ." he began, but she interrupted.

"Keep the beast still."

Whitford turned, saw the horse stumble toward them, and hurried to its side to halt its progress, but the hoofbeats did not cease. Indeed, they came on, muffled and steady in the darkness.

"Who goes there?" she called. Her voice trembled. She stiffened her spine, ashamed of her weakness. "Who—" she began again, but then she saw it, a pale apparition, bigger than life, bearing down on her from the tattered fog.

She stepped back, ready to flee, feeling the age-old terror grip her throat like calloused fingers. *I didn't mean to hurt him. I didn't mean—*

"Me lady," rumbled a voice from the darkness, "is aught amiss?"

She realized then that she had pressed her fist to her chest, as if to keep her heart from bursting. She lowered it slowly, grappling for courage. "Who comes?" she asked.

" 'Tis Sir Banyon of the Celts," came the answer from the darkness. When his steed took another step, she could almost make out his features, could almost believe he was harmless.

"Has there been a mishap, me lady?" he asked

and rode into the shifting beams of her lantern.

The golden light caressed him, gilding his hair, shining in his azure eyes, as if the clouds had scuttled away from the moon to herald his approach, like a wayward angel come to earth.

But she had little use for angels. Indeed, she wanted nothing more than to be left alone. She glanced in the opposite direction, hoping for help from another front, but she was being ridiculous of course. Few would be as foolish as she. Few would hazard uncertain roads to flee from a golden-haired knight whose smile shone like a beacon in the darkness.

"I fear my beast has injured himself," she said.

The Irishman settled back against the cantle of his saddle. Candlelight stroked the width of his neck, casting shadows in the hollow of his throat. For a posh, London buck, he seemed strangely natural there in the lonely darkness, as though he'd done far more than ride Hyde's circuitous course to ogle and be ogled.

"On yonder log?" he asked, though he did not turn to look away. And in truth, it would do him little good, for 'twas difficult to see one's own feet.

"Yes," she said and watched him dismount, a fluid dance in the darkness, though his steed did not look like a willing partner and pinned its ears against its poll.

43

"You should not be traveling so late, lass," he said, approaching her. "There may well be dangerous men aboot."

Lithe and lean, he stood a full ten inches taller than she and outweighed her by a good five stone. She tilted her head up at his approach and held her ground.

"My thanks for that advise, sir," she said. Her tone was wondrous sincere, testimony to years of careful training. She must remember to be grateful for the old man's harsh tutelage someday, but the gelding's pain was increasing again. She felt it as a dull ache in the back of her head. "But for now perhaps assistance would be more appropriate than warnings."

She saw the flash of his smile in the darkness.

"Me apologies, lass," he said and bowed with a sweep of his hand toward his mount. "Might I offer ye a ride to yer destination?"

"No." Training be damned.

He straightened abruptly. She could feel his surprise.

"But you may take my driver," she said.

"Yer—"

"Whitford," she called, but he was already beside her, his brow, the only unmarred portion of his face, furrowed. "You must ride with this gentleman to Arborhill to fetch another steed."

"Nay."

"No."

The two men spoke in hasty unison, surprising her with their mutual passion. She raised an imperial brow.

"M'lady," Whitmore said, stirring restlessly. "I cannot leave you here alone. I cannot."

"He is right, lass," burred the Irishman. " 'Twould be unforgivable folly to abandon ye. Chivalry insists that I stay at yer side." He grinned. "However distasteful the task might prove. Yer driver can take me own mount and—"

"No." She'd spoken faster than she'd planned again and drew a careful breath now, clasping her hands in front of the pearlescent drape of her skirt. The mists that curled about her knees like silvery fronds matched it to mystical perfection. "I fear that will not do."

"I'll not leave you, m' lady," said Whitford, and shifted a distrustful glare toward the Celt.

She would have laughed if the pain in her head were not beginning to pound with such vicious insistence.

"Very well then, monsieur," she said, and turned regretfully toward the Irishman. "We've little choice then but to hitch your steed to my conveyance."

"Though I would dearly love to oblige, I fear me

destrier can be a bit peevish and will na carry a cart."

She gave him a scowl for his antiquated verbiage. "Luckily, your *destrier* will not be asked to tote some ramshackle dog cart," she said, turning primly away and holding her skirt from the mud. "If you will kindly remove his gear, we shall be on our—"

"*Her* gear."

She swiveled her head toward him impatiently. "I beg your pardon."

" 'Tis a mare."

She turned her gaze back toward his mount. The beast stood a good seventeen hands at the withers, had hooves the size of dinner plates and a baleful glare that might well quell a seasoned gunner.

Their gazes met, anger shining like dark lightning in the equine eyes. " 'Tis an Eddings brougham," she mused.

"Me apologies," said O'Banyon, eying her in the shifting light, "but I fear it would na matter if the carriage be crafted of purest gold by the king himself. The steed be a mite . . . opinionated and will na carry a conveyance of any sort."

She held the animal's gaze a moment longer before speaking.

"You are wrong," she said and turned brusquely

back toward the knight. "You may place your saddle at the back of my carriage. Whitford." She glanced toward her driver. "Fetch my wrap, please. The night grows chill."

The men eyed each other distrustfully, and for a moment she thought they might refuse, but finally they turned to their assigned tasks. She waited an abbreviated second, then hurried toward her gelding. He raised his head a painful inch.

"I am sorry, *mon petit*," she whispered and stripping off her gloves, set her hands to his brow.

Pain battered her, but in a moment it was gone. Ebony dropped to his knees, then rolled peacefully onto his side and lay still, his kindly eyes closed.

Silence echoed in the night. Tears welled hot and bitter in the grubby girl's emerald eyes, but the cool countess remained unmoved.

"What happened?"

Fayette jerked at the intrusion, but the countess of Colline turned with regal slowness toward the Irishman and pulled on her gloves. "I think the beast is dead."

Whitmore stood halfway between her and the carriage, her shawl drooping in her hands. His gaze met hers. She pulled hers away with an effort. "Hitch up the mare," she ordered and pacing to the carriage, managed to mount unassisted.

47

The cushion felt strangely unstable beneath her. She placed her hands against the black leather, steadying herself. There was no pain now. Just regret, and fatigue, as heavy as a tether weight in her soul.

Time slowed to a crawl. Reality blurred. She was small again, and weightless, alone but unafraid. In a heavy liquid, floating.

"Are ye unwell, lass?"

She realized foggily that the Irishman was facing her from the opposite seat and wondered how long he had been there, how much he had seen.

Scattered wits skittered back into place, marshaled by sheer will and abject necessity.

"I am fine." Her voice sounded distant, but she linked her fingers in her lap and straightened her back against the tufted seat. "Your steed is properly hitched?"

He gave her an odd glance. "We have gone a good three furlongs since."

Dammit all. She had to gain control, to shake away the cloying cobwebs that threatened to strangle her. "I realize as much," she said, "I but longed to hear you admit you were wrong."

In the flash and sway of the brougham's lanterns, his grin looked to be a cross between angelic grace and demonic pleasure. "Did ye now?" he asked.

"Yes."

He nodded. A narrow braid lay half hidden by the mass of hair that waved gently beside his left ear. Beaded with irregular black circlets, it gleamed like bent gold in the lantern light. How would it feel against her fingertips?

"Verra well then, lass," he admitted, "ye were right. She was as gentle as a lambkin in the traces. How did ye ken?"

She gave him a negligible tilt of her head, though even that was difficult. "Because I wished it to be so."

He laughed, the devil at play. "Do ye always get what ye wish for then?"

She gave him the smallest shrug. "I am the countess of Colline." Not Fayette, alone and frightened in a world she could not understand.

"And never a cloud mars yer glorious sky?"

She lifted a hand, palm up, as if to agree.

"And what of the count?" His eyes gleamed as blue and bright as a summer lake. "Where is he?"

"One gray cloud," she acquiesced evenly.

He watched her too intently, and he sat too close. 'Twas surely not safe.

"I fear he died some years ago."

"As unexpectedly as the gelding?"

She shot her gaze to him, breath held. But his expression was jovial. He was a pretty face with overestimated charms. Nothing more. No matter how her nerve endings sizzled with his nearness.

"I've no wish to discuss either," she said.

He watched her in silence for a second. "Then what shall we speak of, lass?"

She was tired, exhausted really. "Are you so fond of your own voice that you cannot sit quietly for a spell?"

He laughed. "Mayhap Mr. Finnegan is luckier than I realized."

She gave him the slightest edge of a scowl.

"Ye neglected the dance ye promised him," he explained.

So he remembered her words and realized her lie. She must be rid of him, of course, and yet, if the truth be told, he intrigued her. "Are you saying I am difficult, sir?" she asked.

He smiled. "As are many fine things."

"Flattery." She pressed the back of her hand against her forehead and stared wide-eyed. "I fear my poor head shall begin to spin with such words from the Irish cur."

"Hound," he corrected and leaned back in his seat, watching her with a half smile. He had donned the costume of the *ton*—cutaway coat and dark breeches. But there was something different about the way he wore it, something not quite tamed.

"Shall I take that to mean I should keep me compliments to meself?" he asked.

"Not at all." She could barely keep from fluttering her eyelashes. "I find them most exhilarating . . . if a bit unnerving."

"Methinks ye have never been unnerved."

He was wrong there, of course, and yet she could not help but give him the slightest smile.

"I but wonder, lass, why ye felt it necessary to rush from the Regent's grand ball just to avoid the likes of me?"

"Avoid you?" she said and gave him an arch glance. "I fear you give yourself far too much importance, sir. 'Twas simply that I had to leave unexpectedly as my head was beginning to ache."

"Me apologies. I did not ken yer affliction. Come, I shall rub away the pain," he said and suddenly he was on the seat beside her.

Terror pierced her like an arrow. She lurched past him, scurrying to the opposite side of the carriage where she huddled against the corner.

It took her one wild instant to realize he was watching her as if she'd suddenly sprouted fangs.

She straightened, reprimanding herself. What the devil was wrong with her? She knew far better than to scurry away like a flushed debutante. She was the countess of Colline. "I realize, Sir O'Banyon, that you are of Celtic ancestry," she said, still breathing hard, still struggling for normalcy, for calm, "and not accustomed to the ways of civilized persons. But here in the cultivated world . . . we do not accost others without warning."

His eyebrows were somewhere in his hairline. Perhaps, she thought, rather hazily, he was not accustomed to women scurrying from his path like harried rodents.

"Surely ye are na saying I am uncivilized," he said.

She forced a prim smile and calmed her breathing. "Surely not."

"What then?" he asked. "Is me cravat too wide? Me coat too long or is it another deadly fashion sin I have committed?"

"On the contrary, sir, you are perfectly attired."

He lifted a hand. His fingers were long and tapered. There would be magic there. A common magic perhaps, but a magic just the same, and one she had not allowed herself for years out of count.

"Then what?" he asked.

"A wolf may wear a collar," she said, "but he is still a wolf."

For just a fraction of a second, the humor fled his eyes, replaced by something sharp and gleaming, but then he settled back against the cushion and perused her carefully. "Tell me of yerself, countess of Colline."

She spread her gloved hands upon her lap. "What is there to tell, sir? I am what you see?"

"Beautiful, wealthy—so young and fair with form so soft and charm so rare?"

She was honestly surprised. "Poetry, Sir O'Banyon?"

"Yer own Lord Byron has been known to string a likely phrase."

"I do not believe he is *my own* as you say."

He leaned forward, light dancing in his eyes. "Where then were ye born, lass?"

She leaned back, breathless. "What bearing could that possibly have on the situation?"

"I but wonder. What were ye like as a wee lass? Do ye favor sweets? When ye sleep at night, of what do ye dream?"

They were but questions. Casually put forth and easy to answer. At least for most. But to her they were secrets long kept and carefully guarded, lest the truth spill forth and drown her in its dark tide.

She quieted her nerves and watched him. "If you are trying to seduce me, I fear your efforts are wasted."

His eyes crinkled, as if he were smiling in his

soul. "Because ye dunna like the look of me or because ye yet mourn the loss of yer bridegroom."

She longed to tell him it was the former, but she would not tell an unbelievable lie, for it might well cast suspicion on the lies yet to be.

"Fishing for compliments, are you?" she asked instead.

He laughed. The deep rumble of his humor danced in the darkness between them. "Could ye blame me in these chilly waters, lass?"

"Indeed, I could. Besides, there might well be a score of excellent reasons to dislike you other than the shape of your nose or the angle of your jaw."

"Name one then, lass."

"Your tendency to pry into the affairs of others."

He drew back in mock surprise. "Ye think me meddlesome?"

"And vain."

"Nay." He said as if wounded.

"So you do not think yourself superior to other men?"

"Well, aye," he admitted. "But that hardly makes me vain. Only . . . perceptive."

Perhaps she should have been insulted by his vanity. Instead, she found herself tempted to laugh.

"But alas, I dunna pretend to be superior in all things," he assured her, barely sober.

"Oh? How big-hearted of you."

"Aye, well . . ." He canted his head modestly. His single, golden braid fell across the stubbled slant of his jaw. "Size is na amongst those things."

Antoinette willed back the rush of blood to her cheeks, but it was wasted effort. She could control much, but not the flush of embarrassment.

He watched her. Laughter flickered in his eyes. "Ye look all the more bonny when ye blush, lass," he murmured, his deep burr softened as he leaned toward her.

"You should try it, if you've not forgotten how," she suggested, and he laughed as he settled back against the cushions behind him again.

"Tell me, love, how long were ye wed?"

Love. The word tripped so easily from his tongue. She held her hands still in her lap, refusing to fidget. "Not near long enough."

"That much I guessed from yer high color. How did he die?"

"He became ill with consumption."

"I am sorry," he said, and his voice was, quite suddenly, filled with quiet earnestness.

She hadn't expected pity. Nor sincerity. Indeed, she did not want it. "And what of you, O'Banyon, have you never wed?" she asked, her tone brusque. "Or perhaps you are bound to another even now."

He watched her, his lips curved. "Do I look the

sort to leave me bride while I philander with another?" he asked.

"Indeed, you look the sort to leave your bride with a passel of twelve while you philander with *many* others."

She expected him to laugh. He did not.

"I knew ye to be aloof," he said. "But I did not expect ye to be foolish."

She blinked and raised a haughty brow. "I did not mean to wound you, sir. But you *are* known as the Irish Beast, are you not?"

"Hound," he corrected. "And ye have na wounded me. Ye have only disappointed me."

Some emotion twisted in her stomach. Some feeling she could not quite identify. Surely it could not be regret. This man meant nothing to her. He was there to make a conquest. Nothing more. She was sure of it. She had met a hundred others like him.

"What has made ye so cautious?" he asked.

She pursed her lips. Who was he to find fault with her? "Perhaps it is men like you," she said.

He grinned, seeming to forgive her earlier statement. "So yer husband was handsome and charming and virile?"

"My husband was old and bitter and—" Dammit! She almost closed her eyes to her own foolishness, but she did not. Instead, she leaned back and exhaled slowly. She was almost home, and she would not make the mistake of being closeted alone with him again. "There you have it then, O'Banyon, the truth. Are you happy now?"

"Nay," he said and his somber expression suggested that he spoke true. "Na if ye are na."

She forced herself to breathe. "Why are you here?" she asked.

"In truth, lass, from the first I laid me eyes on ye, I could na seem to be elsewhere."

She stared at him. How long had it been since she'd allowed herself to touch, to be human, to be alive, she wondered, but she gave herself a mental shake and laughed out loud. "Tell me, Irishman, do you practice these lines in the mirror so that you can spew them out to every passing maid?"

"Tell me, countess," he said, propping his elbows on his knees to lean toward her, "do ye doubt every word ever spoken?"

"Just when they are issued from men such as yourself."

He shook his head. The expression was almost sad. "Believe this, lass, ye have na met a man like meself," he said and took her hand in his own.

She should have seen it coming, but she did not. Feelings burned like summer lightning, sizzling across her fingers, racing up her arm. She heard his sharp intake of breath. Or was it her own?

The carriage lurched beneath her, its wheels crunching gravel, but the sound was lost in his growl as he moved forward. And she almost did the same. Almost. But in the last second sanity was renewed. She jerked away, scrambling toward the door.

"Cesses!" she spat and fled, tumbling from her carriage and up the cobblestone walkway to Arborhill's silent sanctity.

Chapter 4

❧

"**I**rish!" said the baroness, startled to see him.

O'Banyon smiled. Hiltsglen's wee Fleurette couldn't have looked more surprised if he'd been delivered atop her pickled mushrooms.

She stood in the doorway of her office, the cramped and busy space above Eddings Carriages, a company she had begun on her own and continued to supervise even after her marriage. The idea that her independence must gall the Black Celt's old-world pride lifted O'Banyon's spirits a notch.

"Baroness," he said and reaching for her hand, kissed it.

Her eyes were narrowed when he straightened. "Killian isn't here," she said.

He stepped inside, crowding her back and closing the door behind him. "And what, lass, would lead ye to believe I have come to see the dark Celt?"

He moved toward the window. 'Twas an intriguing spot here above the teeming city. London had grown a hundredfold since his last sojourn there, evolving into a snarled mass of growling humanity.

"If not Killian then what is your purpose?" she asked.

He turned, perusing her office. The new century had burst forth with a thousand clever gadgets that never ceased to fascinate him. "Mayhap I have come to seduce ye."

The baroness stared at him for several long seconds, then settled loosely into a slat-backed chair and laughed out loud.

A tic of irritation niggled at him. "Ye find something amusing?"

"You mostly," she said.

"Ahh." Leave it to Hiltsglen to find himself a wife who did not appreciate good old Irish charm. "May I be asking why, then?"

"First," she said, leaning forward to prop her hands on her much scarred desk, "despite evidence

60

to the contrary, you do not seem to be a complete fool."

He lifted a hand. "Ye are far too kind, me lady."

She grinned a little, but there may have been a rather lethal light in her eyes. "If you so much as touched my skirt, Killian would have your head, but I'm sure you realize as much."

He considered defending his masculine prowess as a warrior, but it hardly seemed worth the time. Hiltsglen was as big as a damned bastion and he'd have righteous indignation on his side. "And second?"

"I spoke to Lucy."

He shook his head.

"Lady Anglehill."

Her meaning dawned on him. It may be that he had acted less than casual when first he'd seen the countess of Colline depart the ball. "Ah."

"Yes, ah. She said you shot out after Antoinette as if your breeches were on fire."

"Yet with a good deal of dignity," he said, but if truth be told, it had rather felt like his lower regions were ablaze.

She laughed. "Did you catch her?"

He found another chair, removed a pile of leather scraps and lowered himself into it. "As it turns out, she be a quick little nipper."

"Is she?"

"I believe she travels in a carriage crafted by yer own clever hands."

"Yes." She nodded. "In fact, we've made two, a phaeton and a brougham, especially for her."

"Why white do you suppose?"

"White?"

"Her carriage, her gowns."

"Oh." She shrugged. She had strangely casual mannerisms, almost as if she had no desire to impress him. Damned Hiltsglen. " 'Tis simply her preferences, I suspect."

"Ye know her well, then?"

"Not particularly. I spent a bit of time in Paris at her estate there."

"Ahh," He grinned. "And that is where ye first saw me, in Jardin de Jacques."

She stared at him, her face expressionless. "That is where I first saw the Black Celt."

"Oh aye." He grinned. "I fear I had forgot that great chunk of accursed stone. Did the countess accompany ye to the gardens?"

"No, I don't believe . . ." she began, then stopped. "Why all the questions, O'Banyon?"

He shrugged. "Curiosity. Naught else."

It was her turn to grin. "It sounds more like obsession."

He snorted. "And here I thought ye to be a sensible lass, but for your choice of husbands, of course."

"So the Irish Hound cannot bear to be rejected."

"The wee lass did na reject me," he countered. "Indeed, she did na even—"

"As I heard it, she took one look at you, conjured up with a poor excuse, and vanished like a puff of gun powder."

He opened his mouth to argue, then shook his head. " 'Tis damned unnatural."

"Vanishing?"

He scowled. She was not so foolish as her spousal choice suggested. "That too. Does she do so often?"

"This is the first. Generally, she's exceptionally well mannered. Though perhaps a bit stand-offish. I do believe she detests you, O'Banyon."

He gave it some judicious consideration, then disagreed amicably. "I dunna believe any lass could detest me."

"I detest you."

"Well . . ." He tilted his head in concession. "I have never once tried to kill *her* husband."

"Simple negligence on your part I'm sure."

He couldn't help but like this woman. "When did her mate die exactly?"

"I say, O'Banyon," she groused, rising from her

chair, "this is the worst excuse of a seduction I have ever yet experienced."

"Aye, well, I don't wish to overwhelm ye with me charms."

"You're doing well then."

"If it means anything to ye, I vow to do me best to avoid killing yer husband in the future."

"How generous of you."

He shrugged, agreeing. "What do ye know of the white countess?"

"She was born in France I believe and married fairly young. If I recall correctly, the count was some years her senior, but I'm not entirely certain. I fear I didn't meet her until well after his death."

"Which was caused by . . ."

"Really, O'Banyon, I knew you to be a murderer and a womanizer, but I didn't suspect you of gossip."

"Aye, well . . ." He shrugged as he rose to his feet. "There seems to be a dearth of hand-to-hand combat these days. I've been searching for a likely hobby."

"So cricket has failed to hold your interest?"

He sighed and glanced out the window, remembering a tattered girl and a lady in white. "My latest opponents no longer wish to play."

Chapter 5

The conservatory was over-warm. It was dirty and humid. It smelled of rotting peat, and there was nowhere in the world Antoinette would rather be. For there was life here. Life that she could touch and coddle and urge to new, lush heights.

Garden succory, for instance. Boiled with black adder bark, it became a bitter liquor that could draw down excess phlegm, but what would happen if she added a bit of wild endive? 'Twas a fascinating question, but just now, she was mixing an elixir.

While traveling down Cornhill she had heard a

child's rasping cough. A bit of dried vervain and sweet cicily should turn the trick. But she would add a few drops of distilled loosestrife to—

Sibylla appeared suddenly at her elbow. Antoinette glanced up, only to find the girl holding out a small, squat bottle. It was made of thick brown glass and contained the essence of loosestrife.

Antoinette laughed out loud, prompting the shadow of an almost grin to lift the corner of the child's cherub mouth. How long had it taken the girl to do so much as meet Antoinette's gaze? Months surely.

Oh, aye, they had made some progress since that first November night. The wind had been bitter cold then, biting with acid intensity as Antoinette turned toward the scruffy girl. The child had been huddled against the rough face of a shabby inn, her face freshly bruised, her eyes haunted.

No words had been spoken. No questions had been asked. Antoinette had merely opened her carriage door. The child's approach had been hesitant, but she had come, climbing silently into the vehicle and shivering like a starved whelp in the corner until the countess draped her velvet cape about the girl's skinny shoulders.

She'd slept then, nodding off against her will, her split lips parted, blowing frosty, shallow breaths into the dark air.

Antoinette called her Sibylla, though the child never managed to give a name. But over the months, she'd gained a bit of weight. And grown. Still, she would not speak. Or allow another's touch. Indeed, she insisted on wearing the same tattered gown she had been found in and could rarely be convinced to wash.

There was the hint of healthy color in her cheeks now and a bright light in her cobalt eyes, but the girl's gaze flickered shyly away and Antoinette turned aside, busying her hands.

"You've a bit of dirt on your nose, child," she said. "Just about there." She pointed to her own face. "Check the mirror and see."

Sibylla turned toward the looking glass that hung beside the door.

The countess almost laughed as the girl stared at herself, for her face was covered in dirt, only the skin beneath her scattered bangs showing her true, fair color.

"Been swimming in the mud again, *ma petite*?"

Sibylla blinked at her. A swell of feelings rushed in on Antoinette. Dangerous, so dangerous, but too late now to change the course of things. The girl had been sent into her life, and she would stay. "Never mind," she said, "I like a child who's unafraid to get her hands dirty. Or her face . . ." She skimmed the child's tattered gown. "Or her clothes.

Or . . . However did you get mud in your ear? It's not yet—"

The door swung open.

Sibylla started like a frightened fawn. Antoinette jerked toward the entrance.

"Good morningtide, countess." The Irishman stood in the doorway. He bowed and turned his sparkling attention on Sibylla. "And wee—" He paused, raising his brows. "God's truth, ye are the grimiest child I have ever yet seen, lass. And I was raised on the dirt paths of Dublin. Congratulations to ye." He bowed. "When I was but a wee lad, me mum told me turnips would grow right out of me pate if I did na wash me ears."

The girl rubbed the side of her head distractedly.

"But she was entirely mistaken."

Sibylla watched him, her eyes as wide as the heavens, her pixie face absolutely sober.

"I could grow naught but carrots, no matter how I tried. Nonetheless, I was a favorite amongst the village steeds."

Sibylla stared at him a moment, and then, like a bit of white magic, the waif's gamin face broke into a cautious grin.

Antoinette looked on, stunned to silence.

"Ahh, lassie," said O'Banyon, watching the girl, "ye look like sunshine itself when ye smile. Tell me, do the wild lads of London follow ye aboot like lampkins on a string?"

Sibylla stared, then shook her head with slow uncertainty.

"Well be cautious nonetheless," he advised. "For they will soon enough. And ye canna trust a lad, na with a bonny smile the likes of yers."

The girl watched him with sparkling eyes.

The countess kept her expression perfectly serene, but inside, Fayette scowled. She had few enough friends and had no wish to share. "I thought I had made it clear to my staff that I was to receive no visitors while I'm in my conservatory," she said, and whisking off her barely soiled apron, stepped out from behind the workbench, barring the girl from his view. "I shall have to speak to them."

O'Banyon grinned. It felt like sunshine in her soul. But she dropped the apron on the bench and lifted her gaze resolutely to his.

" 'Tis na their fault, lass," he said. "Indeed, I dunna think they be yet aware of me presence."

"You've snuck onto my property?"

He shrugged. "It seems to me, snuck is a word reserved for cowards and curs while—"

"Well, you are the Irish mutt are you not?"

"Hound," he corrected, "and I did not sneak . . . exactly." His grin cranked up another quarter of an inch. "I felt it me duty as a gentleman to pay ye a visit."

"Your duty."

"Aye," he said and sobered. He looked like nothing more than a fallen angel, gilded and gleaming even after his descent to earth. " 'Tis worried I've been."

Antoinette pursed her lips. The hours amidst her plants were jealously guarded. Tugging loose the fingers of her cotton gloves, she set them aside, wiped her fingers on a damp towel and carefully rolled down her sleeves. They were white, pristine, pearly. "And what, pray tell, were you worried about?" she asked.

"Aboot ye and the wee lass here wandering aboot alone on the dark streets of London, of course."

"As I have told you before, sir, you are entirely mistaken. Neither I nor my young servant would have any reason to wander *aboot*."

He grinned at her attempted burr. "Indeed?"

"Indeed."

He skimmed her work bench, eying the plants and vials and dried flowers that remained there. "I thought mayhap ye had delivered a tonic to one of the needy souls what live on the east side."

Reaching under the table, she pulled out a new pair of gloves and slipped them on. "I am ever so sorry to disappoint you, monsieur, but I know no one there."

"There was a woman," he said, "In the very midst of the street. I saw her with me own two eyes, na ten paces from me. I was certain she was yerself."

She shrugged and motioned toward the door, away from her sanctuary. Away from Sibylla, for she was yet too fragile and easily frightened. Surely she had only smiled because she was nervous, not because she was charmed. "I am ever so sorry to prove your fallibility."

"She was dressed all in white, much as ye are."

"Would it surprise you to learn that others have been known to wear the color? Indeed, it is quite fashionable in these days of the regency."

He watched her carefully, his eyes alight. "And what of ye, lass?" he asked, and stepping smoothly sideways, addressed the child. "Were ye out at night on the notorious east side?"

Sibylla raised her peaked chin.

"My apologies," Antoinette said, turning to face him. Anger brewed in her soul, but she contained it. "I do not allow others to address my servants."

His brows rose with a snap. "Ye dunna allow—"

"Sibylla, hasten up to the house and assist Mrs. Catrill with the wash."

The girl scuttled sideways and dashed out the door. O'Banyon watched her go.

The conservatory went silent.

"You've something to say, sir?" she asked.

"Aye," he said, examining her for a moment, "she seems a wee thing to be doing heavy labor."

"Does she?" Skirting him herself, Antoinette stepped outside. She sighed with relief when he followed her into the open air. It was safer in the gardens, not so close, not so intimate. "Well, perhaps I think she owes me, since I saved her life."

"Saved her, did ye?" he asked, his gaze holding hers.

She pulled hers away with an effort. "She was quite starved when first I found her in Shoreditch. Indeed, Mrs. Catrill did not think—"

"And what were ye doing in that dark side of town, lass?"

She paused, her mind blanking for an instant. Damn him. He was surely too handsome to have caught her in a verbal trap. Too alluring to be clever.

"I don't believe my business there is any of your concern, good sir."

He shrugged. His shoulders looked broad and capable in his dark serge coat, his legs long and lean, encased in snug breeches and scuffed riding boots. His shirt was open at the neck, revealing skin that was as smooth and solid as polished bronze.

"Shoreditch is not meant for such a delicate lass as yerself. Chivalry demands that I warn ye against traveling there."

"Have you not heard?" she asked, glancing over her shoulder at him. "Chivalry is long dead."

He grinned. Something coiled up tight in her stomach. "Grievously wounded, mayhap, but surely not deceased. Na so long as there be lassies such as yerself."

"Like me?" She was leading him toward the arched wooden gate that closed in her garden.

"Aye, bonny lassies what make men like meself do foolish things."

She laughed. "Forgive me, O'Banyon, but I do not believe I can be blamed for the foolishness of men like yourself."

"What was she doing there?" he asked from some distance behind.

"What?" She stopped abruptly, looking back.

He had paused to caress the bell-shaped blossom of a foxglove. His fingers looked oddly gentle against the velvety bloom, but his wrist was broad, and against his golden skin lay a circlet of braided hair, clasped with hammered steel. "The wee lass what ye saved from surest death. What was she doing in Shoreditch?"

She shrugged and drew her gaze resolutely away. " 'Tis difficult to say for certain, for she does not speak."

He glanced up, surprised, his fingers still gentle on the flower's snowy blossom. "Ever?"

"No."

"Is there aught wrong with her tongue?"

"I wouldn't know."

"She has not seen a physician?"

"She is a servant, O'Banyon." She straightened her back a bit more, though there would be those who would surely say 'twas not possible. "Saved from the dregs of society. She is fortunate to have avoided Newgate."

He watched her, his eyes slightly narrowed, his body absolutely still, as though he could see into her mind. "Indeed?"

She raised a challenging brow. "Indeed."

"Why do you call her Sibylla?"

Damn him. Why the devil could he not leave well enough alone. "I must call her something, mustn't I?"

"Nay," he said and shook his head. "In truth, lass, ye could have left her on the street. Surely it would have been wiser to find another to serve you. She cannot do ye much good. She is mute, filthy, and puny. All but worthless, if the truth—"

"Worthless!" she hissed, but there was no mistaking the gleam of clever trickery in the Irishman's eyes. She drew herself up, cursing silently. "Perhaps you Celts have never heard of Christian charity, O'Banyon."

For a moment she thought he would actually laugh at her. "Perhaps na, love. So why do ye call her Sibylla?"

A pox on him! " 'Tis a name," she snapped. "Just a name. I could not very well call her tattered waif all her life, now could—"

His eyes laughed. He shifted them aside. "Yer potentilla blooms early," he said. "As does your honeysuckle."

She skimmed her gaze from him to the flowers. She had tried to discourage them from cluttering over the wall, but they had become opinionated in recent years.

"And tall," he added. "The vines in Jardin de Jacques did na reach half their height."

"You've been to—" she began, then stopped herself and closed her eyes for a moment. Why the devil was she conversing about flora and children with this irritating Celt? "Shall we be honest with each other, Sir O'Banyon?"

His eyes crinkled at the corners. "If we must," he said.

"Why are you here?"

His lips quirked roguishly. "Because ye are bonny."

Honesty. From an Irishman. God help her. "Well . . ." She roamed away slowly, half hoping he would follow, half hoping he would refuse to be led. "It seems to me there are many *bonny* women in London."

"Aye." He nodded and wandered after her. "But only a very few show up on Aldgate Road, then vanish without so much as good eventide."

"I did not van . . ." she began, twisting toward him, then gritting her teeth. "I was not on Aldgate."

His damned eyes were gleaming like a hunting wolf's. She hated hunting wolves.

"Tell me, me lady, why do ye forever wear gloves? 'Tis a foine spring day."

She tilted her head at him then turned to stroll away, hoping to look casual, as if she spent every afternoon with an ungodly handsome man who made her want to strike him on the head with something good and solid. "Tell me, good sir, whyever would you concern yourself with ladies' fashions?"

"And always white," he continued. "Even in yer plant house."

"Would you prefer I wear lavender?"

"I would prefer you wear naught a'tall."

"What?" She jerked toward him, startled, but his expression was absolutely bland.

"I said I prefer a woman who is naught over tall."

She searched his expression. Innocence shone like evening stars in his eyes.

"Did ye believe I said aught else?"

Who the devil was he? "No," she said. "Of course not."

"Ye are the perfect height," he added.

"Well, I am ever so thrilled to know I shall not have to grow to please you."

He grinned. She felt oddly breathless, strangely off balance.

"Are ye?" he asked.

"No," she said. They were almost to the gate. "I was being facetious."

"Truly?" He drew back slightly. "A lady of yer ilk. I would na have guessed it."

"I am certain there are a good many things you would not have guessed."

" 'Tis true," he said. "I canna imagine why a tender lass such as yerself would be on Aldgate Road."

"Tell me, sir, is there any hope of convincing you that your mystery maid in white was another?"

She lifted the heavy gate hasp. Perhaps she would

have Whitford install a lock, and a bad-tempered dog . . . and a battalion of armed soldiers. O'Banyon stepped up to the fence beside her.

He tilted his head, half smiling down at her. "She looked a good deal like ye, lassie."

"Is it not generally dark at night, especially on Aldgate Road?"

"Me senses are wondrous sharp."

"But most need some light to . . . Senses?" she asked.

"The mysterious lass smelled like ye."

Antoinette drew back slightly, but the gate was behind her. "Are you saying I have an odor?"

"I am saying ye smell like . . ." He leaned forward the barest inch. She stifled a tremble, but she could not halt the feelings that tingled a harried path toward her heart. "The ripening earth," he said, "with just a breath of comfrey."

"I'm afraid you're perfectly mistaken, sir. I haven't worked with comfrey for a week or more."

He filled his nostrils, eyes narrowed. "Five days closer to."

"What?" she breathed.

His eyes smiled. They stood only inches apart.

"Me sense of touch is also quite amazing. Might ye like a demonstration?" he asked and reached out.

She jerked sideways. "I think it's time for you to leave."

He stood very still, watching her, lowering his arm. "A lass such as yerself should never be afeared," he said.

"I am not *afeared*."

"Then why do ye draw away?"

"Why—" She huffed a laugh. "Perhaps in the hollows of Ireland it is proper for men to grope women they—"

"Grope!" he said and took a step closer. She hurried back. "God's balls, lass, who have ye been with?"

She could smell him. She didn't know how or why. Unlike him, she didn't have particularly sharp senses. But she knew he smelled of sharp sunlight and hot desire.

"I've no idea what you speak of."

"The bumbling groper what hath made ye nervous," he said. "Who is he?"

She felt breathless and rigid. "I should slap you for disparaging my honor."

"Verra well."

"What?"

"Ye may slap me if ye wish, lass."

"I . . . I . . ." The world was off-kilter. "What is wrong with you?" she rasped.

He laughed. "Are ye saying ye have been faithful to yer husband's memory, then?"

"That's none of your concern."

"Was he the groper?"

"Get off my property."

"Did ye cherish him?"

"Leave."

"Or was it he what made ye cringe away?" he asked and reached for her again.

"Swear to God." She was breathing hard when she pressed her back against the fence. "If you touch me, you shall live to regret it."

He remained as he was. "Only if ye do," he said and withdrew his hand.

"Go away," she ordered, but her voice was little more than a whisper. "Please."

"And windflower," he said, taking in another breath of her fragrance. "But a wee hint of windflower."

Chapter 6

O'Banyon sat alone in the woods and watched the countess's house. Arborhill was a fine estate. Set but a few miles west of Londontowne, it boasted a venerable stone house and a hundred hectares of rolling pasture.

The night was quiet and still around him. Somewhere in the decaying layers of fallen leaves, a mouse scurried for cover. Banyon heard its harried progress, sensed its winding course, but did not turn from the wrought-iron gates that enclosed her estate.

He was not obsessed though. Hardly that. He

was the Irish Hound, the handsome beast, the golden wolf. He didn't become obsessed.

He was simply curious.

Who was she? Why did she abhor touch? Why were her servants twisted and silent? And why in God's name did she avoid him?

O'Banyon ground his teeth and closed his eyes. Very well then, mayhap he was a wee bit obsessed, but there was something about her ... something ancient and sacred that called to the most primal part of him, and God knew that was pretty damned primal.

When she was near he felt that he was, for the first time in his life, entirely alive. As if every nerve ending was singing with full-voiced energy. He didn't know why.

Oh, aye, she was bonny enough, but as she herself had said, London was not bereft of bonny maids. She was wealthy, of course, but if the truth be told, he had never much cared for coin. It was women he loved. Women and laughter, and curling up near a crackling fire on a cold winter's night. He was a simple man ... in a manner of speaking.

Pebbles crunched on the countess's drive. He stood up, testing the breeze, and in a moment a phaeton rolled away from the house and into sight. Black as the night, it was pulled by a pair of dark horses.

Whitford dismounted to open the gates, then, slipping the reins from the carriage dash, urged the team forward as he walked along beside. In a moment, he'd shut the gates, mounted the conveyance and clicked the steeds into a stately trot.

O'Banyon caught a glimpse of Antoinette inside, her face a small oval in the window, her eyes wide and haunting in the narrow rectangular pane.

And then they rolled away, heading east at a smart clip. There was nothing Banyon could do but follow, keeping to the shadows and wondering about her mission. Did she go to a lover? Did he await her even now?

It was not far to London. But they did not stop at some posh estate, nor did they turn aside at an inn. Instead, they hurried through the silent night. The streets narrowed, the houses became lower and shabbier.

It was more difficult to remain hidden now, but the shadows were deep and the night friendly to one so familiar with the darkness.

The horses' hooves clicked smartly against cobbles and then dirt, steady and unwavering—a handsome pair of matched bays gleaming in the night.

O'Banyon's senses picked up a rap against the carriage roof. The vehicle slowed to a halt. Hidden by shadows as dark as ancient magic, he watched as the driver hobbled from his seat to the countess's door. It creaked open and in a moment she stepped down.

Whitford's voice was little more than a rumble in the heavy silence.

"My lady, I beg you, do not do this."

She responded softly. From his place behind a tilted pony cart, O'Banyon could not tell exactly what she said, but her face looked cool and pale against the night, her gloved hands lost in the folds of her skirt.

The closest horse turned his head as she went past, champing its bit and nickering softly, but otherwise all was silent. Whitford hobbled around her and rapped on the door of a nearby hovel. It seemed a lifetime before it opened. Weak candlelight flickered past the threshold, and then she stepped inside, leaving Whitford bent and alone.

Time dragged past, but perhaps, in reality, only a few minutes lapsed before she reappeared. Murmuring a few sparse words to her driver, she returned to her vehicle and rumbled into the night.

That was it. Nothing more. They returned without incidence to Arborhill. O'Banyon stood for a time in the woods again, watching, listening, but there was naught else to see, naught but the moon shining on the dark metal rail of the fence and the world growing slowly older.

It was early afternoon when O'Banyon entered the livery some blocks from his townhouse. A lad was pitching hay from a nearby wagon onto the dirt floor. Another was cleaning harness. They glanced toward him in tandem.

"Can I help ye, good sir?" asked an old man as he hobbled from a stall. Hanging a leather bridle on a peg near the door, he tilted his head for an answer.

"Aye," O'Banyon said. The stable was filled with the sweet smells of fodder and horse and a dozen other scents as old as time. "I'll be needing me steed readied."

"Certainly, sir, and which horse might that be?"

"The good-sized sorrel with the flaxen mane."

"Certainly, sir. Bailey . . ." called the old man and turned toward the wagon, but the boy who had been there was gone. The gaffer scowled, his wrinkled face perplexed. "Southren," he began, but when they turned in the opposite direction, they saw that the harness lay alone and the lad was just disappearing through the doorway, bare feet flying. "Boy!" the old man snapped. "Come hither."

The lad reappeared more slowly, slinking sulkily toward them.

"Fetch the gentleman's steed, lad, and be quick about it."

The boy shuffled his feet. They were near as filthy as the floor upon which he stood. "I'm unsure which animal that might be, sir."

The old man's scowl deepened, etching grooves like valleys in his withered brow. "We've only one sorrel hereabouts this day."

"Ahh . . ." The boy looked pained. "Sorrel, you say. Well . . ." He glanced in the direction his companion must have taken. "Master Edwards wanted his gelding brought 'round soon. 'Praps I should—"

"What the devil's wrong with you, boy? Fetch—"

O'Banyon cleared his throat. "Southren, is it?" The boy flitted his gaze to him and away. His hair was as red as a sunrise. Freckles stood out in bold relief against his pale skin.

"Aye, my lord."

O'Banyon nodded. "Tell me, lad, did she tear the flesh?"

The old man looked bemused.

The boy glanced toward his employer and back. "Beggin' yer pardon, sir. But she near took my head off."

"Bite ye, did she?"

"Kicked. Both hinds. She's God awful fast for such a whale of a beast."

"Aye." O'Banyon sighed. "She is that. Fetch me a shank will ye, lad, I'll see to her meself."

The boy nodded gratefully and disappeared into a nearby room. He was back in an instant, bearing the leather strap like another might carry a serpent.

O'Banyon took it from him, then marched down the aisle toward the last stall. The Dutch doors were closed. He opened the top one and peered inside.

Luci stood with her tail toward the door. Bending her heavy-crested neck, she gazed at her would-be master through a forelock that reached the curling summit of her nostrils. O'Banyon had at first thought the long, golden foretop made her comely and coy. And perhaps at times it still did, but mostly she appeared malevolent and maybe demonic. Following their second fateful ride together, while waiting for his wounds to heal, he had named her Lucifer. But her shifting moods had assured him of her sex. Luci she remained.

"I hear ye be causing trouble again, lass," he rumbled, testing the waters. 'Twas best not to take too much for granted until he'd determined her current mood.

The animal switched her tail with slow disinterest and cocked a gigantic hip. Her hide glistened red-gold and healthy from the light through unshuttered window.

Down the aisle, the second lad had reappeared on timid feet. The three hostlers were absolutely silent.

O'Banyon gave them a grin. "Latch the door behind me," he ordered. "And if I be yet alive when she's done with me, fetch a priest to read me me last rites," he said and stepped into the stall.

In the aisle, Southren rushed to close the door. Then the threesome remained perfectly still, listening. Inside the stall, something hit the wall like a loosed battering ram. Southren jumped back. The mare screamed. A feral growl answered. Another blast shook the stable. There was the sound of rustling straw. Hooves struck the floor, rattling the very earth beneath their feet. And then silence.

The trio glanced at each other and shuffled forward a few tremulous steps. Inside the stall, nothing stirred.

"Are you quite well, my lord?" called the old man. "Or shall I fetch the priest?"

No one answered. The boys glanced at each other, breath held.

"My lord?" he called again.

"Aye," came the growled response.

More glances were exchanged. More breath was held.

"Aye, you are well, or aye, I should fetch a—"

A growl sounded again.

Bailey swallowed. The old man crossed himself. "Good sir?"

Silence echoed like thunder around them. Reaching carefully forward, the gaffer unlatched the top door, then stepped cautiously back.

"All is well," O'Banyon said, appearing in the doorway. His hair was standing a bit on end and his eyes held a strange glow, but otherwise he seemed quite whole. He smiled. "I need but a moment to calm her."

They blinked at him. "Right sir. Of course, sir." The old man bobbed a nod. "Shall I have Bailey fetch your saddle, sir?"

"That would be much appreciated," O'Banyon said and swung the door closed again. "Methinks she missed me."

Near an hour had passed before the mare was saddled and O'Banyon threw the stall doors wide, but all three horsemen still remained, industriously scrubbing at tack that already gleamed with cleanliness.

The Irishman grinned as he led the cantankerous mare down the aisle. The steed's iron-shod hooves met the cobbles like the slow, heavy strike of a smithy's hammer. "There be times when wee Luci here can be a mite fractious," he said. "But she'll na harm ye."

"Of course, my lord," said the old man.

"Unless ye come within striking distance," Banyon added, and leading the beast into the open air, slipped the reins over her head. The sorrel shifted an evil eye toward him.

O'Banyon growled. Luci flipped her tail and turned away, casual as a turnip. "Good day to ye," Banyon said, and mounting, reined the mare onto the thoroughfare.

Hacks clip-clopped past. Luci pinned back her oversized ears and shook her head.

An open curricle spun by. Two identical young women, dressed in identical gowns, with identical expressions of glee, sat across from a scowling matron. They giggled and whispered something behind their identical ivory fans. O'Banyon gave them a grin and a truncated bow.

Borough Market's costermongers were in full cry. Milkmaids ambled by with placid cows. Tradesmen hawked every conceivable skill. Baked apples and jellied eels were sold in concert with ice blocks and live rabbits.

But O'Banyon soon left the hustle and bump of

prosperous London behind. East End looked different in the light of day, but he had no trouble finding the hovel where the countess had stopped just the night before.

Issuing a terse warning, he dismounted distractedly and led the moody mare to the door. The portal was warped and slanted, set askance on bent hinges. He rapped once and waited. Down the street, a boy appeared, eyes wide in his dirty face.

"Lad," he called. "Might ye tell me who lives here?"

The child remained frozen for an instant, then turned and ran, dirty feet flying beneath tattered breeches.

O'Banyon rapped again. Footsteps sounded from within, and finally the door opened on rusty hinges. An old woman stood there, bent and gnarled.

"Yer pardon, mistress," he said, "I believe an acquaintance of mine was here last eventide."

The old woman gave a jerk of her head, eyes bloodshot and beady in her creased face. "And who might you be?"

He gave her a bow. "Me name be O'Banyon, lass, of the fighting Irish. 'Tis pleased I am to meet ye. Do I have the proper house? Did a lady come by during the night just past? She is—"

" 'E's dead," she croaked.

O'Banyon felt the air escape his lungs. "Yer pardon, mistress."

"Cush is dead. Dead and gone. She'll get nothing more from 'im," she said and closed the door in his face.

Chapter 7

O'Banyon strode down the uneven street toward the livery. The stately stores that lined Cavendish Square were placid compared to the bustling open shops of Borough Market, but his mind was still whirling. What the devil was happening? Why had the countess visited the hovel in East End? What had she done there?

He'd spent a poor night wondering just that . . . and dreaming, dreaming of an ethereal lass with sable-dark hair and fairy-green eyes. But well before dawn the apparition had changed into something horrible and beautiful. Something he could not fight, could not hope to conquer. And yet he *had* fought, had battled as if his very soul were at risk. For indeed, it was. He'd awakened in a cold sweat, breath rattling in his lungs, fingers clinging to his scattered bed sheets.

It had taken him some time to calm his charging senses and realize all was well. He was whole. He was free, not forever trapped in ancient stone and misty shadows. Not doomed to an eternity of nothingness. But neither was he in his own time and place.

Hiltsglen had been given a mission, a quest to right a supposed wrong done centuries past. And that quest had drawn him unscathed from dark curses cast long ago.

But what of himself?

Rising from bed, he had prowled the confines of his townhouse, his mind racing.

Some hours later, striding past a plumassier's shop, he was still plagued with questions.

Why was he here? Oh, aye, he knew why he had been cursed; no woman likes to be turned aside—especially if she is powerful and vain and the *only* maid he had ever refused. Indeed, he knew why he had been *twice* cursed—bad luck there. He should not have been so close to Hiltsglen when the dark master sought revenge for the Celt's betrayal.

But why had he arisen from the darkness precisely when he had? Was his awakening simply in concert with Hiltsglen's quest, or had he too been appointed a task?

And what of the white countess? Why did she travel alone to dark sections of the city only to leave death behind? And why did she avoid his touch? 'Twas unnatural. Oh aye, some would have said *he* was unnatural. Indeed, *all* would have said he was unnatural if they knew the truth of his strange double life, but even so, maids were still drawn to him.

Why was she not? Why—

Might she be the reason he had been called to the here and now? Black magic had brought him here. Mayhap it was his task to see that that same sorcery never harmed another. Could *she* be the quest? Might he have been brought here to prevent some terrible evil?

Perhaps her bonny face hid a black soul. It had happened aplenty in years past. Indeed, he thought, but his troubled musings skittered to a halt as a narrow wisp of a girl flitted down the stone-laid walkway. Her frock was ragged, and a stubborn streak of dirt marred her cheek, but her eyes were gleaming as she slowed beside a nearby carriage. Stepping onto the busy thoroughfare, she approached the dark cob hitched to the conveyance, then opened her tiny hand to expose a plump root.

The mare tilted her elegant head to gaze at the girl from behind rectangular blinkers then nipped the fat tuber from her shrinking palm. The child wrinkled her turned-up nose, and it was not until that moment that O'Banyon was sure of her identity, for none but wee Sibylla made him smile just to look at her.

"Lass," he called, keeping his distance lest she shy away.

She glanced up, startled, and stepped closer to the mare.

O'Banyon winced. "Ye must na stand too near the steed, lass," he warned. "It may strike out."

She blinked, eyes wide in her gamin face, one hand curled tight in the mare's black mane. It was then that he noticed her bare toes, curled only inches from the horse's iron-shod hooves.

"Careful lass," he warned, but in that moment, the animal turned and lapped the girl's cheek with her tongue.

Lifting one tiny shoulder, Sibylla giggled, and it was that noise, that sunny ray of glee that stopped him in his tracks, for it was the very essence of unfettered happiness.

Worries crept a little further toward the back of his mind. 'Twas difficult to fret in the light of such a wee pixie's joy. "I've rare seen such houndish affection in a steed," he admitted, "but still, ye must be cautious, lass. The beastie may yet misstep and land on yer feet." He strode forward to whisk her from harm's way, but in that instant, the girl shimmied sideways. Grasping the mare's hame with grubby fingers, she hooked her toes atop the wooden shaft and scrambled upward. In less than a heartbeat, she was perched atop the animal's back like a Moroccan's pet monkey, her scathed, knobby knees just visible beneath her rumpled hem. Her hair was knotted and her gown rent, exposing one skinny arm. And yet, despite her shabby appearance, she looked, he thought, just as he imagined a wee fairy might, bright eyes gleaming with mischief and hair . . . well . . . instead of being adorned with fair blossoms, there seemed to be a twig sticking out at a jaunty angle. Strangely, it made her only more appealing to an Irish rogue so far from home. Indeed, it made his chest ache at the beguiling sight of her.

"Or mayhap ye'll trod on her toes," he said and gave her a tilted smile. "Tell me yer tricks, wee one, for I've a surly mount yonder what needs a firmer hand than me own." He nodded toward Luci, who flipped her flaxen tail in irritable agreement. "If I feed her plump roots from me hand do ye think she will lap me cheek like a much-loved pup?"

The girl's eyes were round when she shifted her gaze to his fractious destrier, rounder still when she turned back to O'Banyon with a slow shake of her elfin head.

He grinned. "Mayhap ye be right. I shall save the treats and me fingers with them. And methinks I shall retain the charm I wear just to be safe."

She blinked at him, uncertain.

"Ye see," he said, raising his arm to show the braided horsehair that encircled his wrist. "I have crafted a circlet from her tail."

The girl's eyes got rounder still as she stared at the simple bracelet.

"She be the fiercest beastie I know. It seems but wise to keep a bit of her power on me own person."

Sibylla rubbed her own tiny wrist.

" 'Tis clear though that ye've already harnessed the power of the steed," he said, indicating her sturdy perch. "But tell me, lass, do ye oft venture into Londontowne of yer own accord?"

Her toes curled, finding a firm resting place above the tug buckle. Her cherub's mouth hitched up a notch. She shook her head.

"Nay? So this be a rarity," he said as if musing. "Mayhap ye have run short of pipe tobacco and have come hither to—"

She shook her head again. The entangled twig bobbled.

"Nay." He stroked his chin, thinking hard, eyes narrowed with the effort. "Then perchance ye need a bridle to tame some wayward steed and have traveled here to—"

Her shoulders were hunched now. The barest hint of humor shone in her ever-blue eyes. Ahh, lassies, they were a wee bit of heaven, wrapped in happiness, alive with hope.

"Well, then, ye have traveled alone here on an important mission with the Prince Regent who has summoned ye hence—"

Again she was shaking her head. The tiniest giggle escaped her lips.

He stood entranced by the sound for an instant, a hardened warrior out of place, caught fast by a child's charms. "Ye are na here to see the prince?"

A silent negative answer.

"But ye are alone?"

She shook her head. Her grin peeked forth. She curled her fingers near her mouth as if to hide it away.

"Then where be yer servants, me lady? Surely they should be aboot, making certain ye are safe."

She bit her berry-bright lip and flicked her gaze toward a nearby store.

"Ahhh, so they be off buying ye a grand new costume. Well then, if ye'll excuse me, lass, I shall reprimand them sternly for leaving ye astray." The mare turned to nuzzle the girl's bare leg. "And ye in such dire danger," he said, and giving her a stately bow, turned toward the stone façade.

She watched him go as silently as she had watched him stay, a tiny slice of utopia amidst a contrary world.

The door creaked quietly when he stepped inside. He felt foolishly breathless as he skimmed the interior, but the countess was not there. Not that he had hoped to see her of course. He only wished to learn answers to the questions that plagued him, but the store's only customer was a skittish young maid who was even now hoisting a large, wooden box from the counter.

Still, chivalry was a hard master to shift. "Might I help ye with yer burden?" O'Banyon asked.

The girl jerked her eyes toward him and away. "No!" she said, not glancing up.

"It looks a mite heavy for a wee lass like yerself," he countered, but she didn't address him again. Instead, she hefted the box and scurried away, out the door and down the walkway.

He watched her go. From across the street, a bent and twisted Whitford hurried from a harness shop toward her. O'Banyon tensed, ready to fly to her rescue, but when she raised her sky-wide gaze to the gnarled hostler's, there was no fear in her eyes. Not fear. Certainly no revulsion. Not even when his hand brushed hers with tender shyness.

Indeed, it almost seemed that she smiled.

O'Banyon scowled. These London women were an odd lot. It wasn't as if he himself had been about to poke her in the eye with a sharpened quill. But she had fled him much as her mistress had done—

"Never mind her," said a voice.

Turning, O'Banyon spotted a woman behind the counter. She had a long face, much-stained teeth, and bright, fire-quick eyes.

"She's like that with everyone," said the matron. "Even devilishly 'andsome gents what offer assist."

Flattery. More welcome than a spring-fed oasis in the deserts of the infidels. He turned toward the merchant. "Is she now?"

"Indeed."

He approached the counter. "And what is she like with sharp-minded maids with pleasing eyes?" he asked.

She laughed. "Ahh. Just as I thought—a charmer, not to be trusted, but oft to be admired," she said.

"Astute and outspoken." He grinned. "Might I have the pleasure of yer name, lass?"

"I am Mrs. Fritz," she said, coming around the corner of her counter.

"And I am honored," he responded and reaching for her hand, kissed her knuckles.

She eyed him narrowly as he straightened. "Mr. Fritz is in the back room even now."

He tilted his head. "I be fair warned then."

" 'Twas not a warning," she said. "I was hoping you was a man what likes a challenge."

O'Banyon laughed out loud. Her eyes gleamed in return.

"What can I help ya with, gov'nor?"

He glanced about the shop. Bottles and bags crowded boxes and barrels, covering every possible surface. Searching for an excuse for his presence there, he spotted a sign that boasted miracle results. "I've had a bit of a cough of late," he lied. "I was hoping ye might have somemat to soothe it."

"A cough ya say."

"Aye."

"Rasping or soggy-like?"

Soggy-like didn't sound very manly. "Rasping."

"I've just the thing," she said and striding toward the back of the store, picked up an amber bottle with a brown label. "This'll peel the hair right off 'n yer chest."

He raised a brow. "In truth, lass, 'twas na quite the results I was wishing for."

"Well, I can't tell ya much about the countess."

He stared. "What countess?"

Striding back behind her counter, she watched him with arch interest and nodded toward the door. "She's the reason ya offered to lighten the girl's load is she not?"

"Nay. I was but being chivalrous and—"

"So ya wished to converse with the maid about the wonders of the universe?"

"She seemed a mite small to be hefting such a—"

"Dense as a parsnip."

"Yer pardon."

"The girl. There's something amiss in her noggin." She touched her own pate. "Ya wouldn't know it to look at her, I'll grant. But her father was a right mean bastard. Pardon my language. Back-handed the poor child once too often." She shook her head. " 'E died too easy if you're wantin' my opinion."

"Died—"

"Shortly after the countess hired him on."

Something squirmed in O'Banyon's gut, but he kept his expression bland. "What countess?"

She scoffed as she lifted her apron and scrubbed at a nearby bottle. "Don't act daft with me, gov'nor. It don't suit. She hired him to do a bit of odds and ends about her estate up there at Arborhill. Only he didn't last a fortnight."

"What happened?"

She shrugged. "Up and died 'e did."

"Was he unwell?

"Not that I knows of. But he drank like an Irish lord, beggin' yer pardon, and acted worse after. Who knows what he poured down his gullet after she paid his last fee. Still, it were a shame, him leavin' his girl with no prospects. Perhaps the countess felt responsible."

"How so?"

"It was her money what sent him on that last spree wasn't it now? In fact—"

The bell at the door tinkled musically.

Mrs. Fritz stopped in mid sentence. A tall woman stepped inside. It took O'Banyon only a moment to identify her.

"Lady Anglehill," he said in unison with the proprietress.

"Mrs. Fritz," said the countess. "Sir O'Banyon." She shifted her gaze from one to the other.

"How . . . frightening, the two of you together."

Fritz sniffed. "I've no idea what ya mean."

"I mean, a woman of your age and intellect should know better than to flirt with the likes of a roguish Irishman," said the lady, skimming her gaze to O'Banyon.

"I don't know whether I should be flattered or insulted," Mrs. Fritz said.

"I'm fair sure I'm insulted," O'Banyon countered.

"I'm certain it would not be the first time," Lady Anglehill said and turned toward the shop keeper. "Now, what did you tell him of the countess?"

"The countess?"

"Don't act daft with me, Fritz," she said and turned her steady attention on O'Banyon. "He may be as alluring as dark chocolate, but we don't know a bit about him and he's obsessed with poor Antoinette."

Fritz's eyes narrowed in happy concentration. "Obsessed, ya say?"

He shook his head. "I've na wish to disagree with a handsome maid such as yerself, me lady," he said, "but I am na—"

"Chased her right out of Prinny's grand affair just this week past."

"Indeed?"

"As if he were entranced."

"Believe this," he said. "I am na the type to become easily enamored. Not by a countess or any other."

"I witnessed his hasty exodus with my own eyes."

"I had other reasons to leave so hasty."

"Indeed?" intoned the two women in unison.

"Aye."

"So it is not truest love?" Anglehill asked.

He scoffed. "Yer pardon, me lady," he said, sketching a bow, "but if the truth be told, I favor maids with more . . ." He glanced her up and down. She would stand six feet tall in her stockings. Her heeled slippers added three inches if they added a hair. "Substance."

"Substance," she repeated dryly. She was not, he thought, a woman to accept roses without checking for the thorns.

"Aye."

"Then you would not be interested to know she will be attending the masked ball this Friday eve."

He shrugged, but his stomach had twisted up hard at the thought of seeing her again, of feeling the titillating power of her presence.

"She dances divinely."

He smiled.

"Lord Bentley is hoping to get up the nerve to ask for her hand in marriage."

Something knotted up hard in his innards. "Bentley?" he asked.

"A dumpy little man with a paunch and bad teeth. But he has a goodly fortune put aside."

He could think of nothing to say. Nothing at all. What the devil was his problem? He'd had something to say since he'd breathed his first breath.

Lady Anglehill smiled. "Perhaps he will ask her at the ball."

He planned to deny his feelings again, to protest, but the women were watching him with identical expressions of needle-sharp curiosity.

He gave them a shallow bow. "Me congratulations, lass, 'tis rare I've witnessed such cruelty in the fairer sex," he said instead.

The countess laughed. "Then you've not been about London long, my lord. But you cannot blame Lady Colline," she said. "She's been without a spouse for quite some while, and perhaps she yet hopes for children. Bentley may be well past his prime, but he seems virile enough to—"

O'Banyon was never quite sure, but he thought he may have growled.

In any case, the women's brows shot up in happy unison.

"Did you say something, sir?" asked the countess.

He calmed himself, eased open his fists, and gave her a carefully civilized smile. "I was but wondering where this ball might be held."

"Oh. If I'm not mistaken . . ." She smiled back and swept a bit of invisible dust from her sleeve. " 'Tis at my estate."

The world went silent. He searched wildly for his gift of gaff, for his charm, for some errant word. Nothing came.

"Would you, perchance . . ." She paused, staring at him, her expression all innocence. "Might you wish to attend?"

He refrained from baring his fangs. The wellbred might think it unrefined. The astute might think it deadly. " 'Tis most generous of ye to ask, me lady."

Silence again.

"Is that an acceptance or a regret?"

He gave her a bow for her wit and her cruelty. "I can hardly say nay to a lady of yer charms."

She laughed aloud, throwing her head back in a most unfeminine manner. "Very well then, Sir O'Banyon. I shall look forward to seeing you in but a few days."

He nodded and turned toward the door. Retreat was oft a hero's best choice.

But Mrs. Fritz thumped the tonic bottle on the counter, propped her hand on a hefty hip and scowled. "That'll be half a crown," she said.

Chapter 8

Antoinette surveyed the ballroom. Masked revelers were everywhere, milling, gossiping, laughing. She nodded regally to a gentleman in a Pan mask. He nodded back, stubby horns bobbing.

It should have been amusing, of course. Should have been a happy sight, the carefree wealthy at play, but behind her feathered mask Fayette shuddered.

Her throat felt tight. She shouldn't have come. Not tonight. She was weak and alone and hideously hungry.

She turned toward the refreshment table, seeing

it in sharp focus through the slanted openings of her disguise. Delicacies of every sort were spread across the lavishly clothed surface. Cucumber sandwiches, raspberry creams, tiny crystal bowls filled with currant fool. For a moment she was tempted almost beyond control to snatch up a half dozen of the creamy desserts, to shovel them into her mouth, to gorge herself until the black memories faded like old scars. But she would not.

She curled her gloved hands against her skirt, hiding the tremble.

No one knew. No one suspected. To them, she was Lady Colline. Not a grimy child with an evil secret.

But someone was watching her. She felt it like rancid breath on the back of her neck. She glanced behind, muscles stiff, searching.

"Care to dance, my lady?" asked a man too close at hand.

Fayette shrieked in terror, but the countess turned with smooth aplomb, forcing herself to breathe. To prolong the charade.

"My thanks," she said. Her would-be suitor was dressed in black, as were most other men, but he wore the mask of a jester. The unearthly expression looked ghoulish and terrifying. In her mind, she scrambled beneath the table, hiding behind the cloth, shivering in her rags, hoping they would leave her be. She'd done nothing wrong. Nothing. Antoinette's hands shook again, and it was that weakness that made her nod, made her take the risk, yet again. "Yes," she said, "I thought none would ask."

He laughed and raised his hands. She braced herself against the impact and met them with her own gloved fingers. Their palms touched. She held her breath. But there was only a skittering of pain, only a shadow of disquiet.

"Do I—" he began, then paused. Inside his idiot's mask, his mouth remained open for a moment. Though his gait only became marginally smoother, she felt the change in the quiver of her muscles—that lessening of tension, that fluidity of step. "Do I know you?"

" 'Tis difficult to say," she countered. "Are you acquainted with many swans?"

He laughed, sounding young and free despite the gray hair she could see above his collar. "What a grand ball this is." He twirled her about a elderly couple. She drew her elbow breathlessly against herself, lest she brush them.

It seemed an eternity before the waltz came to an end.

"My lady." Her partner bowed. "Another dance?"

But she shook her head. Weakness. Her refusal

was a weakness, but she would allow it this once. "I fear I've not your energy," she said and it was true. Already she felt drained, though he was unaware of the exchange, oblivious to the fact that his step was lighter, his movements quicker.

"Then I shall fetch you some refreshment to replenish you," he said. "Wait here."

She nodded simply, watched him go, and turning, faded into the crowd. The balcony doors were flung wide. She headed for them, focusing hard, doing her best to keep from touching the other revelers.

"Good eventide."

She turned toward the speaker.

He wore a wolf's mask and dark breeches. She forced herself to halt, to give him a brief nod. "Hello."

"Might I beg a dance?" His voice was slightly slurred behind the mask. Probably drunk. Safer then. Alcohol masked reality. She considered refusing, but he was already reaching for her. She braced herself. Their hands met, but there was no pain. Nothing. Yet perhaps she was wrong. Perhaps there was a shiver of feeling she could not quite identify. She raised her eyes to his as he swept her across the floor.

Her feet felt light. Her head the same. Why? "Do I know you?" she asked.

"That may well depend," he said. The conversation was strangely reminiscent of the one only moments earlier, but the feelings were entirely different, new and fresh and breathtaking. He leaned slightly closer. "On whether you are speaking biblically or otherwise."

She stumbled, but his arm was strong against her back, bearing her up. They floated past another pair, standing still in a bright blur of color.

"What did you say?"

"I but wonder if you mean basically, or on a deeper level," he said.

She found herself staring into his face, but his mask hid all except his eyes, which gleamed down at her, as bright and feral as a creature of the night's.

"The Irish mongrel," she whispered.

"Hound," he corrected and gave her the slightest tilt of his head. The crowd spun past.

Anger spurred through her. She had made herself clear. She had no wish to see him. No wish to touch or be touched, yet here he was, with his arm laid with heart pounding intimacy against her back. She could not bear it. Dare not stand for it. "I thought perchance you had returned to the caves of your homeland?" she murmured.

"I beg your pardon."

"I thought you had returned by cart to your

homeland," she said, gaze hard, lest he think her naïve. Lest he think her a fool.

His eyes laughed. "I had pressing business here," he said.

"Indeed?"

"Aye," he said and pulled her a half an inch closer, so that his hip brushed hers.

She fought the emotions, held back the fear. "Then you must surely get straight to your task," she said. "I've no wish to hold you here against your will."

He grinned behind the mask. She could feel it in her soul.

"There is na reason to fear me, lass."

"Fear you?" She almost pulled away, almost stumbled to a halt, but he kept her moving, kept her lost in the haunting sway of their bodies.

"I admit I am na one of the tame lap dogs what people your world, but I will na harm ye."

"My good sir . . ." She caught his eyes in a steady hold. "I am sorry," she said.

"And for what might ye apologize, lass?"

"For allowing you to believe I have some sort of interest in you."

His steps never faltered. His blue-fire gaze held hers in an entrancing blaze. "Ye mean to say ye dunna?"

"I most certainly do not," she said. "And for

115

that you have my deepest apologies, for you are probably not so . . . rustic as you seem."

"Rustic," he said and twirled her in a breathtaking arc.

It took a moment before her world settled back into place, but she resolutely found her voice. "If the truth be told, I am considering Lord Bentley's suit."

"Lord Bentley," he said. His tone was level, but perhaps if she listened carefully, she could hear the hint of a growl.

"His grace has honored me by asking for my hand in marriage."

They spun again, wildly, so that her soul seemed to quiver, throwing them closer still.

"The title 'his grace' implies that he is a duke," she told him, her tone measured, as if she spoke to a wayward bumpkin, and not a knight—a knight with sapphire eyes that seemed to see through her burning skin and into her very soul. "The highest rank of the British peerage."

"Does it indeed, lassie?" His voice was almost a caress. The sound shivered across her skin.

"Yes," she said and blinked as she stared up at him. "So tell me, Sir O'Banyon, of your pedigree."

He never missed a step. His hand was firm on

hers, his movements as graceful as a hunting beast's. "Me mum was a weaver."

She almost tripped. "A weaver," she said.

"Aye."

She did not glance about, but she knew there was not another in this posh assemblage who would admit such lowly antecedents. "And your father?"

His gaze never wavered. It felt like loving fingertips against her face, as if he knew the truth and cherished her anyway. She clawed back the weakling feelings he engendered, straightened her back.

"And what of your sire, sir?" she asked again. "You did know him, didn't you?"

They spun again. She tightened her hand against his shoulder to keep from flying into dark oblivion.

"I believe he was in your king's army."

"You believe?"

"He died," he said, "before I was birthed."

"Oh." She felt a stab of pain near her heart, but she would protect her own, survive, conquer. "I am sorry."

"That he died, or that ye insulted me mum?"

"I did not mean to—"

"Aye, ye did," he said. "And ye did na yet ken

117

the half of it. The truth is, she killed him when I was yet in her womb."

She stumbled violently, her throat tight with tension. "What?"

He drew her back up. The taut muscles of his shoulder shifted rhythmically beneath her grip.

"To me own mind, death seems too mild a response for the rape of a wee lass," he said. "But mayhap I be out of fashion."

Fayette whimpered, but Antoinette held herself perfectly straight. "I did not—"

"She and me aunties nurtured me," he continued.

She could not help but wince, but she was masked, she was gloved. He would not know. "Alone?"

"They were a lively trio and doted on me something fierce."

O'Banyon as a child, not hiding beneath a fetid fallen log, not quivering in a hole. But happy. Loved. Carefree. Laughing in that way that made the world shine with joy. Smiling as though he knew her secrets and did not care.

" 'Twas a hardship for them to be sure," he said. "She died when I was but four and ten." His hand held hers just so. His body moved with fluid grace, his oaken thighs brushing hers, sparking midnight feelings. "I thought her as bonny as a wild rose till the day I put her in the ground with her wee cross upon her breast."

The girl inside the countess cried, unashamed and unabashed. The woman said nothing. *Could* say nothing.

"As bonny as ye mayhap," he added, tilting his head a bit.

"Forgive me," she whispered, though she did not know how the words escaped. They should have been kept behind her careful mask. Should have been safe in Fayette's trembling hands.

His gaze caressed her. His hands held her steady. "Verra well, lass. If ye tell me of yer childhood."

She felt herself blanch. Felt her knees tremble, but she moved as she should, as she'd been taught, like a princess. *For God's sake, girl, are you a washer woman or an heiress?* The old man's voice snarled harsh and cold in her memory.

"She was a lady in waiting in the French court," she lied. "The queen's cousin by marriage."

"A beauty to challenge all the flowers in Paris?" he asked.

Beautiful and kind and so long gone. She had left her only daughter at too tender an age. *Take care of my Faye,* she had whispered to her grieving husband. But he had failed, succumbing to fever and sorrow just days later. "Not particularly," she lied. "The queen did not care to be outshone."

"What was her name?"

"Her name?" She remembered the lessons, of course. Remembered the old man's every word as if her very life depended on it. But it yet hurt to tell the lies she'd been taught. To defile the fragile memories. "Lady Reneire." Fayette shook her head, denying the lie.

"And her given name?"

"Beatrice."

"A foine name," he said. "And it 'twas she who named ye Antoinette?"

No. "Of course."

He was watching her. Too close. Too hot. Too intimate. "There are times when it suits ye," he said. "But there are times when ye seem entirely different, like a wee, small—"

She jerked out of his arms and stumbled to a halt, bereft at the loss of his hand in hers. The room spun around her.

"Lass?"

The door. Where was the door?

O'Banyon pulled off his mask and touched her arm. Feelings sparked like lightning through her. She jerked away.

"What is it?" he asked.

"Nothing."

"Ye hurt."

She stared at him, heart pounding. "What?"

"What troubles ye, love?" He stood very close, almost touching, but not quite, and yet she could feel his nearness like a warm caress. "Tell me. I shall make it better if ever I can."

She shook her head and backed away. "You can't," she rasped.

"What is it?"

"I need . . ." Touch. Warmth. Love. An image sparked in her mind, a picture of them together, skin to skin, heart to heart. He was laughing as if the world were not terror and darkness, as if he could cast her life in happy sunlight simply by holding her in his arms. The sound of his laughter rumbled through her system like silver magic. But it was not real. She trembled, breathing hard.

"Come." He drew her toward the doors. Air wafted across her cheeks, but her arm burned beneath his hand. "Sit."

She felt a bench against her legs and did as commanded.

"Remain here. I shall return in a moment."

She nodded. He dropped his mask beside her and turned away, and yet, from the back, he looked no less the wolf, his tawny hair agleam in the light of a thousand lanterns.

There was something there. Something different. Maybe as different as she. Maybe this time she could trust. Maybe . . .

But inside Fayette sobbed, her voice broken, her heart bruised.

Antoinette forced herself to stand, to move quietly toward the door, toward safety.

She was not a fool. She would not trust. Not now. Not ever.

The crowds seemed to crush in on her, but she hurried through, holding her skirts aloft, barely breathing, barely seeing.

"My lady."

Her vision cleared. Whitford stood before her, his ruined face creased with worry.

"Take me home," she whispered, and just managed to pull herself inside the safe confines of her carriage.

Chapter 9

❧⟋⟍❧

They were coming for her.

Fayette shivered, wriggling deeper into the swamp. Fetid smells wrinkled her nostrils. The mud was cold, numbing her arms, paralyzing her legs. Something slithered against her side. She almost screamed. Almost cried out. But there were worse things than wriggly creatures in dark holes. Far worse.

Voices. She could hear them. Men's voices, deep and sinister, coming for her, whispering. Lies.

She hadn't meant to harm the boy. He had fallen. That was all.

Aye, he'd said cruel things. Nasty things. Unforgivable things. But—"There she is."

The light shone in her eyes, blinding her, freezing her.

"Non!"

Antoinette awoke with a start.

Her breath rattled in the cavernous bedchamber. Her hands were wet and trembling, gripping fast to the bed linens. Her lungs felt tight, as if she were drowning.

Men. Lanterns swaying against the midnight darkness. Coming for her.

A strangling noise issued from her throat. She cowered against her pillows.

They were soft against her back, soft and warm, and it was that sensation, that reminder of safety that finally eased the tension from her throat.

All was well. She scanned the space between herself and the window. A score of plants cluttered the room, cascading from her wardrobe, climbing up her bed frame. She drew a deep breath of the earthy scent of life, but the room seemed hot and close.

She pulled the linens aside. They tangled about her legs, pulling her down, dragging her under, but she was coherent now. Awake. Safe.

Still, her legs felt unsteady as she crept from her bed. The floor felt cool against the pads of her feet, and the wall, when she touched it, felt rough and real, solid and hard against her fevered fingertips.

Outside, the moon looked down from its tattered bed of clouds, and her garden reached toward it, worshiping its somber countenance.

The garden. It called to her, pulled at her.

The stairs were all but silent beneath her bare feet. The arched door opened silently. Night air washed soft and kind against her cheeks. She drew in a deep, reverent breath.

All was well. She was grown. She was safe. She steadied her hands against her thighs, warm beneath the fragile fabric of her night rail.

Vines laced the arbor under which she passed and leaned lovingly toward her. She brushed a thumb across a fat bud. Feelings shivered through her. Scents of nightshade and wintergreen quickened her senses.

She was safe. None would come here. She was the countess. Wealthy, regal.

The roses bobbed at her passing. The maidenhair waved a gentle frond. Peace settled tentatively into her trembling soul. There was no place like the garden. No place so right, where she could touch life, where she could bury her hands in the soil and feel the very essence of the earth stir her soul. Here she was accepted. Here she was herself—not a make-believe countess in a small girl's trembling body, but a woman, strong and whole. Here she was—

"Beautiful."

She jerked around. A shadow lay across her stony path. They had come! They had found her. She stumbled backward.

" 'Tis a splendid bit of garden ye've got here."

He didn't approach. Didn't strike. Her breathing slowed. Her mind settled. 'Twas the Irishman with the golden hair and magical hands that stood before her. 'Twas just the Irishman.

The world went absolutely silent.

"I did na mean to startle ye, lass."

"Sir," she said, and found that her fingers were curled into her night rail. She eased them open. "You are on my private property in the very heart of the night." Her voice sounded steady to her own ears—a marvelous testimony to years of training . . . or abject terror.

Think, child. What the devil is the matter with you? Do you long so for the hangman's noose I've snatched you from?

"Aye," he said and took a step forward. She crowded back, though she told herself not to. He stopped, studying her. "I was concerned for yer well being."

Courage! She drew it around her like a mantle, pulling her shoulders back, standing straighter against the virgin's bower that trilled over the wall behind her.

"I am ever so grateful," she said, "but as you can see, sir, I am perfectly unharmed."

He remained exactly as he was, his face etched by moonlight, his hair gilded against his beautiful throat. It was not until that moment that she realized he wore a tunic of sorts. Open at the neck, with sleeves folded up above his elbows, it was tucked into what looked to be a broad-belted Celtic tartan. For one wild moment she wished it were light so that she might better see the corded strength of him in his native garb, but the weakness passed, almost making her laugh at her own foolishness. Almost. But he was watching her, examining her, close and silent.

She shifted nervously. "So there is little reason for you to stand about like a poor imitation of some ancient statuary," she said. Fear was giving way beneath the nudge of anger and something else, something rich and primitive and strangely hopeful.

His teeth gleamed like ivory when he smiled. "But I'm fair familiar with ancient statues, and chivalry demands that I stay a bit longer, lass. Ye should na be unchaperoned while dressed aught in the midst of the night."

"If you can remember," she began, her tone

honed to a fine point. "I am on my own property, behind a wrought-iron fence with my servants within shouting distance. Surely only the most depraved would dare bother me here."

She could see the etched beauty of his dimples dance in his moon-shadowed face. His chuckle trembled through the night, as seductive as quiet in the midst of chaos. "Mayhap ye are right. But 'tis impossible to guess what depraved souls might venture forth to catch a glimpse of ye in yer midnight beauty."

"On the contrary," she said, watching him, "I believe I can venture a fair guess."

His laugh was virile and full of life, making her ache with a longing she would not put a name to.

He sobered slowly. The garden went quiet.

"I've na come to hurt ye, lass," he murmured finally.

And strangely enough, she believed that. "Why have you come exactly?"

"That be a fine question."

"Perhaps you could try to think of an answer on your way home."

"And leave ye without a champion in the dark of the night?"

Without a champion. The phrase seemed strangely out of place amidst England's cool-headed gentry, like a leftover memory from the days of knights and chatelaines—old fashioned and tarnished, yet somehow hopelessly alluring. "Tell me, sir, what has brought you here from your homeland?"

"I believe she was called the *Merry Maiden*."

She gave him a slanted smile and strolled toward the garden's exit, but he stood between her and the gate and lifted a hand toward the iron chairs nestled beneath a constellation of moonflowers. She glanced toward the house, but he did not press, did not step closer, and finally she acquiesced and settled cautiously into a chair. The metal felt cool and smooth against her thighs. She pressed her gown against them.

"As you well know, sir," she said, "I was not inquiring about the ship's name. I was wondering about your purpose for coming here."

He sat upon the second chair, facing her at an oblique angle. "Why are ye na wed, lass?"

She did not need the darkness to hide her surprise. For she was, once again, the master of her emotions, as cool as the paving stones beneath her bare feet.

"It is, I'm certain, ever so kind of you to concern yourself with my well-being," she said. "But I assure you, my reasons for remaining independent are my own."

"Thus I should shut me mouth and keep meself to meself?" he asked.

"In so many words," she said. "Yes."

He laughed. She watched the moonlight play across his golden features, watched it dip humor into his lean cheeks and flash across his feral grin. " 'Tis fine advice, lass," he said and leaned forward so that his elbows rested on his knees, "and yet I find I canna."

He was closer now. Within reach. She scooted her feet back a wary few inches.

"Perhaps if you but tried harder," she suggested.

"In truth, I have tried. But to no avail. Indeed." He narrowed his eyes as if puzzled. "I've na had this trouble afore in the whole of me life."

"This trouble of accosting women in their homes?"

"Accosting." He made a face. " 'Tis a poor choice of words, me thinks."

"Me doesn't."

That grin again, unfettered and alive. Something unfurled gently in her stomach.

"It may surprise ye to hear this, but some maids find me passing fair."

"Do they?"

"Aye."

"Then why are you not *passing* your time with them?"

"I have been," he said. "For some good while."

"You, sir, are rather vain for a man who needs

to skulk about in the dark in an attempt to speak to women."

He laughed. "Mayhap I be vain," he said and leaned back slightly. The moonlight shadowed his eyes and shone on the width of his chest, covered as it was in soft, simple garb. He did not look elegant now, but earthy and touchable and solid. "But mayhap there be reason for some pride. 'Tis impossible for ye to judge if ye dunna come to know me better."

"In my experience men have little need of reason for their vanity."

"And what has yer experience been exactly?"

She raised a careful brow, knowing how she would look—regal and cool against the backdrop of her adoring garden. "Are you asking who I've taken to my bed?"

"Nay," he said. The night went quiet but for the sound of singing frogs. "I but ask who has wounded ye."

She sat very still, remembering to breathe. "I fear I must insist that you leave now, Sir O'Banyon."

"Was it yer husband?" He was watching her closely, like a hawk in flight, like a wolf, intent on its kill.

"I fear I am growing rather chilled. Indeed—"

"Then 'tis me own duty to see ye warmed," he said and suddenly he was crouched before her.

She tried to shy away, tried to draw back, but there was no room. He reached forward. His hands touched her bare ankle.

Life sizzled through her. Her head dropped back at the sharp slash of feelings.

"God's balls!" he rasped and jerked away. "What the devil was that?"

She stifled her breathing, straining back in her chair. "I've no idea what you're talking about."

He stared at her from one knee. "This," he said and reached forward again.

But in that instant her senses burst free. She scrambled to her feet. The metal chair clattered to the stone pathway, but she was already skittering away.

"*Cesses, Irandais!*" she hissed. Her breathing was out of control again and her diction had lost its polish. She knew it and yet there seemed nothing she could do.

Fayette was back at the helm, eyes wide in her gaunt face. "Be gone before it's too late for ya," she warned and lifting her gown, galloped for the house.

Chapter 10

"'T would na be a good day to challenge me, lass," O'Banyon growled. His steed flipped her heavy tail but did not bare her teeth when he stepped into the saddle.

The cobblestones clicked beneath the mare's giant hooves. A gentleman on a chestnut stallion passed to their right. Luci flashed him a coy look from the corner of her eye, but the other mount gave her one nervous glance and hurried past, long legs lifting high.

"Aye, ye and me," O'Banyon said, "we are all but irresistible these days."

Luci shook her head in constrained frustration,

and O'Banyon chuckled, but the weight of his thoughts soon dampened his humor, for there was much he did not understand.

What had happened on the previous night? He had but touched the white lady's ankle, had but caressed the merest inch of her skin when lightning had struck him.

Oh aye, women were magical. That he had learned many long years hence. But they usually didn't make his heart stop dead in his chest, like the strike of summer lightning.

And whilst it was true that it had been some time since he had enjoyed a fair lassie's favors—say a few hundred years—that hardly explained the ripping feelings that had burned through him at the merest touch of her skin.

She was comely. He would grant her that. And the fact that she wanted naught to do with him may have only sharpened his interest. But there were too many inexplicable events. Too many uncertainties. What was it about her that drew him with such agonizing force, such unearthly vigor?

A shiver shook him, though the day was warm.

But nay. He was being foolish. He was not in the dark ages when the druids danced naked beneath waxing moons and wailed to forbidden gods.

'Twas a new age. A refined age, with marvelously clever carriages and grand balls and golden orbs that chased the darkness back like the morning sun.

But not here. He glanced about. The grand estates and lofty storefronts had given way to rumpled hovels and squalid poverty.

Would the poor never change then? Would they forever live in shadow and hunger?

On the corner of two muddy streets, a narrow cottage leaned in drunken disarray toward the alley.

He remembered the place. He had passed there but a few nights before—the night the girl had been accosted by thugs. The night he had seen the vision in white. The only night his passions had pushed him past control in several months.

He turned his mind aside. Where had he been exactly? The details were somewhat blurred, for it had been dark and he had been . . . bestirred.

But there . . . The wee lass called Sibylla had emerged from that alley. Of that he was certain.

Skirting a puddle, he turned Luci into a pockmarked opening too narrow for a carriage. The houses here were naught but hovels. An old man leaned against a crumbling wall and rolled uncaring eyes upward at O'Banyon's approach.

"Good morningtide," he called.

The old man was silent.

"I be wondering if ye could give me assist."

Still nothing. Time or hard drink had robbed the old man of animation.

O'Banyon reached into the pocket of his silver-shot waistcoat and drew forth a gold florin.

The old man's eyes widened.

Long ago, when O'Banyon had plied a claymore like another might a lute, he'd saved his hard-won gold and hidden it carefully away for any eventuality.

But none could not have foreseen this future. Nor the need to take it from its hole so many long years later.

"Some nights ago there was a wee lass come hither into this alley," he said.

The old man's gaze never left the coin.

"Might ye remember her?"

"There are many lassies," said the gaffer, his tone raspy, as if unused for too long a time. "Some live. Others die."

"She was dressed in rags, but she had a smile like the sunrise. Did ye see her?"

The grizzled head shook the slightest degree.

"Mayhap she ventured into one of yonder hovels."

"I sleep beneath a wagon," the old man intoned,

nodding jerkily. "Until the rain wakes me. Or the cold. Even now it grows chill at night."

O'Banyon gritted his teeth. "There was a maid also," he said. "Dressed all in white, she was. Bonny as the—"

"I dreamed of a great lady in silver," gasped the gaffer.

"Aye, well this was true life. Did ye—"

"She stood just there." He pointed a gnarled finger toward a spot past the other's shoulder.

"Aye," said the Irishman, tempering his excitement. "That was where she stood. But did ye see where she went?"

"Dreams are not real."

"What of the girl? Did ye see a girl?"

The old man shook his head. Dullness returned to his eyes. His arm trembled, but he still pointed as if habit kept him alive long after hope had passed.

O'Banyon pressed his mount forward, and leaning from the saddle, folded the coin into the twisted fingers. The rheumy eyes shifted upward, tears glistening.

By evening, O'Banyon had knocked on a score of doors, had questioned countless people. But none had seen the girl or her mistress.

Had he dreamed it then? Was he as daft as the

old man? Was the girl he had found in the alley not Sibylla but just another tattered waif lost to poverty? Was he losing his mind?

Most probably. He glanced up, only to realize he had arrived at Briarburn, Hiltsglen's home, just as the sun was setting. Beside the manor house, the gardens bloomed, laid out lavishly beside a towering statue of an ancient warrior astride a half-rearing steed. The Black Celt.

O'Banyon stared, transfixed. Unchanged for five hundred years, the Celtic knight remained watching over all, holding the world at bay. And behind him, nearly hidden by riotous greenery, was a wolf-like hound, eyes almost alive, as if he were forever frozen on the brink of battle.

O'Banyon sat immobile as a thousand memories accosted him. Memories of hope and loss and betrayal. He was that hound, in spirit and more. Indeed, his very soul had been encased there, trapped, locked away, until suddenly the light of life had fallen on his face once again. Until Hiltsglen's curse had been broken by his wee Fleur and the wolf had been set free to roam once again.

From a nearby paddock, Hiltsglen's giant steed thrust his head over an irregular fence and trumpeted at Luci. She nickered flirtatiously and spread her hind legs, bearing her master abruptly back to the present.

"I've no time for this now," O'Banyon warned and reined her away from the stud, but she was transfixed and did not budge. "Have some pride, mare. Ye'll na—"

"Irish?" The sound of Fleurette's voice snapped his head up. She stood some yards away, her hands filled with roses, her freckled face open and honest. "I fear you've taken a wrong turn."

He leaned back in the saddle, searching for nonchalance and hoping she had not seen his mount refuse his cue. "And why is that, me lady?" he asked.

"The object of your obsession is not here."

He did not rise to the bait, but sat and watched her. She was lively and quick of wit, that was true. But he had not imagined Hiltsglen would be content to settle for the life he now lived—a placid existence with one woman and no battle. Why would any man, when there was such a bounty to choose from? When there were maids with eyes of bottle green? Delicate, ethereal lassies in white who entranced . . .

God's teeth! He stopped his wayward thoughts with a mental curse.

Beneath him, Luci cocked her hips and sent

forth a frothy stream of urine. In his paddock, the dark stallion shook his mane and reared, showing his round underbelly and far more. If O'Banyon had been easily intimidated this would have been the time.

"I've come to see yer mate," he announced, trying his best to ignore the mare's embarrassing behavior, and hoping to God Hiltsglen's wife would do the same.

She watched him for a moment, her face somber, then, "Why?" she asked.

He grinned now, though his mood was far from happy. "The ol' man is lucky indeed to have ye to protect his fair hide, me lady," he said, "but I vow to ye, I'll do him na harm this day."

"Ye've little choice in that regard," Hiltsglen rumbled.

O'Banyon glanced to the left. The Scotsman stood some thirty feet away. Back-dropped by the sprawling grandeur of Briarburn's manor house, he looked out of place in his ancestral plaid and open-necked tunic. Large as oaken boughs, his muscle-bound legs were spread. And from his oversized right hand, an ax stuck out at an awkward angle, almost casual, but not quite so. 'Twas a sobering sight . . . or should have been.

But O'Banyon's spirits lifted, as did his grin.

"Ye'd best be telling yer neighbors to lock up their sheep, lassie," he said, not glancing at the maid. "For it looks as though the dark Celt goes a-reavin'."

"What be ye doin' here, Irish?" Hiltsglen asked.

Banyon shrugged. 'Twas an excellent question. "Is it na the way of elegant gentlemen such as meself to stop by and converse with their neighbors and friends?"

The giant snorted. "Even if we *were* friends, Irish, I've na time to dringle away, so if yer prissy lifestyle has na made ye too much the weakling, ye might come 'round back and fetch a few mites of kindling for the kitchen fire."

"Maybe *ye* can gather the sticks. As for me, I'll be chopping the wood," Banyon said, but when he urged the big mare forward, she refused to move. Indeed, her flaxen tail was cocked to the side and her legs still spread as she gazed adoringly at her would-be lover.

O'Banyon swore in silence and rapped her in the ribs with his heels. She grunted and laid back her ears, but adjusted her stance and lumbered toward the nearby hitching post. Swinging his leg jauntily over her broad croup, Banyon gave Hiltsglen a grin. "Indeed, I suspect I'd best instruct ye in the proper manner of—"

But in that instant the mare's left hind swung forward with the speed and force of a trebuchet, striking O'Banyon square in the knee.

Pain shot like a tarred arrow up his leg. He grunted in agony and hobbled to the side just as the animal swung her head toward the rear.

Throwing out an elbow just in time, Banyon caught the beast a solid blow in the tender hollow of her muzzle.

Hiltsglen's chuckle rumbled through the evening air.

Silently cursing once again, Banyon tied the reins in the ring, straightened carefully, and walked without the slightest limp toward the Scotsman.

But the giant's eyes still gleamed with unfettered glee. "I see yon brute of a mare be too much for ye, Irish. Mayhap me wife could find ye a milding pony what would better match yer foppish attire," he said.

"Or mayhap I could teach ye na to bait yer betters," countered Banyon.

The Scot snorted and turned away. O'Banyon resisted cradling his knee and dropping to the ground like a felled footman, but couldn't quite control the limp. Bloody beast. He'd been thrilled when he'd found a mount reminiscent of the days of yore, when knights rode in full armor into the glory of battle. But just about now he'd be happy as a songbird to trade the animal for a goat and a nice pint of beer.

"Are ye coming?" Hiltsglen asked, turning back.

Banyon gritted his teeth and stifled a groan. In a minute they stood beside a pile of wood that had been cut to size but remained unsplit.

"Well then . . ." Picking up a log as wide as his mammoth thigh, Hiltsglen thumped it atop a level stump. "Did ye have a purpose for disturbing me peace, Irish?" Swinging back the axe, he sent it slamming into the ringed circle of wood. The log cracked open like a dropped egg. He straightened, eyes narrowed. "Or did ye merely hope to ogle me bride?"

"If the truth be known . . ." Banyon shrugged, and retrieving a second axe from a nearby stump, swung it wide with his right hand. The weight felt good against his back and arm, stretching the muscles taut and hard. "I thought mayhap she might wish to ogle me."

Hiltsglen stared, then snorted and set half the log back atop the stump. Once again the wood shattered.

"Ye've always been a lad to dream, Irish. I'll give ye that."

Lifting a log, Banyon set it atop the second stump. "And ye've always failed to believe," he said and slammed the blade into the log's top. It cracked like a melon, leaving the ax reverberating in the wood below. He straightened. "And 'tis that flaw, Scotsman, what snatched us from our own time and place to land us here."

Hiltsglen's gaze was steady. "This be me time now, Irish. And me place is beside yon lass."

O'Banyon shook his head and reset the log. "I did na think I would see the day when the Black Celt . . ." He swung the ax. "Would be bested by a wee maid."

"Bested am I?" Hiltsglen asked and setting his own log, broke it in twain.

"But then ye always had a weakness for the lassies."

"A weakness!" Hiltsglen snarled and cracked another log. " 'Tis ye what could na keep yer wick in yer plaid."

O'Banyon swung. Wood sang. "I may pleasure them. But I ken better than to trust them."

Tossing his ax aside, Hiltsglen tore off his shirt. Muscles bulged like angry serpents as he dropped it and tested the weight of the ax once again. "Some are to be trusted, Irish."

"Aye, some may well be," Banyon agreed, discarding his own shirt. "But the golden lady was surely na one of them. Any cappernoited half-wit should have realized that."

"Mayhap if ye had told me of yer time with her and the . . ." Hiltsglen paused as he eyed Banyon up and down. ". . . troubles what ensued, I would have been more cautious." Lifting the ax, he slammed it into the wood. It jumped and flew.

"I told ye she was not like other women."

"Like other women! She changed ye into a damned cur."

"Only now and again."

Hiltsglen snorted. "Had I seen ye lifting yer leg to the nearest oak, I would have stayed far clear of her, but I had na way of knowing ye were aught but yer usual irritating self."

"I tried to warn ye, ye ungrateful gargoyle." O'Banyon's axe sang. Wood exploded. "But when have ye ever listened to good sense?"

The Scotsman's axe blurred in the air. "Surely na when I listened to ye."

"The true answer be never, Scotsman."

Iron met oak with resounding finality. "I dunna ken what yer whinin' aboot, Irish. She convinced me to turn from our dark master, and aye he was a mite unhappy but—"

"A mite unhappy!" O'Banyon pointed to the statue that overlooked the garden. Even from that distance, it seemed he could feel the wolf's haunting gaze. "Aye, I had me own troubles after me time with the maid, but at least I did not lie with her. At least I was . . . mobile."

"Aye well . . ." Hiltsglen's voice was guttural, perhaps a bit shamed. " 'Tis because of me ye yet live and breathe."

Banyon's muscles jumped and tightened as he swung. "In the wrong time. In the wrong place."

Shards of kindling burst from beneath Hiltsglen's ax. "But breathe ye do, lad. The same would na be true if ye had na been following so close to me heels when our liege spat forth his curse."

"I was but trying to keep ye safe."

"Yet it was me who saved ye."

"Saved me!"

"Aye." Hiltsglen straightened, gargantuan chest rising and falling, eyes narrowed. "Ye have lived these many long years to see wondrous new sights. Me thinks ye but complain because the countess invites another to her bed, while ye roam aboot sniffin'—"

O'Banyon's ax seemed to sizzle sideways of its own accord. The air crackled between them. His blade halted mere inches from Hiltsglen's face. "Dunna sully her name, Scotsman."

For a moment the Celt remained absolutely still, a look of amazement on his broad features, and then he threw back his head and laughed.

Anger roiled through O'Banyon. He gritted his teeth against it, held the spell at bay, and dropped the ax a hand's breadth to poke the Scotsman in the chest.

"Shut yer mouth, Scot," he growled. "Ye look like a braying ass."

Sobering slowly, Hiltsglen lifted his ax and tapped it against the other's. "What's this then, lad? Might the Irish hound be finally leashed?"

O'Banyon swung his weapon in a tight circle, knocking Hiltsglen's away from the other side. "Na leashed, Scotsman," he said as the Celt braced his legs and fisted both hands about the handle. "But unlike ye, I was na raised by wild beasties. Me mum, rest her soul, taught me better than to besmirch a lassie's name."

Swinging up and around, the Scot crashed his weapon into O'Banyon's, driving him back.

"Nay, ye'll na besmirch them," he said, grinning at his advance. "But ye've na qualms against—"

O'Banyon drove forward, swinging hard. His blade struck the other's. Sparks danced in the night sky. Iron rang against iron, until they rested, blade against blade, rasping for breath.

"Dunna say the words, Scotsman."

Hiltsglen laughed again. O'Banyon growled and swung. The Scotsman parried.

"What the devil has come over ye, Irish?" he

asked and parried again. O'Banyon danced backward, fighting hard.

"The devil," Banyon rasped, swinging an upper cut toward the Scotsman who just barely caught it an inch from his crotch. "That may well be the case."

"What be ye blathering about?" Hiltsglen grunted, thrusting Banyon's blade aside.

"The black arts," breathed Irish, swinging again.

"The black arts," Hiltsglen said and chuckled as he advanced, muscles jumping like pugilists. " 'Tis na such thing."

O'Banyon stopped dead in his tracks, mouth open. Hiltsglen's axe whizzed like lightning past his nose. "Are ye entirely daft, Scotsman?" he asked and lifting his ax, pointed it again toward the garden's ancient statuary. "Do ye disremember the Black Celt what stands in yer verra courtyard? You were him!"

"I dunna forget," snarled Hiltsglen, raising his ax again. "But that was long ago, when the world was new and the shadows dark."

" 'Tis still dark!" snapped O'Banyon and slammed the other's weapon aside.

"Na longer." Their axes crashed. Sparks exploded. "Na again."

"How do ye ken? Since when has the Black Celt had such a rosy view of the world?"

"Since . . ." The big man faltered for a moment, and O'Banyon rushed in, slicing sideways, plowing a shallow scratch across the Scot's Herculean chest.

Hiltsglen glanced down in surprise.

"Living soft with bonny yon lass in yer arms has made ye slow," O'Banyon said, grinning. 'Twas rare indeed when a combatant severed so much as a hair from the Scotsman's head. "Slow and weak."

"Weak is it?" Hiltsglen rasped and leapt forward.

There was no time for talk then. Barely time to think. Only to parry and swing and advance and retreat. Metal clashed and sang and sparked and blurred.

The Scotsman had strength on his side. But O'Banyon was quick and wary, with the senses of a wolf and the mind of a troublemaker.

They stood finally, faced off, at an impasse, their weapons met before them as they rasped for breath, muscles quivering and spent, sweat slick against hot skin.

"Tell me, laddie," Hiltsglen rumbled. "How long has it been since ye yerself has been with a bonny lass?"

O'Banyon would have preferred to strike rather than answer, but his muscles quaked at the idea, and his legs refused to move. " 'Tis none of yer affair, Scotsman."

The grin again, so irritating O'Banyon wanted nothing more than to wipe it off his face with the blunt side of his weapon. "So the wee white maid refuses yer advances, does she?"

"The wee white witch."

"What?" The axe dropped a fraction of an inch.

O'Banyon shook his head. "Naught. 'Tis naught," he said and took another swipe at the Scotsman's chest. But it was a weak attempt, set aside by a wobbly blow.

"Ye think the *countess* be dabbling in the dark arts?"

"Nay. Aye! I dunna ken!" snarled Banyon and struck again. Again it was sliced wearily aside. "She is . . ." He struck. Hiltsglen parried. "She avoids me."

"And thus ye accuse her of sorcery?" The Scotsman's laughter melded with the clash of their weapons. "I knew ye to be vain, Irish, but—"

"I can think of none other but her."

They parried weakly.

"Aye," agreed Hiltsglen, seeming to think it the most natural of things.

"She haunts me every dream."

The Scotsman nodded and advanced.

"And when I touch her . . ." Even now, O'Banyon felt the lightning of her nearness. " 'Tis like thunder to me soul. Like a wound to the very heart of me."

"God's balls, Irish," said Hiltsglen, drawing back and breathing hard. "Yer na hexed, ye bloody fool. Yer in love."

O'Banyon felt himself pale. "Ye shut yer mouth, Scotsman."

The other laughed out loud, throwing out his muscled chest. " 'Tis just like a bloody Irishman to prefer to be cursed than besotted."

"I am na—"

"Ye can think of none other even in yer dreams. Ye touch her and are set ablaze. 'Tis na different than any other man what has found his true mate."

O'Banyon scowled and let his ax droop to his feet. " 'Tis how ye felt, Scotsman, when ye first met your wee flower?"

The other didn't speak for a moment, but then he nodded. " 'Tis how I yet feel," he said finally. " 'Tis like pleasant torture every time I look into her bonny eyes or touch her tender—"

"What the hell goes on here?" someone snarled.

The men turned in unison. The Celt's wee wife stood not twenty feet away. She made a comely sight, her legs spread, a pistol held steady in both hands. Unfortunately, the pistol seemed to be pointed rather directly at O'Banyon's head.

"Na to worry, me love," Hiltsglen rumbled. "We were but stretching our muscles."

"Stretching your muscles!" She skimmed her husband's body. Blood was smeared across his chest. His muscles quivered with fatigue. And scattered around them in a thirty-foot radius, was firewood the size of button hooks. She turned her gaze to O'Banyon. Her eyes were slightly narrowed, her mouth pursed.

He gave her a grin. Even that was tiring.

"He's bleeding," she said.

The Irishman shrugged. The ax fell from his fingers with the effort. " 'Twas naught but a lucky strike, me lady."

"Lucky?" She tightened her fingers and advanced.

"Unlucky. Unlucky!" O'Banyon corrected and managed to lift a trembling hand toward her. "Hiltsglen . . ." He shook his head. "He be me best friend in all the world."

"You almost killed him."

"Oh now, lassie," he said, shaking his head and retreating unsteadily. "Ye flatter me, but truly, the Black Celt is all but impossible to kill, na matter how hard I may—"

152

She cocked the pistol. Hiltsglen chuckled and stepped toward his blushing bride.

"There now," he said, reaching out and easing the weapon from her fingers. "If ye shoot him, lass, who will I spar with next time?"

Chapter 11

"How I detest whist," said the baroness of Hendershire. She was plump and fair-skinned. Mayhap her brown eyes were charming and her dimpled cheeks alluring, but at that precise moment, O'Banyon couldn't recall her given name, for she sat directly across from the white countess. "Perhaps I should wear gloves as Lady Colline does, then I might hide my hideous cards inside," she said and threw down her hand.

They were attending a house party at Chitwick Hall. There was always a party, it seemed, a gathering filled with elegant guests and worthless banter. But O'Banyon did not mind. For from his vantage point some tables away where he held his own cards, he could watch and learn.

Love, Hiltsglen had said? Was it possible? He didn't know, and yet, when he looked at her, feelings skittered like June bugs through him, lighting his soul. 'Twas not very manly.

"May I ask why you forever wear gloves, countess?" asked Lady Trulane. She had a sallow complexion and teeth that protruded forward like an aged gelding's. She did *not* have charming eyes, but she was known to spin a lively yarn, and her dogs certainly adored her. Indeed, a small, skewbald cur sat on her lap even now and alternated between licking his backside and giving O'Banyon a jaundiced glare. Dogs tended to dislike him quite fervently. And the smaller they were, the more they disliked him. He could only assume it was jealousy.

"I wear them because they match the color of my eyes, of course," said Antoinette.

"They're white," countered the young baroness.

"As are much of my eyes," quipped the countess. "Or at least I hope it is so."

The others laughed.

"I have always suspected," said Mr. Winters, throwing in his cards, "that her hands have been hideously scarred."

"Like the king of Siam's," said Lady Trulane.

They all turned to her.

"Surely I've mentioned the time I spent with King Rama."

There were moans mixed with laughter. Sometimes the lady's far-fetched tales could meander for hours.

"The countess's hands are not scarred," argued Lord Bentley, approaching with a glass of sherry. He set it reverently at her elbow, which was also covered by her glove. "They are as lovely as the rest of her."

"Thank you, kind sir," said the white lady and gave him a gracious nod.

"You're most welcome, my dear. Is there anything else I might fetch for you?"

He looked like nothing so much as a panting hound, with his drooping eyes and puffy jowls, O'Banyon thought uncharitably. Another minute and he'd be licking her slippers and begging to go out.

Tightening his fingers on his fluted glass, Banyon reminded himself to relax. It wasn't as if the saggy little duke was asking her to bear his children. Although it was entirely possible he was considering the possibility. The hair on the back of the Irishman's neck rose eerily at the mere thought. God's balls. What the devil was wrong with him, he wondered and trumped the others' cards.

He had not played whist before a few months ago. Indeed, he did not believe it had been imagined when last he found sport in the cities of his homeland, but he had a gift for games of chance. Hiltsglen had once suggested it was a devil's gift, and indeed, it had not gained him a host of merry well-wishers and lasting friendships, but he had scars aplenty.

"No thank you, my lord," said the countess. "But you are indeed kind to offer."

"Not at all," said the duke and beaming, drew away to gaze at her from afar.

The evening wore on. O'Banyon won a small fortune and tucked it into the pocket of his wine-colored waistcoat, but it was the gained knowledge he truly cherished, the wee tidbits of information that thrilled him.

The white countess, for instance, did not like sherry. Oh, she sipped it from time to time but only for the sake of politeness.

She favored her left hand, holding her cards in her right.

She had a fondness for the oddly named delicacy called whim wham. He could tell by her expression, though she ate it slowly, by careful spoonfuls and did not indulge in a second.

She did not choose her friends for their handsome countenances. Indeed, the people she seemed to find most amusing bordered on homely—a depth of character which did not make O'Banyon feel particularly secure. There was the countess of Anglehill, with her long, equine features, Lady Trulane whose teeth were slanted and her complexion poor, Mr. Winters, whose face was round and red. On the other hand, Anglehill was as smart as a whip, Trulane had a thousand ready stories, and Winters's wit was as sharp as a High-lander's blade.

And while Antoinette seemed to appreciate each of them, she was polite but formal with one and all. Except, he mused, thinking back, with that quiet ray of sunshine called Sibylla. He had sensed something between her and the girl that he'd not witnessed elsewhere. Something gentle and comfortable, for he had been afforded the op-portunity to observe her in the conservatory for some time before she'd noticed him.

And when she had, she had straightened her back just the slightest degree, as if to add height, as if to challenge the world to see beneath her lovely façade, just as she did now when their eyes met with a velvet clash.

"So you are renting Lady Farrell's winter home?"

O'Banyon turned his attention back to Cecilia.

He had moved from the card table, and though the widow was comely and well endowed, his gaze continued to stray toward the countess in white.

"Aye," he said, disciplining himself to focus on the woman before him. "She was kind enough to allow me its use while I am yet in London."

Mrs. Murray smiled knowingly and took another sip of her claret. Beneath the rouge that brightened her cheeks, there was a ruddy flush, suggesting that this glass was not her first. "I rather doubt it was kindness that caused her generosity," she said.

He resisted glancing toward the countess, though he longed to do so. "And why might that be?"

She watched him with heavy-lidded eyes. "Evelyn's husband is all of fifteen years her senior."

He cocked his head. "I dunna ken what that might have to do with an empty manor house."

"Oh come now, sir," she chided coyly. "I'm sure you know exactly what I mean."

He grinned. "Mayhap," he admitted and reaching for her hand, kissed it, "but that does na mean I've na wish to hear the words said aloud."

She laughed, and in that second he felt the countess's attention flicker toward him. Lightning sizzled along his nerve endings for an instant and then she turned away, distractedly responding to another.

"Then I shall say it," murmured Cecilia. "You are an ungodly attractive man, and any woman who is a real woman would want you in her bed."

He raised a brow.

"Have I shocked you, sir?"

"Can ye na see me blush?"

"No," she said. "Where do you keep it?"

He chuckled. "Ye flatter me, lass."

"Enough to tempt you?"

"Me lady," he said, smiling down at her. "Surely ye ken, I've been tempted from the first moment we met."

"Indeed?" she asked, peering at him through her kohl-darkened lashes.

He meant to answer. In fact, it defied a cardinal rule of flirtation to do otherwise, but at that moment Antoinette laughed. He felt the tingle of the sound in his very soul, and he could not help but turn toward her. Could not help but wonder if something honestly amused her or if, perhaps, she was merely playing the social games of the elite.

Why?

Aye, she was wealthy and well bred. But the same could be said of any of the others who stood in the knot round about her, yet none of them seemed to feel the need to present such a flawless face to the world. Indeed none—

"She would not generate much heat."

O'Banyon turned his attention abruptly back to the handsome widow before him. "Yer pardon?" he said.

Her eyelids were low over her sultry, bedroom eyes. "The countess," she explained.

He canted his head and kept his idiotically chivalrous instincts at bay. The lady in question did not need him to come to her protection—verbal or physical. And sometimes he thought that terrible sad, for he would like nothing better than to lift a sword between her and danger, to right the wrongs he knew in his soul had been done to her, to feel the silver ecstasy of her smile for himself alone.

"She is *not* a real woman," added Murray coolly.

"Then English inventions have advanced even further than I ken," he countered.

She blinked, then laughed when she caught his meaning. "I do not mean she is a machine," she said. "Indeed, I believe she is flesh and blood, I am only saying she would not appreciate a man of your . . ." Skimming him with her lazy eyes, she let her attention rest on his crotch for a moment. "Charms."

He gave her a smile, though the expression felt somewhat tight. Which was foolish indeed, for there was little he enjoyed more than blatant sexual flattery. "And why is that me lady?" he asked.

"She is . . ." She shrugged and shook her head at the same time, a feat that seemed almost more than she could manage in her current state. If he were a gentleman he would offer to fetch her less potent libations. He did not. "Odd," she finished.

"Odd?" he repeated.

"Have you not noticed?" She drank again. "There's something almost . . ." She faked a shiver. "Unearthly about her."

"I've na noticed." It was a lie, of course, but he doubted she meant the words as he did.

She leaned close in conspiratorial zeal. "That's because you're a man."

" 'Tis glad I am ye think so."

She chuckled low in her throat. "Oh, I do indeed," she said, "but like all men, you are entranced by a pretty face and a comely figure."

"I would like to argue but I fear it would only make me sound addlepated."

She grinned lopsidedly. "It is said she has never willingly touched another living soul."

"Ye jest."

" 'Tis true," she vowed.

"Her husband must have been sore disappointed."

Her brows rose sharply. "Not so disappointed as when she killed him, I'd wager."

Something clutched at his heart. O'Banyon squeezed his hands to fists. "I dunna mean to find fault, me lady," he said, "but 'tis such rumors what—"

"Surely you knew—he died the day after their nuptials." She peered at him over the edge of her glass. "The day after she inherited his considerable fortune."

He eased his hands open, calming himself. "I was told he was quite aged."

She laughed. "So you've been asking about her have you? I'm not surprised. But did you know that the old man's natural heir was left with nothing?"

"He had a son?"

"Still does, I would assume Edgar by name. He was left destitute. Not a copper farthing to his name. She inherited everything. Even the ancestral home."

"I dunna think—"

"Well maybe you don't, Sir O'Banyon. But it's true. Ask anyone. Ask *her*. The estate she inhabits in gay Paris should have gone to the old man's rightful heir."

"Then why did it na?"

She shrugged. Her shoulders were pearly white and all but bare above the gathered bodice of her cherry-blossom gown. Her bosoms were plump and fetchingly displayed. O'Banyon could not possibly have cared less.

"Because she bewitched him," she said.

He remained very still, keeping his ancient instincts at bay. All was well. Surely Hiltsglen was right. The age of darkness was behind them. Black magic was a thing from years long past. "Would the crown na interfere with such a transfer?" he asked, keeping his voice steady.

"It is said that she hexed the emperor himself."

"Methinks—"

"Mrs. Murray," called a gentleman, hurrying toward them. He was dressed in a frock coat and buff trousers and teetered dangerously on pink high-heeled shoes. O'Banyon did his best not to stare. "Will you not grace us with a song? You've such a lovely voice."

"Why thank you ever so, Lord Gibbons," she replied, turning away and spreading her fingers across the expanse of her carefully exposed breasts. "I am deeply flattered and shall be with you shortly." She smiled at the speaker, then at O'Banyon. Lord Gibbons bowed and wobbled off.

"Honestly," she said, lowering her voice to its usual husky timbre, "my singing is far from singular. But my other qualities . . ." She squeezed her arms together. Her impressive bosom swelled forth. "Are quite spectacular. Won't you come and . . ." She flexed again. "Watch me sing?"

He forced a smile. "I fear ye would doubt me true sex if I did na," he said and watched as she turned away, laughing.

But he was already listening to another conversation.

". . . Thursday next," said Lady Trulane. She stood between the baroness of Hendershire and Antoinette—the countess of Colline, the white lady, the enchantress. Was she also a murderer, casting dark spells under a waxing moon, floating about her garden like an ethereal ghost?

"You must come, Amelia," Lady Trulane continued, addressing the baroness. "The waters' miraculous powers are extolled as far as Dhaka. Why the naib nazim, Hashmat Jang, requested a barrel imported for his bad knees. Bath may be just what you need."

O'Banyon made his way across the room, keeping his strides steady, though he longed to rush even as he longed to escape. He would be a fool indeed to cross paths with a sorceress yet again. Had he not learned his lessons many ages past? Had he not paid the price?

But he was being foolishly skittish. The golden lady of Inglewaer had been known for her dark seductions, while the white countess was . . . Well . . . she wasn't truly known a'tall. Indeed, she seemed to keep herself carefully distant even as she stood well within reach. 'Twas a distance he could not seem to accept.

"In Dublin," he said, approaching the cluster of friends with feigned casualness. "We too have a marvelous cure for any sort of ailment."

"Oh?" said Lady Hendershire, turning to him with a smile. She was small and young and congenial.

Lady Trulane's dog growled low in its throat. She patted it soundly. "And what is that?" she asked.

"Whisky," O'Banyon said and raised his glass in a silent salute.

The women laughed in unison.

"I believe I've heard of it," said the elder of the two.

"There be times when we use it as a kind of preventative medicine," he added, "lest there be trouble brewing."

Lady Colline turned her gaze from O'Banyon to the baroness, her expression serene. If his presence disturbed her calm the least whit, she did not show it in her eyes. "And what troubles you, Amelia?"

From some distance away, Mrs. Murray began a deep-throated rendition of a song O'Banyon could not quite identify. The sound was husky and pleasing, or would have been, had he not been absorbed by the merest breath the countess took. God help him.

"Nothing really," answered Lady Hendershire. "I simply . . . Well . . ." The girl skipped her gaze to O'Banyon and away, blushing prettily. "It's simply that . . . Well, my Edward and I do so long for children."

"Oh." The countess went silent, but did not turn toward O'Banyon. He wondered if she were embarrassed by the topic of birth and breeding, if, beneath her bonny, well-polished exterior, she was squirming at his nearness. "Well, I would not worry. It is yet early," she said. "You've been married such a short while. Less than six months, isn't it?"

"Five months and three days."

"Long enough," said Lady Trulane. "Why, the princess of Kohary conceived on the very day of her wedding." She scowled. "Or so her father would have us believe."

"We do so hope for children," Amelia mourned again.

"Yes, but surely you can wait another few . . . minutes?" said the countess.

The others chuckled and nodded agreement.

" 'Tis not a laughing matter," said Amelia, though she was, in fact, laughing herself. "There might be any number of complications that I've no idea of. I think I *shall* take the waters. I'll speak to my Edward this very eve about it."

"How grand," said Trulane, stroking her glaring pet. "We shall have quite a merry time I'm certain. And what of you, countess? Might you like to accompany us?"

It seemed as if O'Banyon could sense her drawing back the instant they turned toward her, could watch her recoil even though she didn't move. Couldn't the others feel it? Didn't they realize her fragile uncertainty? "Thank you," she said, "but I think not. Though I've heard the waters are a marvel."

"You've heard?" asked Lady Hendershire.

"You mean to say you've not been?" gasped the aging baroness.

"I fear I've not had the opportunity."

"Well, you must come. You must. When I was in Byelorussia, Wit-Rusland, as the Dutch call it, I spent many lovely hours hiking with Mr. Todar Kramer, the great architect of Minsk." She fell silent for an instant, shaking her head. "He was quite an amazing man—could tie seventeen different types of knots. Seventeen. Astounding really. But be that as it may, on one particularly grueling hike I slipped on the mountainside and sprained my ankle. *Madame Truheart*, said Mr. Kramer. He always called me Truheart. I've no idea why. He said, *You must return to Bath and soak up those wondrous waters.* And so I did, and in all honesty, my ankle did not heal one whit until—"

"Yes indeed," agreed Mr. Winters, strolling up to join the conversation. "And when I was exploring the moon with the deputy of Istanbul just this past week, I injured my wrist something grievous. 'Twas a right bugger to heal. Until my marvelous visit to Bath."

There was stunned silence followed by laughter.

"Can I surmise you've not been there either?" asked Lady Trulane wryly.

"In actuality I have," admitted Winters. "But I've been wanting to tell the moon story for quite some time. 'Tis not an easy jest to wedge into a conversation."

"Well, you should come also," she said, though her tone was disapproving as she stroked her sulking hound, "so that you will no longer scoff."

"But I like to scoff."

"So I've noticed."

"Oh, you should come," said the baroness. "And you, Lady Colline. I would dearly love it if you would accompany us. I become overwrought at times, and you have such a soothing effect."

"That is very kind of you to say, Amelia. But I am really quite busy."

"What with?" Winters asked. "The harvest? Tending the dairy? Mowing the meadow?"

"Hush now," Amelia said and laughed as she turned back to the countess. "I know you've much to see to. But you must come. You are always so perfectly serene. It seems as though nothing can go wrong if you are near."

"You expect something to go amiss?" Antoinette's voice was, as always, perfectly modulated, as dulcet as an evening dove's, but there was something unsettled in her eyes.

"No. Of course not. And it's silly I know, but travel makes me tense, and my Edward thinks perhaps that is part of my . . ." She shifted her gaze shyly to Mr. Winters. "Problem."

"I would love to. Truly," said the countess. "But I fear my schedule is such that—"

"Do say you'll come," Amelia begged and after a moment Antoinette acquiesced.

"Very well then, if it means such a great deal to you. I shall look forward to it."

"How delightful. And you must accompany us too," Amelia said, turning to O'Banyon. "My Edward would dearly love to have another man with which to converse. As much as he adores the company of women, he sometimes misses masculine camaraderie when visiting the waters."

"I have oft thought Englishmen were peculiar,"

O'Banyon said. "But never more than now. This place called Bath, is it somewhere near the depths of hell?"

"What? No. Whyever—"

"I can think of no other reason he would avoid the exclusive company of the fairer sex."

"Surely you've visited the waters," said Lady Trulane, but O'Banyon shook his head.

"Then you must do so with us. We leave on Thursday next."

" 'Tis kind of ye to ask," he said. "But I've na wish to horn me way into such elegant company."

"Horn yer way . . ." She chuckled at his choice of words. "Don't be absurd. As I once told the czar, a handsome man can never—"

But suddenly the music stopped. Someone gasped from the adjoining room. The house went eerily silent, then, "Is she quite well?"

"Give her room!"

"Mrs. Murray!"

A good score of people rushed toward the music room, most of Antoinette's party included. The doorway was jammed tight with onlookers.

"Fetch her some water," ordered an elderly voice. "There's a good lad."

"My dear, are you quite well?"

There was a weak murmur. Voices began to pick up, lush at the unexpected excitement.

"Can you sit up?"

Another murmur. More voices chiming in, happy as Christmas to have witnessed such a scene.

"That's better then."

A scrawny lad with straw-blond hair pressed past, sloshing water as he went.

"I'm fine," said Mrs. Murray in her husky strain. "Perfectly fine. How very embarrassing."

Voices swelled back to full volume.

O'Banyon turned toward the white countess. "I did na ken these house parties would be so exhilarating."

"Oh yes," she said. "Once the Regent himself became sick in Lady DeVille's potted palms. I've never seen the *ton* happier."

He watched her closely. "We are all just moments from becoming the beasts that lurk within."

"Are we?"

"Except for yer bonny self, of course," he said. "Tell me, lass, why are ye forever so verra controlled?"

She gave him a cool smile. "Perhaps I don't care to live in the woods with the rest of the pack."

"Ahh." He smiled, for simply being near her made him feel joyously alive. "Then mayhap ye'd agree to ride with me in the open country."

She drew back slightly. "I've no idea how you jumped to such a distant subject, sir."

"It did indeed take a bit of clever maneuvering," he said, moving slightly closer, "but the truth is this, lass, you intrigue me like none other."

"Do I?"

"Aye."

"And so you hope to win my heart?"

"Nay indeed," he said. "I wish only to spend enough time with ye so that I may discover your irritating habits and be happy to see ye gone."

She raised an elegant brow and stared at him in silence, but there was laughter in her eyes. He found that he longed quite fervently to hear it spill from her lips, to see her outlandishly happy. "And how long do you think that might take?"

"That depends entirely on ye, lass. Mayhap we'd best spend a great many hours together so that we might hasten the process."

"But, my good sir," she said, her expression perfectly solemn, "I tire of you already."

He laughed out loud and leaned closer. "That is because ye have *na* spent enough time with me."

"Is it?"

"Most certainly. Ride with me, lass," he said, holding her gaze, "and I will try to dislike ye as soon as ever I can."

"Well, here is something to give you a start," she said. "I do not ride."

He drew back slightly, surprised, though he was

not exactly sure why. Mayhap it was because all of London seemed wild for their handsome riding horses. Or perhaps it was because of the way his own bad-tempered beast had been soothed by her presence. "You jest," he said.

"Rarely."

"Then ye must certainly learn."

She arched a brow at him. "To jest?"

"To ride," he corrected.

"I think not."

"But consider this, lass," he said, leaning toward her with conspiratorial earnestness. "If, on the night your cob was injured, ye had been able to ride a palfrey, ye would not have—"

"Palfrey?" she interrupted.

"Hack," he corrected, remembering the colloquial term. "Had ye been able to manage a hack, ye would na have had to suffer me own loathsome presence in yer own foine carriage."

"A fine point," she conceded, "but had I not spent those . . . loathsome minutes with you, you would not have been afforded the opportunity to begin detesting me."

He shook his head once. "I fear it did little to further yer cause in that regard."

"What a shame."

"Aye, well, 'tis sure to work better next time. I've an extremely short span of attention."

"I'm certain you do, but surely there are a host of others here whom you could . . . dislike."

"None that hold me interest I fear." He moved carefully closer. "Indeed, I must confess, since seeing ye I can think of none other even—"

"Sir O'Banyon. Sir." A tall lord hustled forward, face flushed and coat stretched tight across his belly. "Ahh, there you are. It seems Mrs. Murray has taken a fall."

O'Banyon turned toward him. "That much I had gathered."

"Aye, aye. I imagine you did," breathed the lord. "A bit light-headed is all, I should hope. But she desires to go home straightaway."

"Methinks that might be wise."

"She said the two of you were neighbors of sorts, and that you would, perhaps, be kind enough to accompany her home."

For the first time in his life, O'Banyon resented a lady's request, but chivalry or something like it made him bow brusquely. "Aye," he said. "Tell her I shall be there in but a wee span of time."

The lord hurried away.

O'Banyon turned back toward the countess. "I've no wish to rush ye, me lady," he said. "But might I have an answer?"

"I'm not certain," said the countess, her back straight as a footman's lance. "But I must say I am nearly moved to tears knowing I am the Irish whelp's only interest."

There was anger in her eyes, and maybe . . . just a hint of jealousy. He almost laughed aloud with delight.

"Then I shall surely look forward to teaching ye to ride at the earliest possible opportunity," he said, and not awaiting a response, turned away.

Chapter 12

❦

"Nonsense," said Lady Trulane. She stood before the towering brick of her manor house. Four carriages stood immobile in the graveled yard, horses waiting with cock-hipped patience. "You must ride with us, countess. It would not be the same without you."

Indeed, it would not be, Antoinette thought. It would not be terrifying and stifling and dangerous. She had planned to ride with the others, had convinced herself she could do just that, but that was before she had caught her first glimpse of the Irishman.

Her hands had not been steady since, even

though he stood some distance away, seeming in earnest conversation with Sibylla, who had ridden beside her on the journey there and would travel with Whitford on the return trip.

"I would love to, of course," Antoinette said, bearing up under the gazes of her would-be companions, "but I fear there will simply be too much baggage."

The Irishman was motioning to the girl's arm. She raised it slowly, and with silent sobriety he squatted before her to clasp a simple circlet about her wrist. It looked suspiciously similar to the one he wore about his own broad arm. Who the hell told him he could give the child some strumpet's braided hair?

"Nonsense," said Trulane, snagging her back to the present. "Of course there is ample room. It's an Eddings coach. We could fit a musk ox and a dromedary in if we so desired."

"Then let's do," said Mr. Winters, nodding to his man who just then delivered his bags. "It does sound entertaining."

"Far more entertaining than myself," said the countess and forced herself to refrain from staring at the Irish mutt. But from the corner of her eye she saw Whitford place her trunk atop the giant coach.

"Oh, no. Excuse me, please," she said softly, and hurried to tell him of her change of plans.

But in that moment Sibylla wandered away and O'Banyon rose to his feet. Their gazes met across the courtyard and then he was coming toward her, his strides long and sure.

"Countess."

Her heart did a thump at the deep burr of his voice. She turned slowly, manners insisting that she do so. "Yes, Sir O'Banyon?"

"There is na need to fear," he said.

She kept her body perfectly still. "No, my good sir," she agreed. "I am certain there is not."

"Then why do ye insist on traveling alone?"

How the devil had he heard her conversation? 'Twas obvious he'd been well occupied trying to win over tiny Sibylla.

"This has naught to do with fear, sir," she said. "I am but accustomed to having things my own way."

"And yer way be alone?" he asked.

She tightened her grip on her parasol, glad to have something to occupy her hands. "Perhaps you can forgive me if I've no wish to make the others uncomfortable for the entirety of the long drive."

"Then travel with us," he said, "for surely none could be uncomfortable in yer presence."

It was a cheap compliment, most probably spoken a hundred times to a score of adoring women, and yet a despicable shiver snaked up her spine. She gritted her teeth against the potent feelings.

"Tell me, sir, were you born with that gift for flattery, or is it something you manufacture?"

He watched her for an instant and finally lifted one corner of his satyr's mouth the slightest degree.

"Ye are angry with me," he said.

She raised a single brow. Her back actually ached with her regal stance. "Whyever would you think so?"

His gaze was unblinking. "I did na share her bed."

She knew exactly and immediately what he meant, though she wished to hell she did not. "I am certain that would be welcome, and most probably surprising news to any number of women," she said. "But since I've no idea what you speak of I believe I shall—"

" 'Tis but the fact that we be neighbors that Mrs. Murray asked me to escort her home."

"Of course." Anger coursed through her. Unacceptable and foolish. "It makes perfect sense now. That is just the reason a woman of Cecelia Murray's reputation would ask you to accompany her." She turned away. "Now if you'll excuse me—"

"Ye flatter me, lass," he said.

She pivoted back, lips pursed. It had been a long while since she had been truly angry. Hard emotion was not something she dabbled in. "I am ever so happy to hear that, sir," she said. "Indeed, my poor heart is all but aflutter at the idea."

Laughter danced in his heaven-bright eyes. "I dared not hope for jealousy from such a foine lass such as yerself."

"Jealousy," she said, her tone admirably level.

"She be a handsome woman," he admitted. "Comely of face and pleasing of form, but if the truth be told, 'tis difficult for me to see another when ye are in plain view."

What would happen if she struck him? If she loosed her tight control and punched him in the nose? she wondered, then squelched the idea. It was ridiculous—lovely, but ridiculous. "But I was not . . . as you say . . . in plain view, was I Sir O'Banyon?"

"Ye were," he said, "in me own mind."

Something softened dangerously inside her, easing her tension, brightening her thoughts. But she could afford softness no more than she could anger, so she tilted her head and gave him a smile. "I'm surprised there's room in there for me, sir, what with your high opinion of yourself."

He laughed. "Travel with us," he entreated and extended a hand. " 'Twill be—"

"Non!" she said and jerked away, knowing she had spoken too quickly. *You are not some grubby street waif, snapping off garbled half sentences. You are a lady, or you shall be, fit to marry the likes of me.* "My apologies," she said. "But I cannot." *Why? Think girl.* "I fear I may find it necessary to leave Bath early and I've no wish to disturb the others' pleasure."

He watched her in silence, his expression earnest, his gaze as steady as the sun. "I'll na let ye succumb to temptation, lass," he said quietly. "Na matter how badly ye wish to."

"What?" she rasped.

He raised his brows as if startled by her fierce reaction. "I said, I'll na let meself succumb to temptation. Ye can trust me."

She stared at him. It might just be that she was losing her mind. "I would not trust you," she said, "if you were the last man in all of Christendom."

It felt as though he were looking into her very soul, and though she tried to glance away, she found she could not. "I may well be," he said softly, "for the likes of ye."

She stared at him for several hard seconds, then

turned abruptly away. "Whitford," she called, "I shall be taking my own carriage after—"

"I would sore hate to tell the others that the elegant white countess traipses about her garden in a night rail as sheer as a butterfly's wing."

She turned slowly toward him. "Tell me, Sir O'Banyon, is it true what they say of Satan? Does he indeed have horns and a lengthy forked tail?"

He laughed. "I am na the devil's servant, lass. I but long for yer company."

"No."

"Then I shall accompany *ye*," he said and took a step toward her vehicle.

She felt the blood drain from her face. She couldn't be closeted away with this man. She could barely speak to him in the open air without a desperate, idiotic longing roaring up inside her. It wasn't lust. It was more complicated than that, and simpler, and . . . good God, he was built like an ancient statue, all long hard muscles and . . . Maybe it was a little bit of lust.

"I fear that would not be seemly, sir, without a chaperone to guard my reputation," she managed.

He leaned toward her slightly. She arched back the tiniest degree.

"Neither would it be seemly if I told the others

that ye feared ye could na keep yer hands to yerself if we traveled together alone for so long a time."

"I think, sir, that you may be the first person I have hated for a very long while."

"Come." He chuckled. "They wait."

They were rolling silently on the coach road toward the west, the cushions soft beneath them, the ceiling high and vaulted, their drinks still cool from the time spent in the ice chest that had been packed along.

Antoinette sat next to the door. The broad, square windows were open wide. O'Banyon sat across from her so close they were breathing the same air, all but thinking the same roiling thoughts.

"Lady Glendowne is indeed an amazing woman," said Lady Trulane, stroking a fuzzy white dog with a tongue as long as her forearm. "There is nothing quite so happy as an Eddings coach."

"Or quite so expensive," added Winters.

"Surely with the sale of your marvelous paintings, you can afford to purchase one," said Amelia.

"Well certainly," he agreed. "That and the price of my soul would very nearly afford me this sort of luxury."

O'Banyon chuckled, but Antoinette could still feel his attention on her. Cocky bastard, she thought. Who the bloody hell did he think he was? Some enchanted gift to women?

"What of you, sir knight?" asked Lady Trulane. "Would you sell your soul for an Eddings?"

"Nay," he said, "for unlike Mr. Winters here, I fear me own soul is na worth near enough to purchase tufted seats and brass lanterns."

"Then perhaps you should have married the baroness before your large friend found her," Lord Hendershire suggested. Amelia's husband was not a handsome man, but if his moony glances toward his wife were any indication, he was as devoted as one of Lady Trulane's lap dogs.

"Alas," O'Banyon said. "I fear Hiltsglen had the unfair advantage of saving the lady's life."

Mr. Winters tsked and shook his head. "Women are oft fools for such things."

"Things like strong men who are willing to give their lives for those they love?" Lady Trulane asked.

"Aye, just that sort of thing," said Winters, shivering. "Bloody nasty mess that was, aye? How is it you know the giant Hiltsglen, O'Banyon?"

"We fought together," he said simply.

A soldier? Antoinette would never have guessed it. But maybe she was shortsighted. If she tried she could imagine the roguish Irishman in bright regimentals, but somehow it was easier still to think of him in a different kind of battle, something more elemental, wearing naught but his ancestral plaid, muscles bulging, with a notched sword in one hand as he challenged all comers. And good Christ, when had she become so girlishly fanciful?

"Truly?" Winters asked. "You don't strike me as a military man."

" 'Twas a long time past," said the Irishman. "It seems a hundred years at least."

"We did indeed battle old Bony for a long while. Did you fight under Wellington?"

For a moment something danced in the Irishman's eyes, then, "Nay," he said. "Mostly I fought for me life and the coin me sword could bring me."

A mercenary? Antoinette thought.

Lady Trulane's pet glared malevolently out from behind her mistress's arm at the Irishman. "I met Bonaparte once," she said. "Do you know he's the approximate size of a spring radish?"

"We have common antecedents," said Winters.

The company turned toward him in surprised unison.

"Surely you jest," said Lady Trulane, hating to be bested.

"Nay," he said. "My family was not always as poor as church mice, you know."

"I had no idea."

"Aye, we were once as wealthy as . . ." he paused. "Field mice."

"Well," said Lady Trulane, raising her cordial. "Here's to a reversal of fortunes then."

"Here here," said Winters and clicked his fluted crystal against the other's.

"To loving someone enough to lay down your life for her," said Lord Hendershire, raising his glass, then gazing into his bride's gentle eyes.

"To loving someone," O'Banyon agreed and let his attention flicker momentarily to Antoinette's.

She lifted her glass to her lips. It bobbled slightly between her fingers. She hated sherry. It burned like banked fire.

But so did the Irishman's eyes—burned with promise and challenge and the heady suggestion that love could indeed conquer all.

Images raced through her mind. Images of them together, firelight flickering across his skin as they shared secrets and laughter and more.

God's truth, she thought, feeling panicked, she should not have come. She should have spit in his eye and told him to tell the others whatever he wished.

But that would not have quite fit the image she had tried so desperately to convey for the past twenty some years.

She almost smiled at the thought of their

surprised expressions. The elegant Lady Colline, always refined, always controlled. Surely they would think she had lost her mind. It would almost be worth it to see the look on O'Banyon's face as spittle dripped down his damnably handsome cheeks.

But she would not be so foolish, of course.

Nay, she would remain firmly in control, quieting the tattered little girl in her soul, battling the images in her mind, living a lie.

"To life," she said and emptied her glass.

Chapter 13

꧁ ∽◦◦∽ ꧂

There was truly very little to do in the colon-
naded, moldering elegance of Bath. Very
little . . . except to watch the white lady.

In his mind, O'Banyon did not call her Lady
Colline. Nor did he call her Antoinette. For neither address quite suited her. Indeed, sometimes
it seemed to take her a moment to even recognize
the name. As if it didn't belong to her. As if she
were someone else entirely.

She sat now at a table in Spring Gardens
speaking to an elderly woman and ignoring her
sherry.

"So you've still not tested the waters?" the old

woman was saying and took another sip of her drink.

"No, I fear I have not," said Antoinette. She was dressed in a white gown shot with pearlescent strands. Her gloves extended well above her elbows, almost reaching the delicate silver tassels that hung from the center of her capped sleeves. Her eyes were shaded by the wide brim of a lacy bonnet. "Do you find them to be as spectacular as everyone suggests?"

"Well, I have bathed in Queen's Bath innumerable times and drank enough water from the Pump Room to float His Majesty's man o' war, and yet . . ." She paused long enough to drain half her libations. "I am still old. But on the other hand, I am still alive . . . I believe."

The countess smiled. "Sometimes that is the best any of us can hope for."

"True indeed," agreed the other, but suddenly her brows lowered. "Oh hell's wrath, there's my daughter," she said and draining the remainder of her liquor, hobbled to her feet. "If you'll excuse me," she said, "I go to be berated. Though how I raised a prude, I've no idea."

O'Banyon approached the countess a moment later. An old man with a gnarled staff gave him a nod and a smile, but O'Banyon barely noticed for the countess was all he could see. Setting a bottle of wine and two glasses on the table, he settled into a nearby chair, poured a measure of jewel-bright wine in each, and took a seat.

The countess raised a brow at him. "As you can see," she said, "I've not yet finished my refreshment."

"Nor shall ye," he said. "Tell me, lass, why have ye come here?"

"To Bath?"

"Aye."

" 'Tis a place of some repute."

"Oh aye," he said, "I can see ye are enjoying its rejuvenating waters."

She smiled wryly. "Perhaps I appreciate the relaxing atmosphere."

"In truth, lass, I dunna believe ye can relax."

True, to the casual observer, she might well seem content, at ease. But he was not a casual observer. He was, as Lady Anglehill had so astutely suggested, a man obsessed.

So be it.

"Whatever are you talking about?" she asked and settled back into her chair slightly, as if she were reclining to study him. 'Twas a sign of increased tension and an increased desire to prove the opposite.

He watched and wondered why. Truth be told, most women liked little better than to speak of themselves. Which was most probably also true of men, though he'd never cared enough to find out for certain. "Ye are na comfortable with these companions of yers," he observed.

"Indeed?"

"In truth, the only person you seem at ease with is the wee lass ye call Sibylla."

"I do so hate to argue, sir," she said, her voice subtly suggesting otherwise, "but you are entirely mistaken."

He smiled, loving her. "And ye dunna like sherry," he added.

She swirled the amber liquid. "Perhaps I am simply not a great believer in drunkenness."

He drew back as if shocked and offended. "Whatever do ye find amiss with drunkenness?"

"Forgive me," she said, her tone dry. "I forgot for a moment that you are Irish."

He laughed. "Well, dunna do so again."

Silence settled between them for a moment, almost comfortable, seeming so, if he did not know better.

"Tell me, lass," he said, "what be yer true name?"

She watched him, her brows rising. "Tell *me*, sir, might you be inebriated even as we speak?"

"Yer *Christian* name," he explained. "The one your mum called ye when she put ye abed for the night."

Her expression didn't change, exactly. Indeed, to another, perhaps she would have looked entirely the same. But there was a difference, a shift, though O'Banyon himself could not have said exactly what it was.

"She called me Antoinette," she said.

She was lying. Banyon could not help but wonder why. What would the countess of Colline have to hide from a lowly knight with but one fractious steed and fewer prospects?

"Yer da then," he said, watching her quietly and pretending to believe. "He must na have been so . . . distant."

"You are wrong," she assured him. "We were not particularly close, my father and myself. That is to say, he was kind enough. He simply was not lavishly demonstrative as you Irish tend to be."

Truth to tell, he simply liked to hear her speak. To watch her lips move, to feel the nimble direction of her mind. "Aye, we sloppy Irish," he said, "Na a'tall like ye stodgy French."

She shrugged the slightest degree. "My sire's uncle was the earl of Bayard."

He whistled low, still watching her.

"You are unimpressed?"

"Nay, lass. I am speechless with admiration."

"I doubt you are ever speechless," she said and lifted the sherry to her lips, but in a moment she set it back onto the table with no apparent reduction in volume.

"So then, lass, do ye have sisters?"

"No." She glanced toward the west, where the sun would be setting beyond Bath's stately columns, as if she wished to be gone from such nervous restfulness. "I was their only child."

"And the illustrious earl's nephew did not bounce ye on his knee?"

"Did I not mention he had German blood?"

"Surely he told ye frightful stories at bedtime then."

"Perhaps you don't understand the stoic Germans."

"He was yer da. Ye were a wee bonny lass, given to him like a rare gift from the heavens," he said, watching her. "I shall never understand."

She sat very still, smiling slightly, as if she found him mildly amusing. But there was something else in her eyes. Something carefully hidden. Something that had been hidden for a long while. Something that broke his heart.

"Mab," he said.

"What?" Her voice sounded hoarse suddenly. Her brows lowered the slightest degree over the lush promise of her eyes.

"I shall call ye Mab. The queen of the faeries."

She had mastered her brows; they were arched over her ever-clear eyes again, and her tone was perfectly modulated, but her right thumb jerked slightly where her hand lay on the table. "I am not a faery."

He leaned forward, studying her, trying to understand. "Then what is it aboot ye lassie?"

"Nothing. There is nothing about me." She laughed a little. The tone was light, her expression amused. Her thumb jerked again. "Nothing unusual."

"To a fool or a blind man, mayhap," he said. "But if one looks closer . . ." He did so now, gazing into her eyes, searching her soul. "Ye are magic itself. Ye are—"

But suddenly she jerked to her feet, bumping the table. The wine he'd brought spilled blood red across the linens. "I must go," she said.

"Where?"

"Where you are not," she said and fled.

'Twas less than an hour later that Antoinette stood in the waters, letting them wash, warm and restless around her. She had vowed not to do so, for she had no wish to expose herself in the flimsy dressing gown the attendant had given her. It had been all she could do to keep said attendant from stripping her bare, but she had finally convinced one and all that she was quite capable of disrobing and dressing herself. Minutes later, she had ventured unassisted into Cross Bath, refusing the bulky sedan chairs available to tote her into the spring-fed pool.

She longed desperately for her bonnet and gloves to keep the world at bay, but this seemed to be the only place the Irishman had no intention of venturing. The only place she was safe from his heaven-bright eyes and disturbing questions. Who was he? Had someone sent him? Did he know . . . things he should not know, things that must remain hidden?

"Countess," someone called.

Antoinette jerked toward the sound, chiding herself for her jittery nerves. It was only the baroness of Hendershire who approached, wading laboriously through the steaming waters.

"I am so glad you have decided to join us," said Amelia.

"Well, I could hardly travel all these many miles and fail to enjoy the reputed waters, could I?"

"Indeed not," agreed the girl. "And how do you find them?"

Confusing. Disturbing. Terrifying. She could feel emotions swirling around her like wild dervishes. "Interesting," she said. "And quite unique."

Amelia laughed. "You would have made my mother the happiest woman in all of England."

"Indeed?"

"She so wished for a perfect daughter. One who was forever tactful and elegant and beautiful."

"Then she was lucky indeed."

Amelia shook her head. " 'Tis just what I mean," she said. "You forever know the perfect thing to say. You're always perfectly groomed and perfectly—"

"My dear," called her husband, walking along the stone deck toward them. "I was worried about you."

The girl turned, her eyes immediately lit from within. Edward was a simple man, not handsome or witty or particularly charming. But if he loved his wife any more the condition might very well be fatal. Antoinette could see the adoration in his eyes.

Interesting, she thought. She herself may be perfect, but Amelia was loved.

"Worried?" The young baroness reached up, touching him as he squatted beside the pool. Antoinette watched the caress and felt her heart squeeze tight as their fingers entwined in a simple

197

caress. "I am sorry indeed. But you were sleeping so peacefully. I had no wish to wake you."

He laughed. "My apologies. I did not mean to fall asleep so—" he began, but Mr. Winters interrupted.

"What's this tripe?" he asked. "We are at Bath. Half the beauty of this place is that there is nothing to do but sleep. I do have a question for you, though, Lord Hendershire, if you've a minute."

"I'll try to stay awake," Edward promised and glanced back down to his bride. "Don't stay too long will you, my dear. The waters can be powerful, they say."

"I shall be out shortly," she vowed. Her husband moved away. Her gaze followed him. A sigh parted her lips.

"Something is amiss?" Antoinette asked.

The baroness laughed. "No. Forgive me, please. I am being foolish."

"Are you?"

"I'm just . . ." She laughed again. "As you said we've only been married a very short while. But he would make such a wonderful father."

Antoinette watched her, knowing beyond a shadow of a doubt that she should agree, draw back, stay remote. But there was wistfulness in the girl's eyes—wistfulness and hope and love. "Have you spoken with a physician?"

"Yes." She blushed slightly. "I didn't . . ." She paused. "I didn't tell my Edward. He is certain we've nothing to worry about. But . . ." She shrugged. "I suppose I'm being foolishly impatient."

"What did the doctors say?"

"They can find nothing wrong with me," she said, and scowled.

"But . . ."

The girl smiled, her expression weak. "As a child I contracted a fever. It was quite debilitating." Her brow furrowed, her soft eyes worried. "They think that may have affected my . . . feminine organs."

"Oh." Antoinette drew her hands carefully to her sides. "Well . . . I wouldn't worry. 'Tis far too early to say whether there is truly a problem. And even if there is some small difficulty, today's medicines can do wonders, I'm told."

"Yes." Amelia nodded. "Yes, I'm sure you're right," she said and flickered her gaze away. But not soon enough to hide the bright unhappiness in her eyes. "Look," she said, "Lady Trulane's dear little Cecil is doing tricks. Excuse me, if you will."

"Certainly," said Antoinette and watched the baroness tread her way through the water toward the scampering dog. But in a moment she turned away. She felt sick to her stomach, weak and pale, not up to the task of living. She could not help the girl. She could not risk it. Already she felt drained, as if the waters were taking her strength, telling her secrets. Was there nowhere safe? Nowhere quiet? She wished for nothing more than to be alone, to hide within herself and forget.

But suddenly she heard something, or felt something, or sensed something in that part of her she dare not acknowledge. Danger. She turned breathlessly, skimming the surface of the pool.

But all was well. She was safe. No one came for her. And then she saw Amelia, facedown in the water, her body sinking, her gown floating up in ethereal release, like the faeries the Irishman had mentioned.

"No!" she rasped and jerked toward the girl. But the world dragged at her feet, pulling her down. Everything had slowed to staccato dullness. She lurched forward but couldn't seem to move. Water tugged against her, swelling her sleeves, weighting down her hem. Terror squeezed her heart.

"Amelia!" she rasped and reached for her. The girl felt impossibly heavy in her hands.

Antoinette dragged her toward the surface. "Amelia!" The girl's head broke the surface. Antoinette turned her over. Her eyes were closed, her lashes dark and bent with heavy drops against her pale cheeks. "Wake up!" She slapped her face.

"Please. Wake up," she pleaded, and in that moment the baroness opened her doe-soft eyes with sleepy slowness.

"I was dreaming," she whispered. "I had a baby."

Antoinette's heart clenched, and slowly, reverently, she reached out and touched her face. "You will," she whispered.

Amelia smiled, then turned her head and coughed spasmodically, spewing water from her lungs.

And then the world erupted. People swarmed in—Amelia's husband and friends, talking, crowding, worrying, pulling the girl from the water.

Antoinette backed away, skirting the crowd. Her knees were shaking. Her arms felt as heavy as death, and the world seemed strangely blurred, but she made it to the edge. It took every ounce of her energy to drag herself from the clutching waves.

Escape. She had to escape, before—

". . . amiss?"

She managed to glance up, to lift her face to the glaring brightness of the sun. O'Banyon was squatting before her, reaching for her, his face haloed in gold, like a descending angel. She reached out, but whether to hold him back on draw him forward, she was never sure, and suddenly she was being drawn into his arms, pulled against his chest.

She shook her head, or perhaps she only attempted to do so, for she found that her head had dropped against the sun-kissed skin of his neck, and her body, draped in the sheerest of saturated fabrics, was pressed with intimate tenderness to his.

Warmth. It exuded from him. Enchanting. Forbidden.

She tried to draw away, but when she managed to glance up it seemed they were already at the lodging house.

"Where's your room?"

The question brought a surge of panic. But even that was weak. She failed to answer.

There was the slight sensation of movement, as if they were swimming, as if she were still in the pool. But the waters were as clear as Austrian crystal now and cradled her with strength and caring. And they smelled of peace and stillness and ancient places.

A noise startled her. She managed to glance up, to look around. Rare bits of reality filtered in. A bed. A man's jacket. A walking stick near the door.

"Where?" she managed.

" 'Tis me own room, lass, but ye needn't—"

Fear crushed her. Fayette kicked in wild terror and tumbled to the floor. Panic clawed at her throat, but she could not seem to right herself and lay sprawled near his bed, breathing hard, reality a swirl of chaotic colors in her mind.

"Lass, what is it? What happened?"

"Pars!" The word came out in a spitting hiss.

She saw him frown, but nothing registered, nothing was real.

"Ye needn't fear me, lass, I've na wish to—"

Glancing frantically about, she snatched up the walking stick and held it in front of her. Her arm trembled like bearded barley. "I did no wrong," she rasped.

He shook his head, approaching slowly. Abandoning the stick, she scrambled backward on hands and feet, bumping into the bed and freezing there, cowering against the mattress.

"Lass, please," he said and reached for her, but in that instant she jolted to her feet.

"Stay back!" she warned. "Or I'll kill ya. Swear by all that's holy, I will."

He watched her, his eyes somber, his body still. "Wee Mab," he murmured and reached forward. She crowded away. "Yer safe with me, lass," he murmured. His fingers touched her face.

Feeling rushed in like a burning tide, bursting her heart. She tried to fight it, tried to remain upright, but the darkness was coming for her, blowing in, swamping her, and there was nothing she could do but fall into the haunting mists.

Chapter 14

O'Banyon sat quietly, watching the white
countess awaken—an angel in repose, her
hands as soft as rose petals against the coverlet.
Her fingers twitched the slightest degree. Her
lashes fluttered, dark against her delicate skin.

He waited. He'd lit a candle and sat now in the
semi-darkness, comfortable in the flickering twi-
light, thinking, cradling a metal mug of stout in
steady hands.

And then her eyes opened, the color of hope
against her pale, flawless skin.

She lay unmoving for an instant as her senses

flared back to her and then she scowled, turned slowly and glanced at him.

He didn't move, and yet she jerked as if struck, almost sitting up, before realizing her circumstances. She was naked. After all, he could hardly have left her clothed in her sodden gown. 'Twould have been ungentlemanly.

But perhaps she did not realize his chivalrous ways, for when she settled back against the pillows, she appeared rather stiff, and her lips were pursed. Gentle color diffused her cheeks in a quiet rush. Her fingers were curled tight against the top of the blankets that covered her, but in a moment they relaxed, a silent testimonial to her careful control.

"I've no wish to seem ungrateful, sir," she said. Her tone was a husky melody, denying the sunrise blush of her cheeks. "But might I inquire as to the whereabouts of my garments?"

He couldn't help but laugh, for though he knew not what he had expected of her, this serene formality was certainly not it. Of all the women he'd disrobed, none of them had phrased such a question in quite that manner when they lay naked before him. Setting his stout aside, he leaned forward to rest his elbows on his knees. He did so slowly, cautiously, lest he frighten her, for despite her even tone and deadly steady eyes, he knew now something of her. Still, regardless of his caution, her eyes widened and though she did not draw back physically, she did so in her mind. He could feel it in the depths of his questionable soul.

"Good morningtide," he said.

"My clothes," she repeated. "Where—" But she stopped abruptly. "Morning?" she breathed.

"Some hours yet until lauds if I were to venture a guess," he said.

She shook her head. He'd loosed her hair. It was a dark, sleek contrast against the white pillow casing. Her eyes gleamed vivid green in the wayward flicker of the gilding candle's light.

"Not yet dawn," he explained.

She seemed to assimilate that information, nodded once, then forced herself to relax. Until that moment he hadn't quite known it was possible to do so.

He watched her, fascinated. Women had forever intrigued him, but there was so much more here. Mayhap she was dangerous. Mayhap she was deadly. But just now he couldn't seem to care. He wished to learn every inconsequential tidbit about her—past, present, and future. Perhaps it was a bit early for all of that, though. Perhaps for now he could be content to learn . . . say . . . her given name. "What happened, lass?" he asked. "One moment ye seemed right as daybreak and the next ye looked na stronger than the lass ye had just fished from yon waters."

She watched him in silence, as though she were well above the likes of his irritating blather—and her . . . naked as a song. He liked that in a woman.

"Lass?" he said. "I would but understand."

"As much as I would enjoy conversing with you," she began, somehow managing to purse her lips even as she spoke. "I do not think this quite the proper venue for a discussion. Perhaps, instead, you might return my clothes so that I could journey back to my own quarters."

He watched her, then nodded. "Verra well, lass," he said, "but first ye'd best have a wee bit to sustain ye." Reaching behind him, he retrieved his mug. Some hours ago, he had obtained a plate of sharp cheese and crusty bread. A knife's wooden handle protruded from the loaf, but he had not touched it, knowing she would need sustenance when she awoke.

Their gazes met and melded. There was challenge in hers. She nodded and reached for the mug, but her fingers trembled and the delicate muscles of her lithe arm quivered at that simple feat.

He drew the cup away and set it out of sight.

"As any nidget can see, ye've na more strength

than a swaddled bairn," he said. "Thus I ask again—what happened?"

A flash of irritation shone in her eyes, but only for an instant, as if she were peeved with her own weakness and just as peeved to let it show. "Perhaps 'twas the heat of the water," she said. "I've not fainted before."

"Haven't ye?"

"Absolutely not." She raised a brow. "Regardless what you might think of me, sir, I am no frail flower."

He leaned back slightly in his chair, watching her as he did so. Her cheekbones were wide and high, her jaw gently tapered, and her chin peaked. An intriguing little crease dented its center. Her eyes were sharp and green, slanted up like a curious cat's. It was not the face of a weakling, but seemed most distinctly like the kind of magical countenance one would imagine peeking from beneath an oversized fern in some distant faery glen.

"I'm unaccustomed to the heat," she said, tilting her head slightly as though she were speaking to a child found to be somewhat slow in the head.

"Ahh," he said, amused, despite himself, "the heat."

"Yes."

Perhaps it was something about his tone that

peeved her. Perhaps it was him. He couldn't tell for sure. But she was peeved. That much he knew.

"When I drew you against my chest I thought for a moment you were gone from me," he said, and found, to his surprise, that the memory yet brought with it a strange panicked clenching of his heart.

"Dead?" she asked, humor tingeing her tone. "I did not suspect you of excessive melodramatics, Sir O'Banyon."

He watched her in silence and felt himself relax marginally. She was well after all—safe and unharmed and within reach. "You were as flaccid as a spent buttercup in me hands, lass."

"And because I was . . . asleep, ye thought me dead," she said, and gave him the corner of a smile. "Perhaps, good sir, you haven't had a great deal of experience with the living. Or is it death you are unfamiliar with?"

No. Not death. He had seen its leering maw aplenty. But until she had slipped beneath the water, he had never felt quite that particular flash of undiluted panic in his soul, as if her passing would leave the world bereft of beauty, without hope or light.

Why? Why her? Why now?

And why, by all the saints, had she swooned? She looked to be in perfect health. So there had been little reason for him to assume the worst. The problem could be one of many, he supposed, even . . . His thoughts jolted to a halt. Something feral and unexpected growled in his gut like a hunting beast.

He watched her, trying hopelessly to determine her thoughts. She stared back, her gaze unwavering, like a queen of yore at the helm of her chafing army. Regal as a warrior maid. But regal warrior maids were not exempt from corruption either were they?

"If ye are breeding, lass . . ." he said, his words level as he reached casually for his stout, "you can tell me true."

Her eyes opened wide, and for a moment he thought she would jump to her feet. But she overcame the urge—whether by training or some innate quality, he could not say. "I did not know you were such a comic, sir," she said instead. "Truly, your talents are wasted short of the theater."

He shrugged. "I can but try to entertain on the vast stage of life," he said and found that his hands were gripping his mug with ferocious force. "Who be the father?"

Her face was perfectly back in order, her eyes steady, her lips suggesting just the slightest trace of amusement, as if she found him only mildly

211

interesting. "If I were . . . as you so indelicately put it . . . breeding, do you think, for one moment, that I would tell you of my circumstances?"

"I thought mayhap the bairn might need a da."

The world went absolutely silent. God's breath, what had he just said? Had he lost his questionable mind?

No one breathed. Their gazes were welded tight, neither moving, neither flickering away.

And then she laughed. Not a ladylike snicker or a girlish giggle, but a great blast of shocked amusement.

O'Banyon stared at her, watched her swan-elegant neck arch, watched her fair cheeks dimple, and anger ticked softly into his soul—yet another emotion he had rarely met.

She blinked, calming herself, but still smiling. "Just to be perfectly clear, sir," she said, "might you be offering your services as a father to my fictional unborn, or is this simply a new ploy to coerce me into sharing your bed?"

He wanted to grab her, to kiss her or shake her or . . . something. He wasn't quite sure what. And that uncertainty was different too, for he always knew what to do with women. "It may surprise ye to know, lass," he said, "but never have I found the need to coerce a maid into sharing herself. Never in all me years."

She tilted her head at him, still dimpling. "And tell me, good sir, were many of your conquests coherent at the time?"

He gritted his teeth. "Tell *me*, lass," he countered, "did yer bridegroom truly succumb to consumption or might he have simply preferred death to the sharp edge of yer tongue?"

A flash of emotion shone in her eyes for an instant, but it was gone before he could identify it, leaving her fair countenance back under careful control. "Forgive me if I've been uncharitably harsh," she said. "Perhaps in your homeland women enjoy being accused of fornication and pregnancy beyond the bonds of marriage."

He squirmed a little in his chair. Mayhap he had been something less than charming in this particular circumstance, but if the truth be told, she was driving him mad. "I was na accusing, lass," he said. "I was offering me . . ." What? What the hell had he been offering? Surely not marriage. The last few . . . centuries . . . had been confusing, but he was not addled enough to consider pledging his troth to a woman who turned his guts inside out, whose barbed tongue bit him at every turn. Not to mention the fact that she may very well be a witch! God's balls. "I was merely offering me assistance," he ended badly. "Should ye have a need."

One damned, regal brow rose again. Her lips twitched the slightest degree. "Indeed?"

"As a da," he said. "To the wee one. Na as a bed mate—lest ye misunderstand."

"I shall try to contain my burgeoning hopes then."

He scowled. "In truth, lass," he said, "there have been more than a few who thought I would make a fine da."

"Well then," she said and shrugged. "I am truly sorry."

He narrowed his eyes and tried to avoid the obvious question, but curiosity won out. "And for what do ye apologize?"

"For those wayward ladies who showed so little sense and so much optimism," she said and tugging a linen from the bed, wrapped it about her to sit on the edge of the mattress. "Now, good sir, if you will fetch me my clothes, I shall leave you to your imaginings and . . ."

"Who would ye choose then to help raise yer bairn?" he asked.

She looked for a moment as if she might spit at him. In fact, he rather wished she would. It would be no bad thing to push her past her damned cool demeanor.

"As I believe I may have mentioned, there is no child."

Was she lying? He watched her face. Her expression didn't change a whit, which made him feel utterly daft. He had no reason to think she had conceived. No reason to believe she would even share her bed with a man—any man. Mrs. Murray had said she'd never touched another living being. So why had he jumped to such an illogical conclusion?

Surely he wasn't jealous.

"Then who *would* ye choose," he asked, "if circumstances be different?"

She narrowed her eyes a little, examining him. "Might you be mad?" she asked. Her tone was conversational, without infliction or emotion and echoed a similar query in his own stuttering mind.

He remained exactly as he was, thinking that through, but he couldn't help noticing that her small, bare feet were just visible past the edge of the bed sheet. For reasons entirely unknown, he wanted nothing more than to kneel before them and take them in his hands.

Aye, he may very well be mad.

"Shall I assume ye are telling the truth then, lass?" he asked.

"In actuality, sir, I care very little what you assume." She smiled but there was the flash of heat in it, and in that instant he remembered the

215

feelings that flared through him when they touched.

"Tell me, love," he said, watching her carefully. "Why do ye do it?"

She fussed with her blankets. "Whatever are you talking about?"

Oh aye, she was bonny. But she was also lonely. He could sense that suddenly. Could see it as easily as a tangible wall. Lonely and afraid. But afraid of what?

"Mayhap ye think yerself superior to me," he said. "Mayhap ye dunna even like me. But there seems little reason to pretend ye are na attracted."

She stared at him for several breathless seconds, then laughed again. "I have heard that Irishmen are vain," she said. "Indeed . . ."

But in that moment, he reached out and touched her cheek with his fingertips.

Feelings flashed like fireflies from her skin to his. She jerked, eyes wide. He drew away.

"Do ye pretend to tell me that thus happens with every man you meet."

"I don't know what you're talking about," she said, but her voice had gone breathy. A pulse danced wildly in her delicate throat. He found he longed to touch it, to feel the life of her there where the skin was as delicate as a swan's. But he dare not frighten her more. Far better to engage her wits, to keep her talking, to learn.

"I speak of yer lust for me," he said.

"You, sir, are an arrogant boar."

"Mayhap if I kissed ye, ye would na think so," he said, but suddenly she was on her feet.

"Don't be a fool," she warned.

But she was too tempting, too seductive. He rose and stepped closer, for she called to him, pulled at him, drew him like an enchanted light in the darkness.

"Lass," he murmured and realized, rather belatedly that she had retrieved the bread knife from the loaf and was pressing it quite aggressively against the plaid that covered his groin.

"Not another step, *Irandais*," she hissed. "Or I swear, ya'll wish ya hadn't been born."

Chapter 15

❧❧

Fayette's hand shook, but she dare not lose her weapon, dare not back away.

The Irish barbarian remained exactly as he was, clothed in little but a plaid, watching her, then, "I'll na hurt ye, lass. Na this day, nor ever."

She laughed. The noise sounded hoarse and broken. "Nay, ya'll not. Not so long's I hold the knife at any rate."

"Who are ye?" he asked and made not the slightest move toward her.

She licked her lips. Lucidity settled in a cautious notch. The candle sputtered, casting light and darkness across his sculpted face and spectacular chest. His skin was a golden bronze above the rucked wool of his plaid.

Oh yes, he was beautiful, but perhaps others had been handsome. 'Tis difficult to judge a man's looks when he hopes to kill you.

"Lass?" His voice was little more than a murmured burr in the quiet room, and his expression suggested earnest concern.

She scowled. Perhaps there was no immediate danger here. Antoinette drew a careful breath. She was safe. She was well. And she was acting like a lunatic. She forced a laugh and drew the knife away. It took all of her hard-won strength to do so.

"Have you had so many naked women in your room that you do not remember my name?" she asked and sidled toward the door.

"In truth, lass, ye are the first to threaten me with me own cutlery."

"Truly?" She glanced at him from the corner of her eye, heart pounding like galloping hooves. "I'm surprised to hear it."

Silence settled uneasily into the room, then, "What just happened, wee one?"

"I believe I just . . . reminded you not to take advantage of your position."

"Ye were na yerself," he said softly. "Indeed—"

"Indeed," she interrupted, " 'tis hardly acceptable for a lady of my position to be alone in an Irish wolf's—"

"Hound's."

"Bedchamber. Now, sir, if you'll kindly hand me my clothing—"

He shook his head as if befuddled. "Na a full minute ago ye threatened me manhood with a kitchen knife, and now ye request yer garments as though this were naught but a sunny spring morn by the burn?"

She tried a smile. If felt wobbly at best. "Perhaps you spend your *sunny spring mornings by the burn* naked as a newborn, but I can assure you—"

"Ye threatened me with a kitchen knife," he repeated, exasperated.

She opened her mouth to reprimand him further, then glanced toward her hand and found it was still wrapped around the very knife of which he spoke. It shook. She pressed it to her thigh. "Perhaps apologies are in order," she said and he laughed.

"Indeed ye *should* apologize," he said. "If ye are aboot to make a threat, ye should find a more likely weapon, for 'twill surely take more than a table utensil to keep men from yer beauty if they be bound to take ye."

She stared at him. There was confusion in his

eyes. But there was more—admiration and worry and something else she could not quite identify.

"As for me, lass," he added, "I'll na lie with ye . . ." He tilted his golden head. Candlelight glistened on his hair, on his teeth, on his chest, broad and hard and liberally scared. He looked like nothing so much as some ancient warrior come to collect the spoils of war. "Not until ye be well ready."

She felt strangely breathless. How would it feel to be those spoils? To feel his hands against her skin? "I fear you may not live that long," she said, her voice cool once again.

He glanced toward her hand. "Because of the butter knife or because of yer standoffishness?" he asked.

She almost laughed, for it occurred to her suddenly that he would have no trouble disarming her. He may flirt like a court dandy, but he was built like an ancient sculpture, as hard and etched as polished granite.

"I think, perhaps, Sir O'Banyon, I am not the sort of woman you are accustomed to."

"I admit that most dunna threaten me with castration when I suggest a kiss."

She felt embarrassment flush her cheeks. "How many then?"

"What?"

"Not most," she said. "But a few."

Humor danced in his blue devil's eyes. "In truth, lass, ye are the first."

"Are you going to tell me again how women swoon and fall over themselves when you are near?"

"Mayhap I shall save that tale for a later date," he said, "as the story did na seem to impress ye overmuch."

She glanced toward the door, feeling foolish, for she too had learned to flirt, to flit away foolish hours with foolish men. But somehow she had suddenly forgotten all. Was it something about him that brought out these strange primal instincts? Or was it something else, some danger she could not quite see. "My apologies," she said. "I do not usually—"

"I dunna mind yer anger," he said, sober suddenly. " 'Tis yer fear I canna abide."

She turned her gaze fretfully toward the door again, feeling the terror well up again.

"Ye are na strong enough to best me in a foot race, lass," he said softly. "Na whilst wrapped in those linens leastways. Thus, we'd just as well sit a bit so that ye might tell me true what ye be afeared of."

"Afeared?" she asked, and tried quite desperately to imbue her tone with hauteur. She barely managed audible.

"Someone wounded ye," he said. "I but wonder who it was? And why."

She stood frozen, struggling against memories seeped in age and pain. But she drew herself straighter and pulled the sheet more tightly against her body. "No one wounded me, Irishman. I am simply not accustomed to finding myself without my clothing . . ." She gave him a single nod. "In a virtual stranger's bed chamber."

"There is na need to fear me," he repeated.

"So you have said, and I assure you, I do not. Indeed—" She stepped forward, and in that moment he did the same, and suddenly they were inches apart.

Reaching out, he slipped his hand behind her neck.

Life came to shuddering halt, trembling on a breath, and then his lips met hers. Feelings soared like loosed doves, circling wildly. Thunder clapped. Lightning struck.

He drew back.

Her neck felt strangely weak. She could barely draw a breath, could barely remain on her feet. Feelings tore at secret places inside her very soul.

As for the Irishman, he seemed temporarily stunned, his lips slightly parted, his eyes half mask.

"Lass," he murmured and reached for her again, but she managed to skitter shakily away.

"Don't touch me," she breathed.

"Is that how it feels for ye each time?"

"I don't know what you're talking about."

"Aye, ye do, love. I speak of magic."

She laughed, but the sound was wild. "You flatter yourself, sir. Just because you have a winsome face and—"

He touched her arm. Her head jerked back. Her body ached with need. 'Twas too much to ask of her. She'd been too long alone, too far from humanity and hope and light.

He drew her toward him.

"Please," someone whispered.

Was it him? Was it herself?

"Please what?" He whispered the words against her face.

Fire sung in her veins.

"What kind of magic do ye possess, lass?"

She shook her head. He touched his fingertips to her face, smoothing back her hair. Need ripped through her. She was breathing hard.

"Surely it does na always feel thus."

She licked her lips. His hand was warm and firm against the back of her neck, imprisoning her, burning her alive, making her want and need and dread.

She should run, she should scream. But he called to her, pulled at her, drew her like the doomed moth to the golden flame. She could do naught but kiss him. Naught but slant her lips against the paradise of his.

Magic engulfed them, burning on contact, throwing them high, near ripping them apart.

"Mary and Joseph," he murmured. For a moment, she almost thought he would loose her, but instead he drew her closer, so close in fact, that their thighs brushed, their bellies lay flush, one against the other.

Colors sprang alive in her head, a wild kaleidoscope of painful pleasure.

"Is this love then?" he breathed.

She watched his lips move, watched him watch her, and she kissed him again, because she could not resist, because she was weak beyond words, lost and hopeless.

It was false what they said about lightning. It did indeed strike twice. Her lips burned with it, her body trembled.

"Because I dunna . . ." He paused, looking shocked and weak and disoriented. "I dunna ken if I can survive it, lass."

"Try," she whispered and let the sheet fall away like water between them.

His gaze was like a crash of thunder on a

darkling night. Like the taste of rain against her parched lips.

"Sweet Mary," he whispered. His voice was hoarse and parched, his gaze unblinking.

Silence settled around them, hot and breathless. His nostrils flared like a wolf on a scent, like a wild beast testing the breeze, searching for its mate.

Lifting his hands with slow reverence, he smoothed them down her arms. She shivered violently in their wake and dropped her head back, closing her eyes, letting the feelings take her. When she opened them, she saw that he was watching her again, his gaze as sharp and clear as daylight.

"Hiltsglen told me 'twas like this," he said and skimmed his knuckles across her belly.

Feelings clamped up hard, curling down to her very toes.

"You discussed this," she murmured, barely able to force out the words as she reached for him, "with the Scotsman?" Her fingers trembled when she touched his chest.

He moaned deep in his throat. The sound called to the deepest part of her.

He was gritting his teeth. She slipped her hand across the hard velvet of his chest. His muscles jerked tight beneath her fingers, as if she burned him, as if he were branded by her touch. She ran her fingers down the hillocks of his ribs and for a moment the world seemed faint, but she found that her back was against the wall now and that he supported her, one hand on each side of her body, holding her still, holding her up.

She rested her head against the wall, breathing hard. Just breathing, watching him.

"You are beautiful," she whispered.

He laughed. The sound was little more than a growl of feral longing. "You think so now," he murmured, but the sound seemed broken, almost pained. His arms trembled beside her. "But if I dunna leave soon, I fear—"

"You?"

He watched her from inches away and it seemed almost that she could read his mind, could feel the thoughts unfurl inside his head.

"I do not believe you fear anything," she said and leaning forward, kissed his chest with a tenderness born of wonder.

"Lass, I must leave—"

She kissed him again. The world crumbled beneath them.

He opened his eyes slowly.

"But I fear I canna."

She ran her knuckles down his abdomen. He

quivered against her. She shivered in return. "Stop me," she pleaded.

He laughed again, his eyes wild with emotion. "Na if it kills me."

Fear trembled through her. She caught her gaze with his. "I don't want to hurt you," she breathed.

"God's truth, I would na care," he gritted and crushed her with a kiss.

The world exploded. She didn't know when their lips parted. Didn't know how he became naked, but suddenly he was, as naked as she, as beautiful as a symphony, as warm as sunlight against her skin.

"Stop me," she breathed.

"Stop *me*," he begged, but she could not, would not. She had waited a lifetime, had lived it alone, had been cautious, wise, hiding, waiting.

For what?

For this?

This moment when life exploded.

They were on the floor. It felt cool against her back. Heat flared inside her. Need reared like wild horses in her soul. Her wrists were trapped in his hands. His thighs, bunched with corded muscle, were between her own.

She moaned.

"Sweet Mary," he groaned and reared over her. She held her breath.

"Hello," someone called and pounded on the door.

Antoinette snapped in a breath. O'Banyon growled low in his throat.

"Hello. I am ever so sorry to wake you, sir. But I search for the countess." It was Mr. Winter's voice. "I fear she's gone missing."

They were staring into each other's eyes, inches apart, inches from ecstasy. *Ten* inches, to be precise.

She opened her mouth, perhaps to speak, perhaps to shush him, she didn't know, but he was already shaking his head. His single braid brushed his jaw. Something like pain showed in his expression. Something like dread.

"I am mad with worry." Winters pounded again. "Open up, sir. I must speak with you."

O'Banyon lowered his head. She could already feel his kiss, and knew beyond a shadow of a doubt that she was lost, but her lips parted at the last instant.

"Please," she whispered.

He stopped. Feelings sizzled like pitch fire along her nerve endings. The world waited in silence, and suddenly, as lithe and smooth as a hunting beast, he rose to his feet.

She lay alone on the floor. He burned her with his eyes, and she let him, let him fill himself with the sight of her. Indeed, she may have arched like a wanton feline, may have flushed beneath his heated gaze, but finally he reached down. Their hands met, fire on fire. He gritted his teeth against the pain and drew her up beside him.

His desire brushed her thigh. She felt the burn of it to the core of her being and shivered at the contact, but he was already handing over her gown, motioning her behind the door. It physically hurt to move away. Something ached deep inside when he pulled the sheet about his waist.

They stared at each other, and for one sparse second she almost flew back into his arms, but she did not. It seemed like a death march across the floor to the wall.

"O'Banyon," Winters called again.

"A moment." The Irishman's voice was deep with desire, low with impatience. Muscles bunched hard and eager along his forearm as he gripped the sheet near the rippled strength of his waist.

He yanked the door open.

Mr. Winters gasped and drew back, then laughed with nervous relief at his own skittishness. "Oh!" Antoinette could see him through the crack of the door, watched him flicker his gaze toward the candle. "You're awake."

"Aye." O'Banyon's voice, usually so glib and congenial, was rough edged and hard.

Mr. Winters glanced about. "I'm sorry to wake you. Might I come in?"

"Nay."

"Oh." He seemed immediately flustered. "I'm sorry. I didn't mean to . . . That is to say. Bad timing on my part, I'd say." He reddened.

"Is somemat amiss?"

"Yes. Yes, indeed. 'Tis the countess. Lady Trulane went to her room but she was not to be found and . . ." He stopped abruptly, his eyes going as wide as his mouth. His gaze darted to the side, and for one panicked moment Antoinette was sure he could see her, flattened as she was behind the door. "Oh dear," he said. "I . . . That is to say, I didn't realize the two of you—"

"Did you check her carriage?" asked Banyon.

Silence for a moment, then, "What?"

"The lady seemed distraught," said O'Banyon. "Mayhap she traveled home already."

Winters paused. "Umm."

"I left her in her room sometime hence."

No one spoke for several seconds.

"Then she's not . . . That is to say, you haven't . . ."

"The countess?" O'Banyon said, his voice rising a bit as if just now understanding the other's meaning. "A bonny lass, I'll admit," he said. "But a bit cool for me own tastes."

"Oh."

"Mayhap I should have stayed a spell with her, but I met an eager maid earlier in the day and—"

"Oh. Of course. Yes." Winters cleared his throat. "Then you've no idea where she might have gone off to?"

"Where is it ye've looked?"

"In truth, I came here straightaway, knowing you were the last to see her."

"I've na idea where she might be. But if ye'll wait a bit I'll ask me . . . companion."

Winters cleared his throat. "Very well. Yes. Of course. I shall wait."

O'Banyon closed the door. Antoinette stared at him, heart pounding in her throat.

He reached for her hand. She shook her head and drew her arms tight against her chest. Emotion flared in his eyes, but in a moment he nodded and turned away. She followed behind, her gown damp and chafing where she'd scraped it over her shivering skin.

"He will be gone in a matter of moments," O'Banyon murmured.

The world felt strangely surreal.

"I shall go with him," he added.

She managed a nod. He turned away before

dropping his blanket, but she could still see the plum-tight head of his pride past the muscled slope of his hip. She turned away, face burning as he wrapped his plaid about his waist.

"We shall search the stables," he whispered.

She refused to look at him.

"Go to the garden," he ordered. "Find a likely spot and settle in."

"The garden?" she breathed.

He turned with a scowl. " 'Tis the only place in all the world ye are at peace. Surely yer friends will know to look for ye there."

She could do nothing but stare at him.

He reached for her. She watched his hand, breath held, but at the last moment, he curled his fingers tight into his palm and backed away.

The very air seemed to sizzle between them, but then he was gone, leaving her weak and trembling in his wake.

Chapter 16

❧⸺❧

The journey to London seemed slow and torturous. Lady Hendershire sat close to her spouse, her face pale, her husband's worried. Pryor Winters seemed almost as concerned about the young baroness. Only Lady Trulane was her usual loquacious self, telling tales of dignitaries and statesmen she may or may not have met once upon a time.

As for O'Banyon, he sat in silence, listening distractedly to her ambitious stories as his mind spun in ever-widening circles. The white countess sat directly across from him, and yet it seemed as if a black abyss lay between them, as if he had not held her in his trembling arms only hours before. As if the world was yet as it had been before they'd touched.

O'Banyon watched as Hendershire squeezed his bride's hand and inquired quietly about her health. Amelia smiled weakly, assuring him all was well, but she was not a skilled liar. Even O'Banyon could tell that something was amiss. Each time they struck a bump, her face seemed to grow a shade paler while the hollows beneath her eyes etched deeper.

"I wish you had taken some breakfast," murmured the lanky baron.

"Please." His wife's voice was weak. "I'd rather not think of food just now."

"Perhaps it was something she ate yesterday eve," said Lady Trulane.

"Yes," agreed Winters, glancing at the countess and away. "That is probably all that is amiss."

"I must admit the collared eel looked a bit suspect," said the baroness. "Indeed, once when in Brussels I . . ."

O'Banyon let his mind shift away. Mayhap wee Amelia had indeed eaten some unfavorable tidbit, but perhaps it was something else entirely. Something inexplicable.

Black thoughts tangled in his mind.

Amelia, though small, had always seemed

healthy—always seemed lively and bright, until the countess had touched her, until the countess had pulled her from the waters. It was at that moment that Antoinette herself had become weakened. Why? Memories stormed in, midnight dark against his soul—endless loneliness, mind-bending confusion. Sorcery was real. Sorcery was evil and terrifying. Even now he felt the blackness close in around him, as if the carriage were being crushed inward, stealing his air, drowning the light. He fought against it, but it was not so simple as battling a warrior. Even with Hiltsglen, O'Banyon had been afforded some hope, some possibility of success. 'Twas sword against sword then, muscle and wit pressed to the limit in honest combat, but how could he fight what he could not see? What he could not understand?

How could he fight beauty itself? He glanced at her, his gaze hopelessly drawn against his will.

Who was this woman who drew him like a siren's song? What kind of power did she possess? Was it the usual magic controlled by a beautiful maid as Hiltsglen had suggested, or was there something more, something sinister, something he dare not contemplate. There were times he was certain she was all that was good and right with the world, when her smile overwhelmed him, when her beauty undid him. But other times . . . Perhaps more lucid times . . .

Uncertainty ate at him, gnawed at his mind until the rough roads gave way to the cobbled, gaslit streets of London.

The coach rumbled to a halt. The company disembarked, their farewells subdued in the waning light of day. Everything in O'Banyon insisted that he accompany the countess to her waiting carriage, that he question her until he learned the truth. But truth was a slippery thing, and if he knew anything, he realized he was not quite sane where she was concerned, was not able to keep his wits, to refrain from touching her, though his very life might well be forfeit.

Far better then to return alone to his own abode. To spend the night in solitary reflection. Or so he thought. But morning shed little light on the situation.

Afternoon found him restless and irritable. 'Twas said that the lads on Bond Street found some relief in pugilism, but O'Banyon did not quite trust himself to such dramatic sport. Thus, he saddled Luci and visited Hendershire's estate to inquire about the young baroness's health.

"I'm certain she will be entirely healed in a few days' time," said the baron, but his eyes looked tired, his cheeks gaunt.

They sat alone in a high-ceilinged parlor surely grand enough to house a queen. "She is eating then?" O'Banyon asked.

"Yes, yes, she eats," said the baron, then closed his eyes and turned toward the long, narrow window that overlooked the bustling thoroughfare below. "But if the truth be told, she cannot keep it in her stomach." His voice faded. "And she grows weaker by the moment." His hand shook as he wiped it across his face.

So this was the face of love, O'Banyon thought. In truth, he had no use for such anguish. Far better to enjoy the pleasures of a host of lovely lassies than to agonize over one. Yet he could not put the white countess out of his mind, could not forget the sunlight of her eyes, the silver of her laughter.

Who was she? What powers did she possess? He feared he knew, but it could not be so. Not now. Not again. But there was an unearthly pull to her, an unnerving attraction that drew at his every fiber, that left him hard and sweating in the night, fraught with frustration and unanswered desires.

He must learn the truth, before it was too late. Before he was lost again.

The cobbles clattered beneath his mount's cadenced hooves as he left Hendershire's estate.

Hyde Park was awash with polished carriages

and handsome horses, stepping lively, going no-where but round and round.

Ladies glanced his way as he pressed his steed in amongst the others. Gentlemen scowled at their partners' floundering interests. Pleasantries were exchanged. Flirtations were renewed, but the one woman he longed to see was not amidst the throng. And indeed, without her, the world seemed strangely bereft, hazy and dim as if the light of the sun had been somehow diminished.

". . . haven't seen you about for several days."

O'Banyon brought his attention back into focus. Mrs. Murray gave him an arch glance from the scarlet seat of her tilbury phaeton. The hood was folded back so that the evening sunlight shone on her carefully coifed hair and pearl ear bobs. A footman in bright livery stood at her horse's head and resolutely avoided eye contact.

"Indeed," she said. "I am not entirely certain you are here even now."

He smiled and bowed over Luci's arched neck. The mare jigged beneath him, hopefully eyeing a steed half her size. Was that the way of the world, then? To forever want what you could not have? But nay, that had never been true of him in the past. He had been happy with any number of maids. It had never been a chore to give a comely maid his undivided attention. So—

". . . elsewhere."

And damn it, she was speaking again.

"Me apologies," he said. "What say ye?"

She gave him a careful smile. "Dare I ask to where your mind has wandered, Sir Banyon?"

He leaned toward her, gathering his wits. Beneath him, Luci arched her neck and gave a girlish nicker. "Places that said aloud tend to get me face slapped," he said.

Mrs. Murray laughed and glanced through her lashes at him, not entirely unlike the longing glance the giant mare sent toward the stunted stallion.

"Intriguing. Tell me, Sir O'Banyon, are you free this afternoon? I will be hosting a small gathering at my home in Nettle Heights."

"Indeed? How small?" he asked.

She tilted her head slightly. "If you come . . . there shall be . . . let me think . . . just the two of us," she said.

It should have been an irresistible offer, but a tantalizing image was teasing his mind's eye— dark hair framing a pixie face, slanted eyes watching him with sharp-edged intellect, drawing him closer, pulling at his soul.

He felt cold sweat trickle down his spine. He straightened it with an effort. "Two be me favorite number," he said.

The lady gave him a satisfied nod then slapped the reins against her horses haunches. For a moment 'twas a race to see if her footman would regain his place at the back of her carriage. He bumped inelegantly into his seat, holding on tight as they whirred past a crested brougham and out of sight.

Though O'Banyon stayed some while in the park, the time seemed poorly spent. Dour and dissatisfied, he turned the sullen mare toward home. But it was not much later that he found himself on a quiet road a short distance from Arborhill. From a gently sloping hill framed in bracken fern and horse chestnuts, he could see the wrought-iron gates and grand entrance to the countess's estate. She was there. He could sense her presence, could feel her allure like a silken cord, drawing him in, pulling him under.

His body felt tight and hard with desire. He gritted his teeth against the temptation, almost spurred his mare forward, then, cursing, turned his mount toward Nettle Heights. The traffic blossomed, then thinned as he left the posh whips and carefully coifed ladies behind. In the heart of London, millers and cobblers earned their livings much as they had for hundreds of years. But now they rubbed shoulders with a host of perfumers and button-makers and drapers. Indeed . . .

"Sir."

O'Banyon glanced up, shaken from his dark reverie. Mr. Winters sat a blood bay gelding, watching him from but a few feet away.

"You look quite lost."

"Lost?" O'Banyon brought himself back to the present with an effort. "In thought mayhap."

"Well, you must do a fair amount of that," he said. "Thinking that is. 'Twas quite clever of you to suggest looking in the garden for the countess."

"Na clever a'tall," he countered. "I was but trying to get ye from me chambers in the quickest possible manner."

Winters laughed. "Ahh yes, I believe I owe you an apology for the ahh . . . interruption."

O'Banyon shrugged. " 'Tis said that absence but makes the heart grow warmer."

"And did it?"

"The lass was na cold," he said and refused to think of the woman with whom he had truly been engaged. The woman whom he could not forget, yet could not touch.

"I must admit that for a time I thought you were with the countess herself."

Worry jolted through O'Banyon, though he assured himself he had no particular reason to protect the lady's reputation. Indeed, 'twas entirely possible the world needed protection from her and not the other way about, and yet, despite everything, he wanted nothing more than to guard her, to hold her, to make certain all was well and safe in her world. "In truth," O'Banyon said, "I fear she has little interest in the likes of me."

Winters grinned. "Aye, well, I would not take it too much to heart, Sir. Lady Colline is . . . well . . . let us simply call her unique."

"Aye. She is that."

"Some find her cool detachment . . . unnatural. But for myself, I do not believe in such nonsense."

O'Banyon felt his muscles tense. Felt himself grow bitter cold. "What nonsense might that be?" he asked.

Winters laughed. "The stories about her . . . unusual qualities," he said. "But then, I find the aversion to touching another completely understandable. Humans are such smelly beasts. Well, I must away," he said. " 'Twas grand indeed to see you once again."

"Aye," O'Banyon agreed, but his mind was spinning as he pressed his steed into a canter. Answers. He needed answers before it was too late, before he was lost entirely.

It was only a short distance to Nettle Heights now. Mrs. Murray's aging doorman showed no expression as he invited Banyon inside. The same could not be said for the lady herself as she entered the drawing room where O'Banyon waited.

"Why, sir," she said. "I am delighted to see you have had the good taste to accept my invitation." They were alone in a chamber that outsized the entirety of the hovel he had known in his boyhood, but he failed to appreciate its grandeur, or even the periwinkle gown that displayed his hostess's bosom with such eager openness.

"Despite what some say," he countered as he assembled his thoughts and kissed her hand, "I am na completely without wits."

She smiled and dipped her gaze down the front of his form. "Or other fine qualities."

" 'Tis good to ken ye think so," he said, but he was chafing with impatience, wrapped in tempered anxiety.

"Well . . ." She took a seat and motioned for him to do the same. "I'm certain I'm not the first."

"Nay," he agreed, "but na every lass realizes me fine attributes whilst I am fully clothed."

She stared at him a moment, then threw back her head and laughed. The tone was brassy and unbecoming. He scowled at his uncharitable thoughts.

"I like a man who recognizes his gifts."

"I am fond of women who recognize them as

well," he assured her and tried to find his footing, to relax, to enjoy the moment.

She laughed again. "I admit that I was somewhat concerned that you had become interested in another."

She indicated the fragile glasses that held wine on a silver tray nearby. He took one.

"Another, me lady?" he asked.

"There have been rumors of you and the countess of Colline."

He tightened his hand on the glass. It felt cool and hard beneath his fingers. Not unlike the hilt of a fine blade. "I enjoy a good rumor as much as the next man if ye care to share," he said.

She smiled, watching him closely. " 'Tis said you have become enchanted."

He drank but did not taste the wine, for his thoughts were spinning madly. "Ye dunna look like the kind to believe in ghosts and hobgoblins, me lady."

"Then you do not find the countess . . . unusual?"

"Truth to tell . . ." He shrugged. The movement felt oddly stiff. "She shows suspicious little interest in me."

She laughed. "Oh . . ." she tsked. "You poor thing. I imagine that is unusual indeed for a man of your . . . naked charms."

245

"Aye well," he said with a tilt of his head, "she's not had an opportunity to see me charms."

"One of the few?" she asked, arching a brow at him and rising to her feet.

"Mayhap you've got the wrong impression of me," he said.

She closed the double doors that led into a cavernous ballroom. "I very much doubt it," she said, turning back. "I know men quite well."

But what did she know of the countess? "I might yet surprise ye, lass," he said, glancing up as she approached.

She shrugged as she sank to the seat beside him. "I admit, you have shown surprising good taste in coming here."

"Me thanks."

"You see . . ." She drank, nearly emptying her glass. "I think you are being modest."

"It seems rather unlikely."

"I believe the countess may very well be interested in you," she said, and, reaching out, unbuttoned his shirt.

Uncertainty tangled with worry. Desire growled low in his gut, but it felt strangely off beat, not quite right. "What would make ye believe thus?"

"As it happens, I know women quite well also."

But the countess was more than a woman. She

was light and music and hope bound up in a fragile—

He gritted his teeth and jerked his mind resolutely to the lady beside him. She was handsome and ripe and eager. Just the sort of woman he had admired for as long as he could recall.

"I am intrigued, me lady."

"As well you should be," she said and slipped her hand beneath his shirt. "Perhaps . . ." She eased her fingers across his taut muscles, but no scissor-sharp feelings sliced along his spine. No inexplicable sensations shivered across his skin. Could it be that the age-old curse had truly been broken? That the burning moments he had spent in his natural form while in the throes of passion with the countess had not been a fluke or his imagination o— "If this day goes well . . . I might introduce you to a few of my . . . friends."

She squeezed his nipple. He held his breath, concentrating, but nothing happened, no growling changes, no sharpened senses.

"I am certain any friend of yours would be a friend indeed," he intoned. Might it be that he could once again find pleasure where he would?

"Indeed." Slipping to the floor, she settled between his legs, tugged his shirt from his breeches and finished off his buttons. "Sir O'Banyon," she said, letting her gaze skim his crotch. "You may be the first man of my acquaintance who has not oversold himself."

Rising on her knees, she lapped her tongue across the muscles of his abdomen.

He sucked a breath between his teeth. "Careful, lass," he said. "Or ye'll make me blush."

She was squeezed between his thighs, her half-bare breasts pressed against the heat of his groin. "I rather doubt you even know how, sir," she said and wriggled slightly so that her bosom caressed the bare skin above his belt.

Still all seemed well. He was human. He was man, without even that preliminary tingling at the base of his skull. Slipping an arm about her back, he drew her closer, pulled her up.

Her lips met his, warm and eager. He splayed his fingers through her hair and kissed her without reserve. Full charge ahead. 'Twas now or never. He would forget the countess and her haunting eyes, would put her from his harrowed thoughts.

Mrs. Murray's breasts were soft against his chest, but she was breathing hard when she drew away. "You weren't lying," she murmured, face flushed and eyes alight. "The witch hasn't enchanted you."

She was hastily undoing his pants.

"Witch?" he breathed.

"The countess," she said.

"Witch?" he intoned rustily.

"Yes." She was tugging at his trousers. "I thought you knew."

It wasn't until that moment that he realized the truth—indeed, he *hadn't* changed. Not a'tall. He was perfectly flaccid.

"God's balls!" he growled and jerked to his feet.

She ran her gaze down his body. "Truly?"

"Me apologies," he said. "I fear I must away."

"What?" she asked, rising too.

"I must go."

"This instant?"

"Aye. Something has arisen," he said.

"That was supposed to happen."

Damn right it was. But it hadn't. And he sure as hell was going to find out why.

Chapter 17

❝What the devil have ye done?"

Antoinette jerked about, searching the darkness of her garden. "Who's there?" she asked, and though she tried to hide it, he heard the tremor in her voice. Indeed, he reveled in it, for she had every reason to feel fear.

"Ye dunna ken who I am?" he asked.

"An intruder?" she guessed. He could see her back away a cautious step, her face an alabaster cast in the moonlight.

Anger roiled through him like thunder. "Ye dunna even know?" he growled and strode forward. "When all I can think about is—" He stopped both his words and his movement, his voice softening to a low rumble. "What have ye done?"

She clasped her hands in front of her. Even in the darkness, he could see that she was fully dressed. Her gown glowed pearlescent in the moon's silvery light. Her gloves reached nearly to the sleeves that capped her delicate shoulders. "I fear I've no idea of what you speak," she said.

"I think ye do, lass." He stalked slower. She was not an adversary taken lightly. He knew that now. Mayhap he had underestimated her in the past. But no more.

"I am quite flattered by your faith in me, sir," she said. "But I fear I must disappoint—"

"I felt nothing!" he snarled.

"Whatever—"

"Mrs. Murray!"

She straightened her spine like a beleaguered squire and refused to back away another step. Damn her. Damn her and all who dabbled in the black arts.

"She is a handsome woman," he said.

"Is she?" she asked.

"Aye," he growled. "She is that. Handsome and eager, yet I could na . . ." He paused, feeling suddenly idiotic. Perhaps he should consider it a good trade. After all, he had remained in human form despite the nearness of a willing companion. But if the awful truth be told he'd far rather be a damned beast than an impotent man. "Whatever ye have done, ye shall undo it."

"If I had any idea what you were accusing me of, I would surely have an answer. But as it is, I fear I must bid you goodnight," she said and turned away.

He caught her arm.

Feelings spurred through him like an enflamed poker, jerking back his head, galvanizing his body, but he kept his grip tight on her arm.

"That," he said through gritted teeth. "That is what I accuse ye of."

She shook her head, but she was backing away again, keeping as much distance as possible between their bodies. And yet she drew at him. Even now he ached to . . .

Devil take it! He did ache! He was not impotent. He was hard. For her. Desperate for her. Aching at the first touch of his skin against her clothing.

"Release me," she hissed.

He shook his head, stunned, frightened, awed. "Release *me*," he countered.

"I don't know—"

"Aye, ye do," he said. "Ye do, lass. Ye've enchanted me. Surely ye know it."

"Are you intoxicated. I've not—"

"Aye," he said. "I am that. I'm besotted at the verra sight of ye. Broken, trapped." He drew a careful breath. Because it didn't feel like he was trapped. Indeed, it felt as if he'd been set free, turned loose to soar with the eagles. "Lie with me," he said.

Her mouth dropped open. "I beg your—"

He gritted his teeth. What the hell was wrong with him? He was the Irish hound, charming, witty, strong. "I need to feel ye against me."

"I've no wish to make trouble for you," she said, "but if you do not release me—"

"I canna," he gritted.

She stood staring at him, silent in the moon-shadowed darkness.

"Lass . . ." He calmed himself with an effort. "I dunna mean to frighten ye. Indeed, 'tis the last thing I wish to . . . Well, mayhap na the verra last. I'd rather frighten ye than . . ." He thought for a moment, but his brain did not seem to be functioning as efficiently as other parts of his body. "I canna think what would be worse. But never ye mind. Suffice it to say there be a host of things I'd wish to do with ye first."

"O'Banyon, I think—"

"Kiss ye," he said and nodded, struggling for the charm he'd once possessed. "God's balls, I need to kiss ye." Damn it all, if he could not be charming, perhaps he could manage lucid.

She was tugging at her arm, trying to break free. From him! What the devil was happening?

"Let me go," she said.

He ground his teeth. "If I do, will ye stay?"

"No!"

He scowled. "Ye should learn to lie, lass."

"Listen, O'Banyon. Go home. Sober up. If you insist, we could talk in the morning."

"Talk," he said.

"What?"

"I'd rather frighten ye than talk."

She drew a careful breath. He could hear her in the darkness and found he wanted to step close just to feel her breath against his face. Like a half-witted farm boy mooning over a blushing dairy maid.

"Well, you're in luck then," she said, her words soft and cadenced. "Because you have frightened me."

He steadied himself, tried to release her, found he truly could not. "Me apologies," he said. "I did na mean to."

"Then release me."

His fingers wouldn't move. " 'Tis like this," he began, struggling for lucidity, for normalcy, for a scrap of his old self. "Mrs. Murray invited me to her estate."

"Did she indeed?" Was the fear gone from her tone suddenly? Did it sound rather frosty? Did her body stiffen just a wee bit more?

"Aye," he said, intrigued by her tone, warmed by the potent possibilities. "She did."

"How lovely for you."

He felt himself relax a smidgeon. The raw, open emotion in her voice was like a balm to his tattered spirits. "Me thanks," he said. "I did na think ye would mind, as ye have na interest in me for yerself."

Silence fell between them. He felt her will herself to relax. He felt her fail.

"I am right, am I na?" he asked.

Quiet again, broken only by the deep-throated call of a courting bull frog.

"Lass—"

"Yes," she answered abruptly. "Of course. You are right."

He nodded, though it was not easy. "Thus I accepted her invitation and—"

"I doubt there have been more than a few score there before you."

He almost closed his eyes to the sweet sound of resentment. Instead, he concentrated hard and released her wrist, prying his fingers away with a hard, mental effort.

She stepped back, ready to flee.

255

"I did na say I would be the first, lass," he said. "Indeed, I did na say she could hold a poor candle to the blinding light of ye."

She froze on the edge of escape. "Then why did you go?" she breathed.

"Because I canna have ye."

For several seconds it seemed as though he could hear the beat of his own heart, that it thudded in unison with hers.

"Can I?" he asked.

Silence again, so deep now even the hopeful frogs dare not break it.

"No," she whispered.

He gritted his teeth. "Why?"

"Are you mad?" she breathed.

"Aye." He nodded and chanced a step toward her. She didn't retreat, but remained exactly as she was, staring up at him, eyes as wide as forever. "Aye, I think I might well be. But mayhap . . ." He reached out and touched her face. Feelings flared like Chinese fireworks, jerking his body up hard. "Mayhap ye are too," he said.

"I can't do this," she rasped, her eyes still closed with the hard burst of feelings between them. "I dare not."

"Why? What dire things might transpire, lass?" he asked and stepped closer still.

"Bad things," she whispered. "Terrible things."

"What things?"

"You cannot imagine." Her words were naught but a breath in the darkness.

He slipped his hand onto her neck, reveling in the sharp stab of feeling. "I think mayhap ye are wrong," he said. "For I can imagine quite a lot."

"Can you?"

"Aye." He brushed his thumb across her cheek and tightened himself against the burning pleasure of her skin against his. "Ye, for instance. Naked in me arms."

"O'Banyon—"

" 'Tis where ye belong, lass."

"You're wrong."

"What makes ye believe so?"

"I'm not who you think me to be."

'Twas true, of course. She was not what she seems, but somehow, just now, he could not quite bring himself to care. She was magic, so be it. " 'Tis glad I am to hear it," he said and smiled down at her. The pleasure was almost bearable now. "Because I think ye are a lady far above me own station who has na interest in the likes of an Irish hound such as meself."

Perhaps the noise she made was laughter. But it sounded sadly close to tears.

"I cannot," she said.

Bending down, he brushed his lips across hers.

Just a moment of skin against skin, and yet desire jerked up hard inside him. "Sadly," he said, "I am na above begging."

She did laugh now, breathily, shakily. "Don't beg."

"Please."

"O'Banyon—"

"I'll be the first to admit I have na pride."

"I'm sure you're mistaken."

"Nay." He shook his head and skimmed his hand down her arm. They shivered in unison. "I give it up, gladly. For the briefest touch of me skin against yers. Ye've bewitched me."

"Don't say that," she hissed.

"I must, for 'tis the truth. I fear it may be love."

"No."

"Aye."

"Don't love me, O'Banyon," she breathed.

"I would rather not."

"Bad things will happen."

"Shall I turn into a hunting beast what prowls the shadows by moonlight?"

"What?"

Nothing mattered. Nothing but her, the quick bend of her wit, the bright flare of her voice. "What things?" he asked, but she was shaking her head.

"Leave."

"I canna."

"You can and you must. Before more than your pride is wounded."

"Do ye threaten me, lass?" he asked.

"Yes." She jerked from his grasp. "Yes, I do. Leave now, before it's too late."

"For what?"

"For you. We were not meant to be."

"I think ye be wrong. I think ye be the verra reason I arrived here in this time. Indeed, not in all me days has anything felt so right. So—"

"I'm to wed another."

His world jerked to a halt. "What?"

" 'Tis true," she said.

He shook his head.

"I'll admit you're . . ." She breathed a laugh. "You're more pleasing to look upon than Lord Bentley."

"Lord Bentley."

"But he *is* a duke."

He reached out and touched her face. Joy singed his fingertips. He drew back carefully, lest he combust. "You would give up this magic for a title?"

She backed away. "I would give this up for a song," she snapped.

"Nay!" he said and grabbed her arm.

"Let me go!" Her voice was shrill.

"I canna, lass. This is na something ye find every day. Believe this—"

"Yes it is!" She jerked from his grip. "Every day, with every man."

He shook his head.

"They beg for my attention. For my touch. For my—"

"And ye give it?"

Silence.

"Do ye give it?"

"Yes," she said. "When it suits me."

Anger roared inside him, ripping him open, tearing him apart. "Ye lie."

She laughed. "You wish it were so, *Irandais*, but I will marry another."

"Nay," he said and reached for her, but she jerked away and suddenly she was spinning about and racing through the garden. He gave chase. She screamed.

And then he felt it. The change, snarling through him, bursting free. Feral strength. Wild inhibitions. Shadows lightened. Shapes about him seemed to grow and change.

A noise rang out. Pain ripped through him. He snarled in answer. The countess had disappeared beneath the arbor.

Another took her place. Whitford mayhap. He stood, pistol raised. O'Banyon grinned. 'Twas simply a frail mortal. So easily killed. He gathered his strength, ready to pounce.

"Please." Her plea was like a silent prayer in his soul, but he heard it. He felt it like a sword through his heart, but there was little he could do, for the change was complete. The wolf had come.

Chapter 18

O'Banyon awoke in his bed chamber, groggy, achy, disoriented.

What had happened? Pieces of reality floated back amidst the flotsam of uncertainty. He had gone to Arborhill. That much he knew. He had gone because he could not resist. He was drawn to her, pulled against his will. And she had been there, as fragile as a winter rose, as lovely as the dawn, but with an icy briskness that fascinated him and drew him and scared him to death.

He had gone to ask questions, to demand answers, to clear some of the muck from his head.

He closed his eyes. The muck was still there, only muckier. They had argued. He remembered that and then—

Dear God!

He sat upright in bed.

Pain ripped through his biceps. He glanced down. A bloody furrow had been plowed across the flesh of his upper arm.

Noise exploded in his head. He remembered the sound of a gunshot, but 'twas the memory of their argument that kept him frozen as he was, rigid with terror.

What had happened? Was she well? Was she safe?

Questions stormed through his mind. Answers dragged behind, recalcitrant, groggy.

Bolting out of bed, he was dressed in a matter of moments, was out the door seconds later, his body tense with keeling, ripping fear.

Two carriages were parked on the cobbled boulevard outside Arborhill. O'Banyon wrapped Luci's reins through an iron ring and strode up the walkway. No one answered at his knock. He pushed the door open and paced inside, guts cramped.

"Oh." Mistress Catrill stopped her scurrying pace as she burst into the towering vestibule. "My lord. I suspect you've heard the news."

His stomach yanked up tight. Fear, like bitter acid, ate his innards. "News?"

"Poor thing. Poor thing." She shook her head, distraught and mumbling.

He felt sick. Sick and weak. "What happened?"

"Never 'urt a living soul in all 'er life. It's not right. What's the world coming to?"

"Where is she?" he growled.

"Worser times, that I'll say. She didn't 'ave no—"

O'Banyon grabbed her arms. "Where the devil is she?"

The old woman's mouth fell open, but she nodded sideways, her eyes wide with fear.

It shamed him that it took a moment to gather his nerve, to turn, to stride down the hall, his boot heels ringing like a death knell against the marble tiles.

The door opened beneath his hand. A bed stood against the opposite wall. The blankets were pristine white, the pillows plump, and across the snowy linen dark hair was spread like spun silk. But the face—

He almost hit his knees, almost collapsed there in the doorway, for the face was damaged beyond recognition.

"Jesus God!" The words rasped forth as if torn from him by claws.

The maid's eyes were swollen shut. A jagged,

angry gash ran from her brow to her jaw, and her lips . . . those lovely, bowed lips were split open and weeping.

He clenched his fists and forced himself inside, one painful step at a time. Sickness curdled his stomach. Horror blurred his thoughts. No. It couldn't be. He couldn't have—

"O'Banyon."

His mind jolted to a halt. He held his breath and turned slowly. And she was there. The white countess. As lovely as a song, her breathtaking face somber, her gloved hands clasped in front of her immaculate gown.

"Lass." He was barely able to breathe the word. "Ye are well."

She stood very straight, far back from the bed. "Why have you come?"

He shook his head. "I worried . . . I thought—" He turned toward the bed. "Who—" But then he knew. 'Twas the pixie girl with the grubby face and lightning quick eyes. The pixie girl what had graced him with a smile reserved for so few. "Sibylla," he breathed.

Antoinette stood perfectly still, her hands clasped tight. "Word travels quickly in this city, I see."

"What happened?" It took all his strength to voice the words, for he did not truly wish to know.

The countess's face was all but expressionless, but if one was obsessed enough, if one had studied her long enough, perhaps he could see the spark of something in her eyes. Anger? Blame?

"I do not know," she said. "Doctor Lambert believes she may have been attacked by an animal."

"I may be mistaken," said the doctor and rose from his chair in the corner. It was not until that moment that O'Banyon realized there was another present. He was narrow and short with a balding head that he shook morosely. "The wounds are . . ." He shrugged. "Frankly, they are quite baffling. There are gashes, of course, but there are also—"

"What kind of animal?" O'Banyon's voice was barely audible to his own ears.

The doctor scowled. "That's impossible to say. In fact—"

"Might it have been a wolf?"

"A wolf?" The man studied him quizzically. "This time of year? And so close to the city?"

O'Banyon waited, breath held, head pounding.

"I find it highly unlikely that such an animal would have ventured this close to man. In fact I wonder . . ." He paused, still scowling as he turned toward the white countess. "Indeed, my lady, I must ask, might one of your other servants have attacked her?"

Silence echoed in the room.

"Understand me," he continued. "I admire you for taking these people into your home. Truly I do. I only wish I had the opportunity to do the same, but I often find that ladies of your quality are too . . ." He smiled, pulling his lips back from over-large teeth. "Naïve. And sometimes—"

"You think me naïve, doctor?" Her expression was perfectly placid, but her eyes were bright. With what emotion?

"Perhaps naïve is the wrong word. Trusting, then. Maybe you are too trusting." He lifted a tool from the chair. Black tubes dangled from his hand. "I couldn't help but notice your footman."

She didn't even blink as she watched him.

"What caused his deformities, do you know?" he asked.

"No," she said, and bending slightly, lifted a Bible and a water glass from the nearby table. "We've not discussed it."

He nodded. "I do hate to say it, but sometimes deformed features hide a mind just as damaged. Might he have attacked—"

"No." The countess's voice was firm and quiet.

"You may be—"

"No," she repeated.

The doctor pursed his lips. "Very well then." He tucked his gadget into a leather bag that sat on a nearby console and glanced up. "Might the wounds be self-inflicted?"

"What?" The countess's question was barely a breath in the stillness of the room.

"Sometimes this sort of child . . ." He lifted a hand toward the bed and cleared his throat. "Sometimes they've done things . . ." He shook his head.

"Things?" she repeated.

"She has . . ." He cleared his throat again. "*Had*," he corrected. "She had a sweetness to her face, but as I am certain you're aware, a lovely countenance can hide a host of sins."

She lifted her chin the slightest degree.

The doctor furrowed his brow as if wrestling to convey reason to a lesser species. "As much as it pains me to say it, sometimes people are struck dumb for a reason."

"So you think she is being punished for her sins, doctor?"

"Perhaps." He glanced toward the bed, nodding. "Perhaps she has done evil. In the past, I mean. All in the past. Then, you, in your . . . innocence . . ." He gave her a preening smile. "Take her in. She sees your goodness, but the evil is still in her. And in her soul she wants to do evil again. So she is torn, you see. Torn between right and wrong. A war of sorts . . ." He made a tugging motion with his knotty hands. "Until finally—"

"What the devil be ye talkin' aboot?" O'Banyon asked and stepped abruptly forward. "She be only a bairn with a bairn's—" But in that instant the countess moved between them.

"Thank you for your assistance, doctor," she said.

"If you like I could stay and—"

"No." She lifted the Bible, indicating the door. "I'm certain you've got important duties elsewhere."

"Very well then." His tone was snooty. He bent, lifted his bag from the console. "I am sorry for your loss."

"Loss?"

"She'll not live," he said and strode out the door. "Not through the night."

The world went silent but for the brisk, offended fall of his footsteps.

O'Banyon turned toward the bed. The girl lay unmoving. It took him a moment to find his voice. "Her face is broken, aye," he said, "but I've seen such things heal in the past. Surely—"

"There is damage within." Antoinette did not turn toward him when she spoke. Neither did she tread the floor to the child's side. Instead, she looked out the window toward the garden below. "Broken bones," she said. "Deep bruising that suggests damaged organs, or so says the good doctor."

"The good doctor," he growled, turning toward her, "is a—"

"Countess!" Mr. Winters rushed into the room and stopped short, his eyes going wide as he found the girl on the bed. "Dear God, I heard it was bad, but I had no idea . . . What happened?"

She stood perfectly straight, like a princess facing an armed battalion. Like a warrior queen on a hopeless quest. "We're not entirely certain."

"Not certain? Tell me there was not an intruder in your house."

"No," she said, and for a fraction of an instant, her lips twitched with some emotion so deep she could not quite hide it behind her careful façade. "Mrs. Catrill found her in the gardens."

"Your favorite place in all the world," breathed Winters. "Thank God you were not there yourself," he said and pacing to the bed, gazed down at the small, broken face. "It's terrible. Simply horrible," he murmured, and when he turned, his eyes shone with an artist's sadness. "You've been fraught with such hardships of late. 'Tis unfair that luck should turn so sharply against you."

"I fear this is Sibylla's hardship," she said, but her eyes were empty and lost.

"You've no need to hide your true feelings, my lady," Winters said. "Not with me. I know how you cherish her." He shook his head. " 'Tis too much. Far more than you deserve. You all but drown saving our poor doomed Amelia. Your cart horse dies mysteriously, you—"

"Thank you for coming by, Mr. Winters," she said and lifted her hand again toward the door. "I do so appreciate your condolences."

"I'm a fool," he said, his eyes brighter still. "I've upset you."

"No," she denied, and indeed, her face looked perfectly serene as she stepped through the doorway ahead of them. " 'Tis simply that I need some time alone with my thoughts."

She met Winters's gaze with her own.

"Very well then," he said and nodded sadly. "I understand. Truly."

She bowed with shallow grace, and Winters left, even his footfalls sounding sad as he paced away.

The house went quiet.

She stepped back into the bedchamber, facing O'Banyon.

"My apologies," she said. "I do not mean to be a poor hostess, but I fear I am horribly tired and—"

"What will you do?" he asked.

"What?"

271

"About the wee lass," he said and watched her, every nerve strung tight as the strings of a cross-bow. "What will you do?"

"You heard the doctor," she said and turned away. "There is little I can do."

"Truly?"

"I would like you to leave," she said and faced him. Not a flicker of emotion shone in her eyes now, though her body seemed as stiff as death. "Now. If you would please."

"I did na do it," he said.

Dark brows dipped over evergreen eyes. "What?"

Pain ground at his innards. How much did she know? How much did she guess? "We argued. That much I admit. I became . . ." What had he become exactly. He didn't truly know. Would never know. Would be cursed forever, torn from the things he loved, living a half life in haze and dread. "I was angry," he rasped. "But I would na have harmed a wee sweet lass." Jesus God, his eyes burned with the idea, like that weakling Mr. Winters, brought low by the sight of the girl's torn face.

He turned his stinging gaze to the countess.

"I would na," he rasped, and hoped to God it was true.

"I believe you," she said.

"Do ye?" he rasped. He felt weak and foolish, nearly limp with hope and sorrow.

"If I did not . . . you would know it." Something deadly and bright flashed in her eyes.

He watched her, his mind roiling. "Go to her, then," he urged motioning toward the bed. "Hold her hand, lassie. Speak to her."

She didn't so much as shift her gaze in that direction. "Whatever are you talking about?"

He drew a deep breath, fighting a thousand battles on a hundred fronts. Remembering darkness and isolation so deep he could not breathe, could not hope. But the lass was wounded. What was a little witchcraft where the wee one was concerned. "She cherishes ye like none other," he breathed. "Mayhap if ye call her name, encourage her, ye can yet draw her back from the darkness. Save her."

Silence, then she laughed. The sound was brittle and hard in the dead air of the room. "I didn't imagine you to be a dreamer, Irishman."

He narrowed his eyes, trying to decipher, to understand, to see inside the mask she had so carefully constructed. "Didn't ye?" he asked, his voice quiet lest he disturb the truth.

"People die, O'Banyon," she said. "Every day. Every single day. I do not know what you think of me, but there is nothing I can do about it."

"I think ye be magic," he murmured.

Her brow furrowed abruptly as if she would crumble, as if she would fall, but in less than a heartbeat she was back in control. "You heard the doctor," she said.

"I heard the doctor is a self-important bastard what would blame a wee bairn for her own—"

From the bed, the tiniest scrap of noise arose, a rasping struggle for breath.

O'Banyon turned with a start and paced to the mattress, hands crushed to fists.

It was difficult to look at the battered face that lay there on the pillow. All but impossible to see the open wounds and remember how she had looked only hours before, pixie bright, all but glowing with life.

"Dear Jesus," he murmured. It wasn't his fault. It couldn't be, but his soul burned. He reached for her hand, pale and unscathed with his horse-hair circlet laying limp against her tender wrist.

"Lass," he called and sitting beside her, pulled her hand onto his lap. "Wake up, love. All will be well." Her broken lips were parted, but her engorged eyelids never flickered. The tiny fingers never moved in his. He brushed the bracelet gently against her arm. " 'Twas a gift to keep ye safe, little faery. But I fear—"

His voice broke. He cleared his throat. "Will ye

na come back? Na even for yer lady?" He stroked her fingers, bent against the hardened skin of his palm. "She needs ye, ye ken. Whether she knows it or nay." The smallest tic of movement seemed to jerk in her cheek. Didn't it?

"Tell her, countess," he ordered, still watching the girl's face. "Tell her," he repeated and glanced about, but the doorway was empty.

Chapter 19

❧

"What the devil be ye talkin' aboot, Irish?" Hiltsglen snarled.

"What? Are ye daft?" O'Banyon rasped and tightened his grip on his pint. The tavern where they had met was dark and barren, peopled only by themselves and an old man whose head bobbed sleepily over his brew near the fire. "Have ye heard na a word I've spoke? The wee lass be sore wounded. Knockin' at death's verra door, she be."

"Aye, that much I gather," said Hiltsglen. "But what of the rest of it? Be ye speakin' of . . ." He shook his head, glanced furtively toward the old man and continued, voice lowered to a distant

276

rumble. "Might ye be speakin' of usin' the dark arts to save her, lad?"

"Dark arts?" O'Banyon's stomach clenched at the thought. "Nay. Be ye mad? I've had me share of . . . Nay." He repeated, but in truth he did not know what depths he might plumb to relieve himself of this gnawing uncertainty and draw the countess's wee lass back into the light of day. "I but speak of someone gifted in the art of healin'. Someone what can pull her back from the brink."

Hiltsglen shook his head, brows drawn low over eyes set deep as caverns. "Mayhap she canna be helped, Irish."

"Dunna say that," O'Banyon gritted. "Dunna . . ." He paused, catching his breath, calming his heart. "Ye did na see her face, Scotsman."

"Whose face?" gritted the warrior. "The girl's or the woman's?"

Both. The lassie's, broken and bruised—the lady's, tortured in silence behind cool green eyes.

"She did na deserve these troubles, Hiltsglen," he said.

The Scotsman's scowl deepened even further. "Why come to me?"

"Because ye are the Black Celt," he snarled and curled his arm up tight. "Born to battle. Wounded upon the field. Surely in yer countless years ye met someone what could mend yer sorry hide."

"Are ye daft? A thousand seasons have come and gone since our days of war. Those we knew be long dead and gone. Friend and foe alike. Ye ken as much."

"Aye," agreed O'Banyon fiercely, not knowing what he hoped for, but hoping nonetheless. "Aye, they be gone. But what of their kin?"

"What the devil—"

"These . . . gifts," O'Banyon hissed, his stomach twisting tight. Memories of endless darkness tortured him, grinding at his soul, but he shoved them back. " 'Tis said they be passed from father to son, from mother to daughter. 'Twas the way with the golden lady, was it na?"

"Do na speak her name."

"I shall," he said, "I shall do that and more if it will—"

"Nay!" Hiltsglen growled and lowered his head like a bull set for battle. "Dunna be a fool, Irish. There be naught ye can do to change the course of—"

"I suffered the change."

Hiltsglen paused, brows low over deadly eyes. "What?"

"The night the wee lass was injured." He remained absolutely still, lest he break into a thousand sharp-edged pieces, lest he cry like a bairn at the thought of the lassie's broken countenance. "I was na meself, Hiltsglen."

A muscle twitched in the giant's granite jaw. "Ye think it was yerself what attacked—"

"Nay! Nay." He couldn't bear to hear his own thoughts said aloud. "She was a wee sprite of a girl. Bright and bonny and . . . I would na have hurt her. I would na have. I'm certain of it. But—" Words failed him. He ached in his soul.

"I am sorry," Hiltsglen rumbled. "But I dunna ken what—"

"There be the Forbes," rasped a voice.

The Celts turned as one, then started back. The sleepy old man now stood hunched beside their table, bent like a gnarled oak over his knobby staff.

"Who the devil be ye?" O'Banyon growled.

The ancient shoulders shrugged. "A friend mayhap." He skimmed his rheumy gaze to the Scotsman. "Mayhap more."

"How much did ye hear?"

"About the lassie or the beast?"

"God's breath!" O'Banyon swore, rising rapidly, but Hiltsglen drew him back down with a hand on his arm.

"What do you want, old man?"

He sighed, then hobbling forward, lowered

himself carefully into a nearby chair. "I want what every man of good heart wants, lad."

"And that would be—"

"A happy ending."

"Who the devil sent ye?" snarled O' Banyon.

"Happy ending for who?" Hiltsglen asked and the old man smiled.

"For the Celt and the hound and those of us what look after 'em."

"What do ye know, ol' man?" asked O'Banyon.

"I know a lad," he said, his wobbly voice deep and somber. "Of the clan Forbes. An ancient tribe, they be. Scattered now, and most forgot, but some what have survived still bear the gift."

"Gift?" O'Banyon's gut cranked up tight.

" 'Tis said the ol' laird's lady could heal ye with a glance, could read a man's thought afore they be formed in his head."

"God's breath!"

"He's a good lad. A bit wild, mayhap, with hard days behind him, but good in his heart," said the old man and rising, turned creakily away. "Good in his heart, I'm sure of it."

"Wait." O'Banyon jerked to his feet. "What's his name?"

But the gaffer shook his head. " 'Tis impossible to say what he be callin' himself since her death. But ye, lad . . ." He narrowed his eyes, gazing intently at the Irishman. "Ye'll recognize his ways when ye see him."

"What?" Reaching out, O'Banyon grabbed the old man's shirt. "Why are ye here? Tell me all ye ken?"

"Irish," Hiltsglen said, rising slowly. "Loose him."

"Ride yer great, cantankerous steed to the Highlands, boy. Ye shall find him there."

"Who? Where?"

"Ye might try the village of Teviotton. Or the rugged country to the north."

"Might! Who are ye? Do ye try to be rid of me? Was it ye what harmed the lass?" O'Banyon asked and shook the old man like a doll of rags, but Hiltsglen stepped up and wrapped a fist about his wrist.

"Release him."

"We do na ken who this man be," hissed O'Banyon, his gut aching with premonition. "Indeed, he may well be connected with she what cursed us at the start."

"Aye," Hiltsglen said, his voice dark and slow. "He may well be. Let him go, lad."

O'Banyon loosed his grip slowly, drew a breath slower still. "What do ye suggest, then, Hiltsglen."

"Ye've naught to do but follow yer heart, Irish."

O'Banyon winced. "The lass has verra little time." His voice was quiet, broken. "And the Highlands be vast indeed. If the ol' gaffer would but—" He gritted his teeth and turned toward the old man, but the space where he had been was empty. O'Banyon glanced about. Hiltsglen did the same, but they were the only souls in the tavern. Breaking from his trance, O'Banyon leapt toward the door, but the street was as bare as the inn had been.

Hiltsglen met him on the cobbled walkway outside the oaken door.

O'Banyon shivered. "I hate it when these things happen," he whispered, searching the shadows.

"Aye." Hiltsglen nodded, his impassive face pale in the black night. "But look to the bright side, lad, ye've still got naught but two legs."

"Ye think yerself funny, Scot?"

"Ye be the comic." Silence spilled around them. "What do ye do now, Irish?"

O'Banyon gritted his teeth against the deeds to be done. "I ride," he said.

Hiltsglen nodded again.

O'Banyon turned away, then paused. "Scotsman," he said softly, "if I dunna return—" He glanced down the cobbled street, fighting demons that should have long since been banished. "The white countess, she seems cold, but there is more to her than seen by the world. Keep—"

"I shall make certain na harm befalls her," vowed Hiltsglen. "She will be well upon yer return or I shall die in the effort to keep her so."

O'Banyon reached out. Hiltsglen met him halfway. Their hands clasped and held, bound in an oath as solemn as time.

Fatigue rode O'Banyon like a spurred horseman, heavy across his back and shoulders, cruel in its intensity, but he pushed on, heading north. The grand estates of London had long since fallen behind. Hills reared up ahead, green on green. Villages appeared, each one shabbier than the last until in the end he reached the cool cleanness of the Scottish Highlands.

Time ceased to exist here. Years had been lost in the unending sameness of the days, of reaving and weaving and wining and womanizing. Memories haunted him. Memories of mistakes made, of pain endured, of darkness, unending and intense.

But finally the Irishman sat alone in a bustling tavern. A thousand leagues and a hundred inquiries had brought him here. A group of five sat about a nearby table, well focused on their gaming, one farmer, three laborers, and a young man with seal-dark hair and eyes that spoke of secrets known and kept.

Banyon drank in silence and questioned the same, his soul tortured, his muscles tattered. The Forbes line had faltered through the centuries, that he had learned some days hence, but rumor whispered of a lad descended from the ancient laird's only daughter and a quick-tongued Irishman that went by the name of Liam.

Gut instinct told him this dark-haired boy was that lad. Gut instinct, or blind hope, or some other source he dare not contemplate, whispering quietly from the throes of insanity.

"Can I fetch ye aught else, me laird?" asked the maid that tended the inn. She was built just as a bar maid should be, soft of body and dimpled of cheek, but fatigue or some other ailment O'Banyon refused to consider, left him unstirred.

"Me thanks, lass, but nay," he said, "though I could use a moment of yer time if ye've got one to spare."

Her eyes sparkled, just as a bar maid's should. "Na much can be done in a moment," she said and pulled out a chair. "Though I'm willing to have a go, love."

He smiled. The muscles in his face felt worn. "Yonder lad," he said. "Might ye ken his name?"

She glanced to her right. The boy remained

immersed in his game. "The one with the bonny eyes?"

If he had not been so God-awful tired, he might well have told her that *he* was the one with the bonny eyes. For a moment he felt as old as the earth, beyond years, beyond reason.

"Aye," he said, "that be the one."

"He calls himself Keelan."

"Might that be his given name?"

" 'Tis impossible to say, me laird," she said and shrugged the kind of plump, pale shoulders every bar maid should have. "He does na come here oft. Only now and again for gaming and . . ." She blushed slightly, but did not glance toward the lad. ". . . other things."

He felt as old and battered and pitted as stone. He owned gloves older than this girl.

"Do ye ken what clan he hails from?"

She leaned forward. Her perfect barmaid's bosom bunched prettily. "Me apologies, me laird, but we've na spent a great deal of time discussing his lineage if ye take me meaning."

He almost sighed, like an old man long past such carnal interests. "I was told he had some gifts," he said and eyed the girl narrowly. "Some abilities."

"Oh, he does that, me laird," she said and giggled.

O'Banyon refrained from grinding his teeth. "The gift of . . . sight," he said. "And other things."

"Oh!" She gasped quietly, flitted her gaze to the boy and back. "Well, he doesn't like to talk aboot such things."

He felt himself tense. "What things might that be?"

She leaned toward him. " 'Tis rumored," she said, unblinking and wide-eyed, "there was a lass in Kirkcaldy what couldn't see. Blind her whole life she was, till she met yon Keelan. He said 'twas naught he could do, but she had heard tales and begged him merciless. So he laid his hands on her . . ." She paused, glancing furtively toward the lad and letting the tension build. " 'Tis said she now sees just as right as ye and me."

He scowled, a skeptic by necessity, perhaps. "Did ye know this girl?"

She snorted. "Nay, na I. I've na left the village. 'Twas birthed just down the lane, na half a furlong from where we sit. Big as a bag o' barley I was. Me mum said I near ripped her in twain when—"

"This tale," he said, trying to rein her back to the topic at hand. "Did ye hear it from the lad himself or—"

"From Keelan? Oh no, me laird, as I says, he likes to keep such things hush like."

O'Banyon sat in silence. Perhaps he was a fool to believe. Perhaps he was mad. Many said such gifts did na exist, but many had not lived in the days of the darkness, and many did not roam the streets in another form, with only hazy memories of the dark half-lives they lived.

And time was fleeting. It may already be too late. But he would not believe that. He would not. Too much had been done that he could not make right. This would not be one of those things. "Me thanks," he said and rising to his feet, made his way to the nearby table.

None glanced up at his approach. "Might ye be the lad called Keelan?" he asked.

The boy shifted his attention upward. His eyes were a silvery blue and as bottomless as a highland lochan. "Aye," he said. "That I am."

O'Banyon nodded and braced his legs. Luck and history suggested this may not be a simple task. "I would have a word in private with ye, lad."

"Certainly," said the other, "but as ye can see, I am in the midst of a game. Ye'll have to—"

"It canna keep," O'Banyon said and set his hand to MacGill's black handle where it protruded from his belt.

They stared at each other for a moment.

"Verra well then," said the lad, then nodded to

the others. "If ye'll excuse me for a moment . . ."

There were complaints as he rose to his feet, but no one followed them to the corner of the room.

O'Banyon spoke without preamble. "I am in need of a healer," he said.

Surprise shone like daylight in the lad's eyes. "A healer."

"Aye."

"I fear ye've been misled then, me friend," he said and glanced toward his companions. "If the truth be told, I'm na but a simple tinker what enjoys a bit of sport now and again."

" 'Tis said there was a blind maid in Kirkcaldy what ye—"

"I'd like to help ye," he said, his tone becoming brusque. "Truly I would, but—"

"There be a wee maid in London what gasps for her every breath even as we speak."

"London?"

"Aye."

The boy shook his head and turned away.

O'Banyon caught his arm and leaned close. "I've na wish to tell yer large companions that ye be cheatin', lad."

Their gazes caught and held. Silence encircled them, lean and hungry.

"Me apologies," Keelan said loudly and turned

finally toward his opponents, "but I fear I must away." Shrugging, he pulled out of O'Banyon's grasp and strode to the table where he scooped his winnings into a leather pouch.

"Ye'd na leave without giving us a chance to win our earnings back, sure," said the nearest man. He had the shoulders of a smithy, O'Banyon noticed, or maybe an ox.

O'Banyon stepped forward. He was a peaceable man by nature. A lover and a poet. But battle was poetry of sorts, was it not? "I fear this be a matter of some import," he said.

The smithy rose slowly, his head pulled into his shoulders like a recalcitrant bull's. "So be me money," he rumbled.

" 'Tis sorry I be to disturb ye," O'Banyon said.

"Aye, ye will be," said the smitty, "if ye dunna leave the lad with us."

O'Banyon spread his hands. "I've na wish to cause trouble," he said, "but young Keelan goes with me."

"The devil—" rasped the other and charged, but in that instant, O'Banyon stepped aside, grasped him by his shirt and trousers and slammed him into the far wall.

The blacksmith straightened groggily, turned, then slumped to the floor at their feet.

O'Banyon eyed the group in silence. They stared back in abject silence. "If there be other complaints, now be the time to discuss them," he said.

They shook their heads in unison.

"Come then, lad," he growled.

The boy grinned gamely and ambling to the door, stepped outside.

The night was as black as a witch's heart. Not a single star shone in the inky sky. "Yer quick," the boy said.

Nay. He was slow. Too slow. Time scampered past like scurrying field mice while his own motions felt heavy and lame. His back ached, his eyes felt gritty. "As I've said, 'tis a matter of some import."

"This lass," said the boy. "Be she yer lover?"

"Nay."

"Yer daughter?"

" 'Tis na for ye to concern yerself aboot."

"London be a long way to travel for someone other than—"

"We've na time for questions," O'Banyon said and stepping ahead, pulled open the stable door. "Indeed, we've na time—" he began, but suddenly the world crashed against his skull. Pain washed him like a dark stain. His knees struck the earth. He twisted slightly. The boy stood behind him, a timber held in both hands.

"Sorry old man, but London's not for the likes of me," he said and loosing the branch, backed away.

O'Banyon dropped to one hand. The world swam hazily, but memories were clear now, sharp shards of pain sliced into anger. "Ye'll be comin' with me, lad," he growled, "if yer hopin' to see the light of day."

The boy laughed. "I fear 'tis na yer decision," he said and turned away.

A snarl roiled up inside O'Banyon like a darkling wave. The hair on the back of his neck bristled as senses as old as time stirred to restless life.

Chapter 20

I was dark again. But O'Banyon had returned.
He smelled the scents of Arborhill, the
sweet jasmine, the waxy moonflowers.

Rolling his shoulders, he turned a jaundiced
eye on his companion. "Run and it may well be
the last thing ye remember, lad," he warned.

The Scottish mongrel looked older than his
score of years this night, old and as weary as sin.
It had been a long, hellacious ride from the Highlands. The bruise over his left eye had bloomed
with a host of shining colors.

O'Banyon would have smiled, had he had the
energy. Instead, he turned and pounded on the

door. It sounded hard and solid beneath his fist.

No one answered. He pounded again. "Awake!" he called. "I've brought help for the lass. Awake."

Silence again, as heavy as the night, then, "Who is it? Who's there?" called a faltering voice.

" 'Tis me, O'Banyon, returned from the Highlands. Please, let me come hither."

There was a pause, then metal scraped against metal. The door swung open, revealing a flickering candle and Mrs. Catrill's parchment face. O'Banyon stepped inside, pulling his trophy along behind him.

"I've come as quick as ever I could," he said and nodded toward the lad at his elbow. "With the . . . healer in tow. Please, we must see the wee lass."

Catrill stood with her mouth agape, staring at the young man near the door.

O'Banyon glanced at him. True, the lad called Keelan did not look like one would expect a learned healer to appear? His hair was long and unkempt, his face rough shaven, and in his eyes there was a hint of the devil. More than a hint if the knot on O'Banyon's skull was any indication.

"I fear . . ." she began, then blinked. "Why are the healer's hands bound?"

"There will be time aplenty for explanations

later," Banyon said, pulling Keelan down the broad hallway. "But for now we must—"

"She's dead."

O'Banyon jerked his head up. The countess stepped into the passageway in front of him, her gown pristine white, her face nearly as pale.

O'Banyon stumbled to a halt, his stomach cranked up hard. "Nay," he said and shook his head. He'd been so sure. So positive. Indeed, he'd not slept for an eternity, driven by the certainty that he could make amends, could draw the girl back from death's brink. "Nay," he said. "You're wrong, lass."

Her expression was unreadable in the uncertain light. Her hands were clasped as if in supplication before her pearlescent gown. "Indeed, she died more than a week ago."

"Nay."

"I am sorry."

O'Banyon closed his eyes. The world swayed around him. "Nay," he said again. "I am the one to be sorry."

"Was it your fault then?" she asked.

He couldn't speak, couldn't breathe, but stared at her, soul aching.

"Was it your place to keep her safe?" Her voice was cool, her elegant brows raised above bottle-green eyes.

"Aye," he managed, "that it was."

"You must think yourself powerful indeed," she said, "if you think you can protect all."

"Not all," he murmured. "But if I canna keep safe those I cherish . . ." He turned away, feeling foolish, feeling torn.

"It was not your fault, Irishman," she said softly and turned away.

"Oh?" He took a truncated step toward her. "Who then?"

She glanced over her shoulder. 'Twas not until that instant that he saw the aching sadness. Almost hidden. Almost shut away, and all the more overwhelming because of it. In the past, perhaps he had longed to see emotion in her face, to sense something in her soul. But now it was too much, too harsh, too abrasive. Her perfect features were not meant for sorrow.

He stepped forward, wanting, needing to pull her into his arms. But in an instant she drew herself up, the mask dropping in place, her eyes as hard as polished emeralds.

"I appreciate your labors on her behalf," she said and eyed the young Scotsman who stood watching her in the flickering light. "I appreciate your . . ." She scowled, skimming her gaze to his bound wrists. "Efforts. But I think you would be wise to leave now and not return."

Something scalded O'Banyon's guts. "What's that?"

"She's gone. There seems little reason for you come hither again," she said and pulled her gaze from Keelan to O'Banyon. "Good night."

"What the devil—" he began and stepped forward, but she had already disappeared from sight.

Behind him, the young Scotsman cleared his throat. "Mayhap this be a less than perfect time to mention it," he said, "but ye vowed to set me free should me services na longer be required."

"Shut the hell up," O'Banyon growled. "Lass, come back, ye—"

"Mayhap she is na particularly fond of wild beasties," Keelan suggested.

O'Banyon turned slowly toward him. How much did he know? Oh aye, things had got a bit rough up in the Highland village, but the night had been dark as sin.

The lad stepped back a pace, then remained where he was. They eyed each other in the flickering light.

Keelan swallowed but set his jaw. "Set me free," he said, "and she'll na learn the truth from the likes of me."

Without dropping his gaze, O'Banyon drew MacGill from his belt. The lad stared at him, not quite breathing. Seconds ticked away, and then

O'Banyon reached out and cut the other's bonds. "Go then," he said, and turned back toward the countess.

The boy grinned as he rubbed his wrists. "Where?"

"I care na," said O'Banyon, barely shifting his attention from the door. "To hell if ye like."

" 'Twas na quite what I had in mind. If ye remember, Irish, I lost me coin whilst ye chased me down like a cornered hare. I have na money. Na horse. Naught to eat."

The shuffling footsteps of Mrs. Catrill could be heard in the distance.

"And I'm loath to share me harrowing tales with the ladies of this house," the lad murmured.

"Ye said ye would hold yer tongue."

"I am a bard. As was me father and his father before him," he said, and shrugged. " 'Tis in me blood to tell—"

"Ye said ye were a tinker."

"As I was saying, 'tis in me blood to tell fibs."

"Ye mean to say ye lie."

"Aye."

Mrs. Catrill rounded the corner.

"What happened?" O'Banyon asked, turning toward her.

The old woman's face was creased with a thousand sorrows. "The poor wee babe," she said. "She never awoke from her slumber. Never opened her pretty eyes. She was dead the very next morn. Me lady found her."

"Had she worsened? Was she—"

"Who's to say? She never come to. But my lady . . ." Her face contorted. "I know she seems cold as river water at times. But in my heart I believe she cared for the child. After her death, she wouldn't speak. Couldn't eat. Weak as a lamb, she was, and wouldn't let none of us see the poor babe."

"You didn't see the child?"

"Nay." She shook her head, mourning. "Laid the wee thing in the casket herself, she did, and closed it up tight straightaway."

He tried to assimilate the words, but his mind was fuzzy, his muscles limp with strain. "When was she buried?"

"The selfsame day. The countess couldn't bear to see her lying there." She shook her head. "So still . . . So . . ." She swallowed and lifted her chin. "And what with this heat . . ."

He nodded once and turned away, but in a moment he glanced back toward her. "What of Lady Hendershire?" he asked, his thoughts narrowed to a hard line, his body tight with fatigue. "How does she fare?"

The old woman shook her head. "Only this

morning her Milly told Cook that she worsens. Luck is going poorly."

No more than twenty-four hours had passed when O'Banyon stepped into Brook's Club. He'd slept most of that time, fretted the rest. The room was packed to overflowing. Ladies giggled and fanned themselves. Men laughed and boasted.

But O'Banyon had come for one reason only— to seek answers.

From across the room, he studied the white countess. She seemed particularly effervescent this night. Bright as a star, fresh as a spring blossom. Even from his distant vantage point near the open doors, he could hear her husky laughter.

Five men were gathered around her, but there was not a warrior amongst them. If he so desired, he could break the lot of them. In fact, he longed to do so, to see them scatter like . . .

O'Banyon calmed himself. He was not here to wreak havoc. He was here to learn the truth. To think. Mayhap that was not his finest attribute, but he could not afford to fail. Not this time, for 'twas not his life alone that hung in the balance. There were others at risk. Others he cared for. He was certain of it. Could feel it in the very air he breathed.

"Lord Bentley." He could hear her voice perfectly, could see her eyes glimmer as she gazed directly at one of her dumpy companions. "I am flattered."

But she was not. She lied. She flirted. She teased. Why? 'Twas not like her.

"Sir O'Banyon."

He glanced to the left at the sound of his name. Mrs. Murray stood only inches away. "You yet live."

He bowed. "Did ye expect otherwise?" he asked.

"I rather thought there must be some dire condition that caused your hasty departure from my home," she said.

He had fled her property like a whipped cur. Even now he wanted nothing more than to leave her standing alone, seductive lips curved up at him as he scattered the countess's suitors and carried her like spoils of war from the room.

"Me apologies," he said. "But I had no wish to be tempted beyond me own control."

The countess was leaving the huddle, gliding toward the gaming tables.

"Truly?" said Murray. "And that was exactly my wish."

He smiled. "I am but a simple knight, me

lady. Well beneath yer station. I canna, in good conscience—"

"Beneath," she said and stepped closer. "That might very well be interesting."

She smelled of French perfume. A bit too strong mayhap, but that had hardly bothered him in the past. Her breast touched his chest. Her fingers grazed his arm. Not a flicker of desire warmed him.

He glanced toward the countess. She was standing near Pryor Winters. The man removed the cheroot from his mouth and glanced up from his sport. "Come, countess," he said, his tone expansive. "You can be my luck on this final play." A generous pile of bills lay before him on the table. His face was flushed with success. His opponents did not look so jovial.

"It's true then, isn't it?" Murray asked.

O'Banyon forced his attention back to her. "What's that, me lady?"

The widow held him in a steady gaze. Her lips turned into a strange downward smile. "She has hexed you," she said and turned away.

O'Banyon scowled after her, but a noise from the gaming tables brought him around.

Winters's face looked stricken. His hand shook as he laid down his cards. A young opponent in a dove-gray frock coat whooped with glee as he scooped up his winnings.

The others watched in amazement, murmuring quietly amongst themselves as they wandered away, leaving Winters alone.

"Pryor . . ." Antoinette's voice was as soft as a sigh, but O'Banyon could hear it above all else. "I am so sorry."

"Why?" Winters glanced up, looking dazed. "What have you got against me, countess?" he asked and jerking to his feet, strode angrily from the room.

"Poor luck."

O'Banyon glanced right. Keelan stood near his elbow.

"What the devil be ye doing here?" He hadn't seen the lad since awakening some hours hence, and found he hadn't missed him.

"There was naught to do in yer poor house," he said. "And little enough to eat."

"Then ye must surely make yer way back to the Highlands."

" 'Twas me intent," said the lad, "but I did na expect London's women to be so intriguing."

O'Banyon turned his attention in the direction of the boy's stare. The white countess stood in ardent conversation in a circle of friends.

Something rolled up tight in the Irishman's gut. "Tread softly, lad," he growled.

"Be the rumors true, then?" The boy grinned and drank his brandy. "Is she a witch?"

O'Banyon watched her breathlessly, then turned and slipped into the crowd. " 'Tis me hope," he murmured to no one.

Chapter 21

St. James Park was a picture of pastoral beauty. It was pleasant in the cool-dappled shade of the towering horse chestnuts. Their leaves rustled musically in the breeze. The lawn was lush and soft beneath Antoinette's slippers and she was a good two strikes ahead in a fierce game of pall mall.

She wished to God she were elsewhere.

"I am deeply sorry for my behavior on Tuesday last," said Pryor Winters.

She glanced up. A bevy of so-called friends stood behind her in a semicircle. She could feel their attention against the shivering skin of her back. "Whatever do you mean?" she asked.

"At Brooks," he said, his tone shamed. "I simply . . ." He exhaled carefully. "I lost a great deal I fear."

She watched him, unblinking, unbreathing. Pretense was everything. Panic was fatal.

"I had no right to blame you, countess," he added. "It was foolish and unforgivable."

"I am certain you shall win the funds back," she said. "Luck is an uncertain commodity, and most often present when you least expect it."

"Indeed. And could not possibly be adversely affected by a lady of your quality."

"My thanks," she said, but she could yet feel the others' attention upon her. She couldn't stay much longer in London. Indeed, she must leave soon. Perhaps for Italy. She had a small villa just outside of Florence. But she could not leave yet. 'Twas important that she be here for now, acting as if all was well. As if the nightmares from long past had not come to haunt her once again. Who or what had attacked Sibylla? And why? Was it because of her? Because of fear or ignorance or something even worse?

"I should not feel sorry for myself," he said. " 'Twas my own folly to gamble so impetuously."

Bending, she swung her mallet. The ball rolled across the green and bobbled to a stop inches from the wide wicket.

"Good show," Winters admired. "Mr. Unger, 'tis your turn, if you feel up to the challenge Lady Colline offers."

The Ungers were little known to Antoinette, but the wife already seemed to regard her with quiet suspicion.

Mr. Unger left their companions to take his place behind his ball.

Winters turned back toward Antoinette. " 'Twas naught but money, after all. And we are, the lot of us, far more lucky than poor Lady Hendershire."

Antoinette felt her insides quiver. She tightened her grip on her mallet. "What about Amelia?" she asked.

He shook his head. "Her husband informs me that she is growing weaker by the day."

She felt herself blanch. She should not have touched the girl. Should have yelled for help instead. But she hadn't been thinking clearly. The baroness was drowning. Surely 'twas better to pull her from the water than to leave her be. But she had been wrong before.

"I'm sorry," he said, looking suddenly pale. "Are you quite all right? I thought you surely knew."

"No," she said. "I did not."

"I have heard the lady is ill," said Unger, strolling up. "But I've not quite got the full story of it. Whatever is amiss with her?"

Winters shook his head. "Dr. Lambert has little idea what to make of it."

"Dr. Lambert is seeing her?" Antoinette asked.

"So I've heard," said Winters.

"What's this?" asked Mrs. Unger, approaching from behind. "Wasn't young Amelia on holiday at Bath only a few days past?"

"Indeed she was," Winters said. "Our own Lady Colline was there in the waters with her when first she faltered."

Annette could feel their eyes on her again. Her skin itched with their attention.

"She was lucky the countess was there," Winters added. "Or she would not have survived the day."

"Oh?" said Mrs. Unger.

"Yes indeed. She laid her hands on the baroness and pulled her from beneath the surface."

Mrs. Unger flickered her gaze from Antoinette to her husband. "And the poor girl has been ill ever since?"

"I'm afraid so, but at least she yet lives. And, as they say, where there is life there is—" Winters paused. "Say, there's Lady Trulane." He laughed. "And her infamous hounds."

Antoinette glanced up, heart pounding. 'Twas a small step from here to open accusations, she knew. A tiny step, but she kept her expression serene as she glanced toward Pall Mall. The aging baroness was just dismounting from her coach. Three small dogs accompanied her, rearing wildly at their leashes and pawing the air when they spotted the sport across the park.

"I think I shall give her assist," said Winters. "Mrs. Unger 'tis your turn next," he added and strode across the green toward the busy thoroughfare some thirty feet away.

An uneasy silence fell over the green.

"So, countess," said Unger, clearing his throat. "You were born in Paris, were you not?"

She glanced toward him. Her chest felt tight. "Norway," she lied, remembering the story, the endless lessons. "I lived there for some years."

"Indeed?" he said, sounding pleased. "Wherever do you hail from in that fair country?"

Winters had reached Trulane's coach. He took the leashes from her hand. They lunged against their constraints, tongues lolling.

"I doubt you've heard of it," she said. " 'Tis a small village and far off the usual path."

"I've spent some time in Norway," he said. "Indeed, I traveled quite extensively in—"

But suddenly there was a gasp from the street.

Antoinette jerked her head around. One small dog had broken loose and was dashing across the road, leash flapping like a runaway kite.

Two polished phaetons came spinning around the corner, young bucks at the ribbons, laughing wildly. The dog tried to crowd back, but it was too late. There was a whimper and then the hound lay still as the carriages whirred away.

"No. Oh no!" Lady Trulane's sobs could surely be heard across the globe. They rang in Antoinette's head like a death knell.

She watched the baroness scoop the small, lifeless body into her arms. Watched her lift her watery gaze across the green and knew, without a doubt, that the *ton* had finally found its scapegoat.

O'Banyon gazed across the ballroom. Lady Bevre had assured him the white countess would be there. But she was not. He would know if she were. He would feel it like a pleasant burn against his skin.

And yet, all the rest of London seemed to have come in her stead. Even Prinny was present, corseted and rouged and talking to Mrs. Murray.

Mayhap the widow had set her sets higher than a roguish Irishman who tended to abandon her in moments of high passion.

"Shall I expect ye home this night?"

O'Banyon turned.

Keelan stood only inches away, his silver-blue eyes gleaming as he bounced a pair of bone dice in his hand. "Or will ye be on the prowl yet again?"

Banyon gave him a wolfish grin. "If I hear so much as a whisper that ye've been cheatin', lad, you'll know whether I'm prowling or na."

The boy laughed. "I'm na the one to watch, Irishman."

O'Banyon scanned the crowd again. Where was she? She had not been at her estate. He had gone there, though he had tried to remain home, had tried to believe he was far better without her.

"These English," Keelan continued. "They be an odd lot."

Suspicion clicked in O'Banyon's mind. He turned back slowly. "What are ye saying?"

"Yer friend Winters, he does na necessarily play by the strictest of rules."

"Winters." The world focused down to the boy's face. "He cheats at the table?"

"Aye," said the lad. "He does. And fair well."

O'Banyon stared at him a moment. "He should have employed his talents some nights past then, when he lost all and his pride while gaming."

"Aye." The boy's eyes were unusually bright and sharply focused. "Ye would think he would have. But say, Wolfgang, isn't that your white witch?"

O'Banyon felt it then. That inexplicable stab of pleasure, that hard punch of need. He turned toward the door. She entered like a princess, as regal as a royal swan, as enchanting as a song.

Heads turned toward her, and by slow degrees, the room went quiet, hushed but for a few whispers as they watched her glide in.

"What's that?" The Regent's voice boomed in the silence as he leaned his fleshy face toward Mrs. Murray.

She whispered something, her painted lips a breath from the Regent's ear.

"Dead, you say," said the prince.

His companion nodded.

"My lady," he called, staring across the room at the countess. "Come hither."

Antoinette went without delay, gliding toward the prince to bow with regal elegance before him.

He smiled drunkenly and reached for her hand.

O'Banyon tensed, imagining the lightning feel of her skin against his own fingers, smelling the magic that was hers alone, and awaiting the Regent's reaction. But she was gloved and the prince besotted.

311

He kissed her fingers, then straightened. "I have been privy to some disturbing rumors, countess."

"I am sorry to her that, Your Majesty." Her tone was absolutely serene. "And what rumors might they be?"

He canted his head, gold buttons gleaming on his beribboned waistcoat. " 'Tis said you are a witch."

"A . . ." She raised her brows as if surprised, then, "Oh no, Your Majesty, I believe what you heard is that I was rich."

"Oh?" he said, rearing back to study her.

"Or," she added, glancing at Mrs. Murray. "Maybe 'twas another word that rhymes with witch."

"Another—"

"And begins with a *b*," she added, leaning toward him with a mischievous gleam in her eyes. "Which, I fear, is also true at times."

The prince studied her a moment in silent rumination, then threw back his head and laughed. "Well said. Well said indeed," he applauded.

She sketched a bow and turned away.

There was a moment of stunned silence and then the room fell back into noisy disarray.

Mrs. Murray frowned, stiff backed and silent as

the countess made her way across the floor to the refreshments.

O'Banyon could not help but make his way to her, could not hold back the wild tide of feelings that erupted at the merest sight of her. He could feel her in his blood, could taste the sweet, exotic scent of her like honeyed nectar.

She was bent over the buffet table and didn't turn to him when she spoke without acknowledging his presence. "And what of you, sir, what do you think I am?"

He was caught off guard, and when she turned toward him, her evergreen eyes like purest jewels, he felt lost. Lost and floundering in a sea of hopeless desire.

He couldn't speak.

She watched him. Her face was as unmoved as stone, but her eyes . . . They were filled with a pain so deep he all but drowned. "Do you think I killed Lady Trulane's pet?"

He watched her, engrossed, enchanted.

"And what of Mr. Winters? Do you think I jinxed his game?"

"I think . . ." He paused, fighting himself. But he had already lost. "I think I canna live without ye, lass," he said.

Something sparked in her eyes. Was it hope?

"Do you believe I killed Sibylla?" she whispered.

The world went away, leaving them in silence, lost in each other.

"I believe ye cherished Sibylla like none other," he said.

"That is no answer," she breathed.

"Nay," he said and took the plunge far past caution and into the turbulent waters of uncertainty, "I believe ye saved her."

For a moment, for just the briefest instant, her face cracked. Emotion shone like a beacon in her eyes.

"That is not the consensus here," she said.

"Mayhap ye do na make it easy, me lady."

"Life is not easy."

"Is it na?" he asked and longed desperately to know her, to understand her, to hold her in his arms until all was well. "Even for the countess of Colline?"

"Well, of course," she said and laughed. And suddenly, she was back in absolute control. The white lady without a care, the world at her feet. "For me it is different."

"I would know the truth," he said.

Her gaze held him entranced, but finally she shook her head. "No," she countered. "You would not."

"Is it so awful then?"

She held his gaze then nodded once. "Some think so."

"Mayhap I am different."

"That you are," she said and smiled ever so gently.

He controlled his desires, fought down his needs. "Why do ye let them distrust ye?"

"Let them? You say it as if I can control how they feel."

"If ye but wished ye could make them soar at the sight of ye."

She watched him.

"As I soar," he said.

Her face was sad beneath her mask. "You are wrong."

"And ye are magic," he said and reached for her, but in that moment she jerked back.

"Excuse me," she rasped and turning abruptly away, hurried into the crowd.

"Lass." He rushed after her, but someone grabbed his arm.

"Good Christ, man, have some pride."

O'Banyon turned with a growl.

Keelan raised his brows, but he remained as he was, silvery eyes gleaming.

"If ye've a fondness for that hand, ye'll remove it from me person, lad," O'Banyon suggested.

"What's this then?" asked Mrs. Murray, approaching from the left. "A spat between two Celtic gentlemen?"

"Well, I, for one, am gentle . . . and a man," said Keelan and dropped his hand before 'twas too late and O'Banyon lost his fragile control.

"Oh?" She shifted her arch gaze to O'Banyon. "And what is your friend here?"

The lad turned his gaze back toward the Irishman.

" 'Tis difficult to say exactly," said the boy.

"What are your suspicions?"

"I think he may be a smitten fool," said Keelan.

Mrs. Murray laughed. "I don't believe we've met," she said and lifted her hand.

Keelan bowed over it with a showy flourish. " 'Tis me own honor to meet a lady of yer quality and beauty."

"I am Cecilia Murray. My friends call me Cece."

Keelan bowed, eyes sparkling. "And I am the Forbes."

"*The* Forbes?"

"God's teeth!" O'Banyon rumbled.

Keelan didn't so much as spare him a glance. "Me friends call me Laird."

"Oh?" she said. "Tell me, my laird, do you sometimes wear the plaids of your ancestors?"

"Aye. Quite oft."

She nodded and slipped her arm through his. "I've a question then," she said and led him away.

O'Banyon turned toward the crowd, searching, glad he was not so duped by a pretty face.

Near the edge of the ballroom, he thought he saw a flash of white and hurried toward it. But his quarry was not to be found. He searched the crowd, heart pounding with need.

Outside, the night was as black as sin.

A white carriage rolled away, drawing his attention. He turned and ran. It was elegant and closed. He grabbed hold of the handle and swung up, opening the door as he did so.

"What the devil?" cursed the owner, drawing back in terror. Across the aisle, his wife gasped and clasped the jewels at her neck.

"Me apologies," O'Banyon said and jumped back onto the street.

She was gone, disappeared once again. But he would find her.

Chapter 22

Antoinette hurried to her carriage.

Whitford opened the door, looking up at her from beneath his withered brow. "All is well, my lady?"

Her hands were shaking. "Yes. Quite well."

"We go home, then?"

Home. Where was that? She had many estates, but no home. An abundance of acquaintances, but no friends.

"My lady?"

You could make them soar.

"My lady."

"Take me to Lady Hendershire."

Whitford shook his head and drew back like a gnarled, withered gnome being pressed against his will. "No, my lady. Please. Not that. Not tonight."

"I must," she said.

" 'Tis folly," he argued. "Too much has happened of late. Too much—" he began, but she reached out and touched his face. He closed his eyes as if struck and dipped back his head.

A tremble of power seethed from her, easing readily through the fabric of her skin. "Such loyalty lies hidden within you," she said quietly. "Such sorrow. But you need not worry, Whitford. All will be well."

His tattered eyelids slid up and he forced himself back, but finally he nodded, face solemn as he turned away. Tears glistened on his ravaged cheeks.

Her own heart ached at the sight, but she forced herself to move.

The carriage dipped as she mounted it. The horses snorted as they leaned into their traces. She sat very still then, listening to the clip of the team's hooves against the street, waiting, resting, shoring up her energy like a dike against the tide, until the hoofbeats halted and Whitford made his painstaking way to her door.

It opened on silent hinges. He said nothing, but his eyes pleaded.

She looked away, dismounted the carriage, and made her course up the stairs to a brownstone manse.

She was admitted shortly.

Lord Hendershire joined her minutes later. "Lady Colline." His voice was cheerful, but his face was weary, his eyes afraid behind his careful façade. She knew that mask, understood the price it cost to maintain it. " 'Tis ever so good to see you," he lied.

She didn't offer her hand. She dare not, but nodded instead, then searched his face, but there was little sign of hope. "I have come to see your bride," she said simply, for she was tired, too tired to pretend, to dance and lie and hope he would not know the truth—that she was a monster, a freak of nature, with powers she could neither control nor understand.

He fidgeted, but even that gesture looked weary. "I do so appreciate your visit," he said. "And I am certain you would brighten her mood considerable, but I do not think that would be wise, my lady. She is sleeping now and—"

"Please," she said simply and braced herself to be accepted.

O'Banyon waited in the sweet-scented shadows of Arborhill's garden. She was not home.

That much he knew, but she would come and it would be soon. He felt it inside his shivering skin, inside his soul, and finally he heard the sound of her wheels on the road. He rose to his feet, watching, waiting, breath held.

The carriage rolled into the graveled courtyard. Whitford dismounted from his perch, his face a grotesque mask in the flickering light of the lantern as he opened the carriage door. Voices murmured quietly in the night, and then she appeared, her face a small, bleak oval in the blackness.

She stepped out, slowly, carefully. Her eyes lifted to the mercurial moonlight for an instant, and then she collapsed, falling silently to the earth beneath her.

Terror streamed like venom through O'Banyon's trembling soul. He lurched forward, devouring the distance between them, needing to feel her skin against his, to know she was well, but suddenly Whitford blocked his way. The squat, gnarled body stood like an ancient gargoyle between the Irishman and the countess.

"Stay back," he rasped. A pistol gleamed in the wobbly light of the lantern. "Stay back, or it will not matter if you're man or beast."

So he knew. O'Banyon drew a deep breath, steadying himself against the sight of her so still upon the unyielding earth. "What happened?"

" 'Tis none of your concern, devil's hound."

O'Banyon gritted his teeth but remained as he was. "You've naught to fear from me," he vowed, "unless ye try to keep me from her."

The driver didn't speak, but shuffled his weight slightly.

"What happened to your lady?"

"Leave her before—" Whitford began, but in that instant Antoinette moaned softly.

O'Banyon reacted without forethought, without anticipation, and suddenly the driver's weapon was gone, snatched from his hand and tossed into the darkness.

Striding forward, O'Banyon bent and scooped the countess against his chest. She lay limp in his embrace, her satiny neck a regal arch against his arm. But he could feel the pulse of her heart in his very soul, fluttering softly beneath her perfect breasts.

"What mischief is this?" O'Banyon asked, soul tortured.

Whitford said nothing, but stood his ground, his brow a rumpled furrow of worry.

"Be out of my way then if ye canna help," O'Banyon ordered.

But the gnome remained as he was.

"I'll na hurt her," O'Banyon snarled. "Na if me

322

verra life be forfeit. But I shant give ye the same leeway."

Silence echoed around them.

"What say ye?" asked the Irishman.

"Take her inside," said a voice, but it was not the hunchback's.

The maid called Minetta stepped from the shadows and placed a hand on the driver's arm. He seemed to grow and wilt all at once, his face alight with an emotion almost painful in its intensity.

"Hurry now," she murmured.

O'Banyon strode past them, barely noticing the discrepancy of the maid's delicate beauty against Whitford's hunched deformity.

Mrs. Catrill opened the door. O'Banyon took the stairs two at a time and the others followed, directing him toward the chamber at the top of the stairs. He stepped inside. A pink-shaded candle glowed there, casting its rosy light soft and luminous on a hundred glowing plants. They seemed to reach from every corner, delicate blooms and tenacious vines bowing reverently toward the bed that occupied the center.

"Put her down," Minetta ordered. "Quickly. Before 'tis too late."

He did as told, depositing her on the mattress,

then drawing back, though he found he could not forsake her completely. Could not abandon the soft silk of her hand. "Too late for what?" he asked, searching her face.

No answer was forthcoming. The plants seemed to lean in, as if needing to be near her.

"Too late for what?" he asked again and glanced toward the maid.

She remained at the end of the bed, while Whitford stood like a squat sentry between them.

"You must release her hand," said the girl. "Or she'll not—"

But in that moment the countess's eyes flickered open, evergreen and hopelessly lovely in the pale beauty of her face.

"Lass," he breathed. "Ye are returned."

She blinked. Her brow furrowed slightly as she glanced about her. "Why are you here?"

"What has happened to ye?"

"Nothing." She tried to sit up, faltered. Minetta rushed to the opposite side of the bed.

"Can I help you, m'lady. Can I—" she began, but Antoinette gave her a weak smile and shook her head.

"I am well, Minny. No need to worry."

"He was waiting," Whitford rumbled and cast a dark glare at O'Banyon. "When we arrived here."

His tone was guttural and deep. "Skulking in the garden."

She turned her gaze toward O'Banyon. There was something in her eyes. Perhaps the merest flash of amusement. "Skulking again were you, sir?"

He squeezed her hand, drawing in her beauty, leaning into hope. She yet breathed. Yet spoke. The sun would rise again. "As I've said afore, lass, a knight never skulks," he said.

Her lips tilted up the slightest degree.

"I tried to keep him back," said Whitford. His breathing was harsh in the room. "I failed."

"No." She shifted her attention toward the driver. "Never that," she said softly. "You could not fail me, Whit."

The hunchback's face contorted with emotion, and for a moment O'Banyon thought he might drop to his knees with the force of his feelings. But he remained erect.

"You must do as I ask now though," she said.

Whitford nodded once, his jaw set in a hard line of determination as he stepped forward.

"See that Minetta gets safely to bed."

"My lady—" whispered the maid.

"Nay," Whitford rasped.

"Aye," commanded the countess, her voice

stronger. "Go now. There is nothing for you to do here."

"But what of—"

"And do not worry on my account," she added. "The Irish Hound is not a danger to me. He is only . . . irritating."

They seemed neither amused nor soothed, but finally Whitford took the girl's hand in his. She raised her limpid eyes. Their gazes met like a stroke of velvet and then she followed him slowly from the room. The door closed with seeming reluctance behind them.

O'Banyon tightened his grip on Antoinette's hand and looked into her eyes. "I can but wish I had known such a lady as ye in me own youth," he said.

She gave him a quizzical glance.

"To send me to a bonny lass's bed."

She stared at him unblinking. "There is truly something wrong with you, Irishman."

His soul felt strangely light. "I know, love," he said, "but what of ye?"

Her lips lifted slightly and for a moment he thought she would avoid the issue, but she lied instead. "I am but tired."

He searched her face. "How can it be?"

She scowled.

"That ye have lived for more than a score of years and ye are yet such a poor liar."

She shifted her gaze away for an instant. " 'Tis the truth."

"And I prefer lads to lassies."

She jerked her attention to him.

He cleared his throat. " 'Tis the most outrageous thing I could think of on the moment. What happened to ye, Mab?"

"My name is not Mab."

"Oh?" he asked and skimming his hand up her arm, tugged at the end of her glove. There was little more than a tingle of magic this night.

She tried to draw away, but he held her hand firmly in his own.

"What has weakened ye so, lass?" he asked, slipping the glove slowly from her arm. Feelings bloomed like fragile roses at the touch of skin against skin.

She scowled, watching his movements. He skimmed his fingertips along the crease of her arm. She shivered and tilted her head weakly back against the pillow.

Pleasure threatened to drown him in warm waves, but he held tight against the gentle undertow. "Did ye . . ." He narrowed his eyes, concentrating. "Did ye touch someone what was ailing?"

Something sparked in her eyes.

" 'Twas Amelia, was it na?"

She shook her head, but he ignored the lie.

"There is something about her that drains ye."

"I don't know what you're talking about."

Her glove was rumpled against the delicate skin of her wrist, leaving her forearm bare to his touch. Reaching out slowly, he wrapped his hand about her elbow and eased it toward her hand.

She closed her eyes against the rush of feelings. He felt her pleasure almost as sharp as his own.

"The young baroness takes yer strength," he said. "While I . . ." He stroked her arm and watched her head fall back in ecstatic pleasure. "I would like to say that me slightest touch affects all women this way, lass," he said, abandoning her arm and gripping her gloved hand again. "But 'twould be a foolish lie." Her eyes seemed somewhat glazed. "Why can we na touch without these feelings betwist us?"

"I think you flatter your—" she breathed, but he touched her bare arm again. Feelings sizzled through them. She hissed a breath between her teeth.

He gritted his teeth, feeling life spark between them. "How do ye bear it?" he asked.

She was breathing hard, her breasts rising

beneath the silver-streaked satin of her gathered bodice.

"Tell me true, lass," he whispered, "was it this magic what killed yer husband?"

She only stared, her face pale and her eyes a wide void from which he could not escape.

"Na that I would resent me own death if the same should happen to me. But I would know, lass. Was there this fire between ye?" he asked and reaching out, cupped her cheek with his palm.

Her lashes fell closed, trembling against the delicate beauty of her cheeks. "He did not touch me," she whispered.

He let the feelings take him, let the harsh pleasure grip him in greedy hands until the meaning of her words sunk into his grasping brain. Straightening slightly, he shook his head. "There is much I would believe if spoken from your bonny lips, lass," he said. "But I fear this be too hard a thing to comprehend." He skimmed his thumb across her mouth. She shivered against his touch. "No man could be near ye and na long to take ye to his bed."

Silence entered on slippered feet.

"Truly?" she whispered.

He stared at her, certain for a moment that she must know it to be truth, but her expression was open now, open and lost and whole. "Aye, lass, it is. So I but wonder, why do ye hold yer suitors forever at bay when there be this . . ." He scooped his fingertips across her cheek, bracing himself, but unable to hold back the rush of pleasure that drew him down, pulled him closer until their lips were inches apart, their breath mingled like mist between them.

"No." She shook her head. "Please. Don't do this."

For a moment he tried to obey, but she was more than he could withstand. Their lips touched. Passion arced between them, thrusting them together, and suddenly he was stretched out upon her mattress. Her hand was cupped across the back of his neck, pulling him closer, bearing him down, and at each point of contact, he burned. But he longed for the fire, ached for the pain.

"O'Banyon—" Her voice was a breathy whisper against his skin, her body arched like a fragile flame against his.

"Aye, lass?" he breathed and kissed her neck.

She moaned beneath his caress. "I cannot . . . I must not," she said, but her grip did not loosen.

Their gazes met and burned.

" 'Tis dangerous," she whispered.

"I'll na hurt ye, lass," he vowed.

But she shook her head, her eyes troubled. "Do

330

you not understand, Irishman? *I* am dangerous!"

And he laughed, perhaps because he was insane, had been driven mad by the ferocious intensity of his need.

" 'Tis not a jest," she hissed.

"Nay," he said and kissed her again, because he had no choice, no hope of drawing away. "Ye may verra well be the death of me."

"Don't say that." Her fingers dug into his skin, her gaze bore into his. "Do you hear me? Don't say it."

"Lass, what is it? Is there someone else?" His stomach knotted at the thought. "A jealous lover. Someone who—"

It was her turn to laugh.

He watched her.

"There is none like you," she vowed.

"So ye've na . . ." He drew a careful breath. "Ye've na felt this magic afore?"

She shook her head.

Peace touched him, a quiet so lovely he all but sighed. "Nor I," he admitted.

She raised a questioning brow.

"That is to say, I have . . . lain with a few."

The other brow rose.

"Several," he admitted. "But not for a long while."

"More than a day?" Her tone was jealous.

He felt like singing. "More than a cen . . . decade."

"You jest."

"I do na make light of such things."

She parted her lips slightly as though breathless. His desire did an odd little jig against his abdomen at the sight, but he held himself steady.

"What do we do now?" she whispered.

"We make love."

She scowled. "I don't think—"

"I do."

"But what if—"

He kissed her and found the pleasure just bearable. He trembled with need and braced his brow against hers, holding himself back.

"We shall go at your pace," he murmured.

"I don't have a pace."

He laughed. It sounded crazed. "Let me undress ye," he said and skimmed his hand down her waist.

She moaned. "Can't we . . . do this without trying something so rash?"

He blinked. "Without disrobing?"

"Yes."

" 'Twould be . . . unseemly," he said and eased his hand over her buttocks.

"Unseemly?" She was breathing hard. Her eyes were closed.

"Aye."

She opened her eyes slowly. "Would it be more seemly, if you were naked?"

He thought for a moment. "Decidedly."

Her lips quirked up a quarter of an inch. "Very well."

His desire jerked up hard against his belly. She slipped her hand from his neck. He eased back a few scant inches, watching her, waiting for her. She reached for the buttons on his shirt. The anticipation made his chest ache, or perhaps it was her nearness, her beauty, the power that was hers alone.

Her fingers fumbled on the little wooden spheres.

"Mayhap ye should remove yer gloves," he suggested, but she shook her head and eased the first little orb from its hole.

He almost fainted. "Verra well," he said, seeing the wisdom of her prudence.

She raised her gaze to his. "Are ye well?"

"I shall survive."

Her eyes laughed. The next button fell open and the next until his chest was bare.

Their gazes met with a warm clash of feelings

and then she reached out to brush his shirt aside.

Emotions quivered through him like an intoxicant. He closed his eyes against the hard pulse of need but held steady.

"You are beautiful," she whispered.

He opened his eyes, and bracing himself against the fireworks, reached out to touch her face. She felt tense.

"Ye have na even seen me verra best parts yet, lass," he whispered.

She huffed a laugh, relaxing marginally. Something bloomed inside him. A fragile blossom of joy so painful it was nearly his undoing.

"What ails you?" she asked, worry in her eyes.

"Naught. 'Tis naught."

"Tell me," she said, "or I'll not continue."

He drew a careful breath. "This love," he said and swallowed hard. "I did na expect it to be so wondrous painful."

For a moment she only stared at him, and then she leaned forward ever so slowly and kissed him. Perhaps he died in that moment, perhaps he even saw a glimpse of heaven, but when he next opened his eyes she was scooping his sleeves down his arms.

He sat up, allowing her to slip the shirt down his back and away.

She kissed the tensed muscle of his shoulder. He shivered down to his soul.

"Take your shoes off," she whispered and kissed him again. "So I may see your best parts."

He chuckled.

Her eyes laughed. He kicked off his shoes and stood facing her. She sat up slowly, her legs brushing his. He gritted his teeth against the sensations. Skimming her knuckles down his ribs, she bumped them across the expanse of his scarred abdomen to the clasp that held his trousers.

"O'Banyon—" she began, but he touched her face, halting her words.

"I'll survive," he said. "This I promise."

And he did, even when she loosed his desire, even when she skimmed her hands down his hips, baring his all. He stood before her, hot and hard, waiting, breathless for her pleasure, his desire pressed eagerly against the taut muscles of his belly.

She stared, and then she raised her eyes slowly to his.

Their gazes met. The world went still.

"Say something, lass," he said.

She blinked. *"Incredible?"*

He could not help but laugh, and taking her hands in his, drew her to her feet. Feelings shimmered like desert heat through him, but they were bearable.

"Take off yer gloves," he whispered.

Her body tensed. She shook her head.

"Yer gown then?"

She blinked. "Very well."

"Strange lass," he murmured and turning her about, placed his fingers on her first button. "But me . . ." The first tiny sphere fell open. He continued to breathe. "I have always liked the unusual." He kissed her neck beside the tiny tendril that curled lovingly against her nape. Another button fell free, then another, until her back lay smooth and soft to his gaze.

He drew a careful breath and slipped his hands against her shoulder blades.

Her shoulders felt like rose petals beneath his fingers, her arms like the delicate stems of lilies.

He undressed her in silence, until she was naked before him, bare to his gaze but for her gloves crumpled against her narrow wrists.

Then he stepped back a fraction of a pace. She tried to go with him, but he held her in place so that he could skim the fragile length of her. She was like a fine piece of art, a porcelain vase so perfectly made that he barely dare touch it.

She shivered in the wavering candlelight.

He felt his nostrils flare at the sight, felt a thousand emotions blaze like firelight. Desire, protectiveness, love.

"What now?" she whispered.

"We make love."

"I don't—"

"I do," he said and taking her hand, led her back to the bed. Placing one knee on the mattress, he lowered himself onto it, pulling her with him.

She held back and he released her, letting her take her time as he stretched out upon the blankets beneath him.

Her eyes took him in, skimming his body like a tangible flame. Perhaps a gentleman would have had the decency to be embarrassed, but he did not. Indeed, he lifted one brow and smiled at her as the heat of his erection danced against his skin.

Her eyes snapped with a mixture of fear and longing, and for a moment, he actually thought she might run, thought she might snatch up her gown and flee, but instead she eased onto the mattress beside him. The softness of her thigh brushed the tensed muscles of his. He guided her on top, until she straddled him, until she was poised above him.

"What—"

"Make love," he rasped and bracing himself on his elbows, kissed her.

Everything was perfect then, everything was ordained. They touched and smoothed and arced in a haze of misty magic.

He skimmed his fingers over the peak of her budding breast and she arced into him, baring her heart.

There was nothing he could do but take her hips in his hands and ease slowly into the hot depths of her. They hissed in unison, and for a moment O'Banyon actually thought he had been wrong, that he would indeed succumb to the liquid heat of feeling her around him, pulling him under.

It was she who moved first, who rocked into the aching length of him. He reciprocated with a tortured growl, then feared the change had begun, but it had not. It was himself as he had not been for a hundred plus years. Perhaps as he had never been.

They rode together on the building tide. Her hands felt like brands against the flesh of his chest. Her knees hugged him, holding him close, riding him hard.

Tension bloomed and roared. O'Banyon gripped her thighs. Her luscious lips parted. Her body tensed and arched. He felt the release like a volcanic eruption, spewing forth every bit of strength from his muscles until he felt drained and exhausted.

And then she fell, soft and sated against the thrumming hollow of his chest, their heartbeats melding, their bodies limp.

He could barely draw a breath, could not, in fact, lift an arm. She had emptied him, had taken his all, and he fell, limp and spent into the soft darkness of sleep.

He awoke well after dawn and reached for her, needing her, but she was gone. He knew it in his heart before his mind fully accepted it. She was gone and he was alone.

Chapter 23

〜✦〜

"**W**hat do you mean, she's not returned?" O'Banyon asked. He stood taut and edgy before Arborhill's broad, double doors.

It had been two days since last he'd seen her. They had been the longest days of his life, stretching out before him in bleak agony, as vast and hopeless as the endless hours of darkness behind him. Oh aye, when she had failed to return, he had told himself how lucky he was to have the spell broken, to know that he could once again enjoy a bonny maid's charms without becoming embarrassingly hirsute. Indeed, he had intended to do just that.

Instead, he had returned to Arborhill before evening. And on the following day. And the next.

"She's not returned," said Mrs. Catrill. "Since 'er exodus some days past."

"Where did she go?"

"As I've told you before, sir, my lady did not mention her destination."

O'Banyon gritted his teeth. "When will she return?"

"I 'ave no way of knowing that. Now if you'll excuse me . . ." she said and shut the door.

He left then, returned to his townhouse. The night passed in grinding slowness. He spent the day asking for her, swallowing his pride, pressing others for any clue of her whereabouts. She owned property in Paris of course, and a villa in Italy. Perhaps she had gone there. But she had not. He was certain of that, could feel it in his soul.

Keelan watched with interest as he paced the length of his sitting room. God's arse, why couldn't he manage to lose the boy as thoroughly as he had lost the countess?

"Can't you simply . . ." The lad leaned back in his chair, watching him. "Do what ye do?"

O'Banyon glared at him. "I've na idea what ye speak of."

"I think ye do."

"Well ye be wrong again," he growled. He wore his plaid and naught else, thinking his ancestral garb would make him feel more himself. It did, if himself was an unkempt Irishman with a feral growl in his gut and an aching need to dismember someone. "Are ye certain she left no message with ye concerning her whereabouts?"

"She being . . . ?"

"The countess!" O'Banyon snarled, and the boy grinned.

"Ahh." He paused, then, "Nay, I am quite certain I would have noticed had she come to me door."

" 'Tis na *yer* door,"

"Aye well, I believe I would have noticed had she come to *yer* door also. But she did na, did she?"

O'Banyon lowered his brows. "Mayhap now would be a likely time for ye to begin yer journey home, lad."

"So the Irish Hound can lick his wounds in private?"

"What be ye yipping about?"

The boy shrugged. " 'Tis fair plain to see, she is na coming back to ye."

He twisted toward the lad, his hands fisted, his jaw clenched. "Get out," he ordered.

Keelan but raised his brows over well-amused eyes. "What did ye do to her to make her so distraught?"

342

"I'm warning ye—"

"I hope ye did na harm her. I would hate to think I'm sharing—"

"Get out!" O'Banyon roared and dragging the lad from his chair, all but tossed him from the house.

Anger poured through him like bile as he paced again, but it was anger laced with fear, with unmitigated terror. Where had she gone? And why had she left? Their one night together had been magical.

But perhaps it had not been so for her. Perhaps he had been so immersed in his own ecstasy that he had failed to consider her pleasure.

But no. She had moaned in his arms. Had writhed beneath his touch, but could that not be for dual reasons?

She was gone. That spoke volumes.

Yet even now he could feel the satin of her skin against—

Snarling a curse, O'Banyon ripped open his door and stormed from the house.

London was dark and dangerous. His mood was the same. He prowled the streets, asking questions, searching everywhere. But there was no trace of her.

It was well past vespers when he found his bed. Sleep took him finally, but nightmares haunted his dreams. She was there, just out of reach, watching him. The room was dark. She was alone, lying on her side. And suddenly, like the magic that was hers alone, she was naked. Her skin gleamed, gilt ivory in the flickering candlelight. She smiled, that secret seductive expression that made him ache with desire. He tried to go to her, but suddenly he was elsewhere and he could do naught but look on. Another man was in her bedchamber. Another paced across her room, sat upon her bed, looked down at her, his back toward O'Banyon.

Her eyes widened, as if she just now recognized the intruder. She cowered away. The man raised his hand, and now there was a knife clutched in his fist.

"Nay!" O'Banyon awoke with a start. His chest felt tight, his skin clammy. His fingers were curled like talons against his bed sheets.

"What the hell happened to ye?" Keelan stood in his doorway, nearly unseen, but not unknown, not with O'Banyon's heightened senses. He could smell the scent of him. Could taste his own terror on the air.

"Get out!" he growled, but the lad leaned a shoulder against the door jamb and chuckled.

"Jesus, Irish, 'tis time ye set this behind ye, is it na? She's gone. Well out of your reach."

"Get the hell out!" O'Banyon warned, but the lad stepped into the room, shaking his head as he came.

"Forget about her. She's surely forgot about ye."

A growl issued low in Banyon's throat. He eased onto his hands and knees. The blankets slipped away from his naked body. "Tell me, lad, do you wish to die so young?"

The boy shrugged. "Na particularly, nay, and mayhap she does na either. Mayhap 'tis why she escaped ye. Mayhap 'tis why she chose another."

O'Banyon could feel the change rip though him, could feel the bite of anger roar along his spine. "Get out of my sight."

"She is probably moaning in his arms even now. Glad to be rid of ye so that she might—"

But suddenly O'Banyon leapt. He heard his own growl, heard the boy's yelp of surprise, and then he was gone, just managing the door before the change was complete, before he was leaping down the road.

The darkness of the night suited him well. Fear and anger drove him like a whip.

He was at her estate in a matter of minutes, but she wasn't there. He knew it immediately, knew it through the pads of his feet. But she had been. He could smell her exodus, could taste her retreat. The carriage had taken her away. There, to the north.

Lifting his head, he gazed into the distance . . . and felt her fear in the marrow of his soul.

The cottage in the woods was quiet and dark, lit only with one flickering tallow candle, but Antoinette liked it thus. She was alone here. Well, nearly so. Perhaps she could be happy with this simple sort of life. Perhaps she could be safe, undisturbed.

But O'Banyon's face lit her memory. Feelings shivered through her, a magic so potent and heady that her heart seemed to swell—

But she wouldn't think of that. She couldn't afford to, not for his sake and not for hers.

She was an anomaly, a danger. He was . . . She didn't know what he was. Magic of his own sort, surely.

A sound scraped against her window. She jerked her head in that direction, but 'twas naught more than a branch against the panes. The wind was picking up.

She paced the confines of the cottage. She was well away from the city, away from eyes that watched her with calculated knowing. Faces that turned to watch her walk by and whisper behind her back.

She glanced toward the window. A man's image flashed there.

She gasped. But the apparition was already gone, disappeared, replaced by nothing. Blackness. Her limbs felt weak.

What was wrong with her? She was simply imagining. All was well. She was safe, hidden here in the woods. Alone to level her thoughts, to find her bearing. Even Whitford and Minny had gone. But not without duress. She had sent them on, saying she needed them to prepare to return to Florence, but they knew the truth.

Something squeaked from the kitchen. She caught her breath and turned toward the sound, her muscles wooden. All was silent. 'Twas a mouse surely. Nothing more. They had come aplenty since the cottage had been left empty. Perhaps she should get a cat.

Retrieving the candle from the nearby table, she lifted it high and almost laughed at her own wayward thoughts as she turned toward the kitchen. Just what she needed to set tongues wagging—a cat. Perhaps she could get a tattered broomstick as well or—

"Hello, countess."

She jerked back with a gasp. A shadow stepped into the room. The candle bobbled in her hand, spilling wax across her fingers.

Mr. Winters's face glowed in the flickering light.

"What are you doing here?" Her voice was

nothing more than a whisper of shock, unrecognizable in the ensuing silence.

"I was worried about you," he said, but his smile was crooked, his eyes strangely bright.

She straightened her back, willing away the fear, but it was there, lodged in her soul, a heavy weight on her heart. And once again she was in the swamp, fear filling her lungs until she could barely breathe. "How did you know I was here?" she murmured.

"How did I know?" He spread his hands and approached. "I know much, my love. I know, for instance, that your name is not Antoinette."

Fear skittered like hunted deer up her spine. They'd found her. But how? "I fear you are intoxicated, Mr. Winters." She turned away. The candle bobbled again. She flickered her gaze across the room, searching for a weapon. Anything. "I think you'd best leave."

"Leave." He laughed. "When I've gone to so much trouble to get here?"

She raised her chin. Sickness clutched her gut. "Whitford will be returning in a short while," she said. "He will—"

"Ahh yes, Whitford," he said. "Your . . ." He opened his eyes wide, his lips quirking mockingly. "Minion."

He'd left a pistol on the table, had insisted that she keep it. But she'd put it away, buried it in a drawer.

"Tell me, countess," he said, "was he deformed before you met him, or was that your doing?"

She jerked her gaze toward him, remembering these taunting tones from long years past. A gangly boy calling her witch, his lips curled in derision. But that was far behind her, another time, another person. Not herself at all. "I don't know what you're talking about."

She was close to the drawer now, nearly there.

"I'm talking about the black arts, countess."

Dread ripped through her. She turned toward him, breath held. "I'm afraid you've gone quite mad, Mr. Winters."

He laughed. "Perhaps. But I am also right. I know who you are," he said and took a step toward her.

Fear stalked her, treading softly, tickling up her spine. But she had felt fear before, and it would not help to run. Not now. 'Twas too close. Too real. She set the candle on the table. Wax spilled onto the wood in an erratic pattern. The flame hissed and flickered.

"Your name is Fayette. Your mother was a milliner's daughter. Your father was a . . ." He laughed. "Nobody."

349

She swallowed. Memories swamped her. She held them back, fighting them down. "I have heard that strong drink can cause all sorts of hallucinations," she said. "But I did not expect you to imbibe so heavily when—"

"They died when you were but five years of age."

Her breath stopped short. Her hand was inches from the drawer, but she could not move, could not function. She was too small, too weak.

"My only question is whether 'twas you who killed them."

She couldn't speak. Couldn't think.

"They knew of course. Indeed, the entire village knew you were . . . different, but 'twas not until after their deaths that it became . . ." He shrugged. "Problematic."

She shook her head, barely able to manage that much.

"You can hardly blame them. Times were hard in Sternbrough. No one wanted a scrawny girl with eerie ways. But they fed you, didn't they? They fed you . . . until you killed the miller's son."

"*Non*. I didn't do it." She was shaking her head. Her hair was matted, her hands cold.

"Yes, my dear. In fact you did," he said.

She was small again, small and alone. "*Non*. 'Twas an accident." Memories crowded in like hungry rats. He'd taunted her, teased her, his face red as he called her a witch. Still, she hadn't wanted him dead. "He fell. That's all."

The laughter again, but was it Winters's or the miller's son's?

"You were driven from the village."

"I didn't mean him no harm."

"Of course not. Witches have to survive too."

She jerked her gaze to his. The world fell silent. She shook her head. Her hands felt clammy. She could smell the heavy odor of the swamp where she hid. "I'm not a witch."

"That's not what the old man believed, is it?"

She felt her face contort at the torch of memories. "He hated me."

"Hated you!" he snapped, then laughed. The sound was loud and harsh in the flickering darkness. "He hated everyone. And everyone hated him," he sneered. "But at least he did not plan to disinherit his own son. Not until you bewitched him."

Not a soul whispered. Not a spirit moved. Understanding dawned with slow certainty in Fayette's shuddering soul. "Edgar," she whispered.

He laughed, throwing back his head. His teeth flashed with carnivorous glee in the candlelight. "So you've finally recognized me."

She tried to back away, but the table was behind

her. She shook her head. "I didn't ask for your inheritance."

"No, of course not. A witch does not ask. The old man was more than willing to steal from his son. From his only heir!" There were tears in his eyes.

"You despised him," she whispered.

"Of course I despised him," he hissed. "He was a contemptible, withered old bastard who reeked of smoke and onion." He shivered delicately. "I couldn't wait for his death. That is, until I realized you'd convinced him to give everything he owned to some little guttersnipe whore who'd come begging at his doorstep."

She shook her head. "I asked him to make amends with you."

"Was that while you were seducing him? Little Fayette. Six years old, but you knew how, didn't you? Girls like you are born with the knowledge."

She felt sick, dirty, shamed to her core. She hadn't slept with the old man. He hadn't touched her, but if he'd asked, if he'd insisted . . . What would she have done to tame the hungry monster that gnawed at her guts?

The monster growled now, like a hunting beast, consuming her. Eating her from the inside out.

"It took me years to figure it out," Winters said. "Initially I believed the old bastard had actually found some titled fool willing to wed him. Indeed, when first I saw you after his death, I didn't recognize you as the ragamuffin girl the servants had taken in years before."

"Anna . . ." She remembered the old woman's kind face, remembered, and felt tears well in her soul. "She gives me muffins from her own plate. They taste like laughter."

"Anna." He nodded. "The old ogre. Half witch herself. So she took you in, and then you worked your wiles."

She shook her head.

"You wheedled your way into the old man's bed."

"He didn't never like me. But he . . ." She lifted her gaze to Winters, seeing the old man instead in the young man's eyes. "He hated you."

He gritted his teeth.

"Still and all, he wanted you back, Edgar. He tried, invited ye to Colline."

"As if I were a guest!" he snarled. "As if it were some great favor. Like I was on trial, to see how I would perform. When the estate should have been mine. It all should have been mine." He strode forward. "But he had you." He hissed the words. "In his bed. In his mind." He tapped his skull. "Poisoning him."

"I don't want to live no lie," she whimpered, but the old man struck out with his crop.

You'll do as I say, girl, or you won't want to live at all.

"Tell me, Fayette, did the two of you laugh behind my back as you concocted your scheme?"

She shook her head. A welt stretched angry and red across the back of her hand. It stung like fire.

"Was he chortling up his sleeve the whole while he paraded you before his damned blue-haired friends?"

"They don't trust me. I ain't one of them. Let me stay in the kitchen with Anna. I can cook—"

You'll not cook, child. And you'll not eat. Not unless I say so.

"My only question is, how did you convince that stunted little Bonaparte to agree?" He shook his head. "You must be powerful indeed,"

"Secrets," she whispered.

He scowled.

"M' lord has secrets about the emperor. Secrets he don't want aired."

The room was silent for a moment and then Winters laughed. "So the old bastard blackmailed Bony himself." He shook his head. "Perhaps I didn't give him enough credit." He narrowed his eyes. "I would not have thought he had the balls to train a whore to be a lady and blackmail the grand *First Consul* in one swell swoop."

"I ain't no whore."

He laughed.

"I didn't want to hurt you."

"Truly?" he asked and pulled a knife from under his coat. "Because I dearly long to hurt you."

She pressed back against the table, her heart dead in her chest.

"Think, my dear. I'm sure you'll figure it out."

"His will."

He laughed. "What else? You've got no heir. And even if you did . . ." He shrugged. "Stupid old bastard let the inheritance revert to me in the . . ." He smiled and advanced. "Unlikely event of your death. Apparently he didn't give me much credit. Thought I'd roll over and die. But I've had years to think about it." His face contorted. "Years shut away in a hovel, painting like a hermit. Living like a pauper when I should have been . . . Well, it doesn't matter now. Because it will all be over soon," he said and stepped toward her.

"No!" she screamed, and jerking about, snagged the pistol from the drawer.

He stopped dead in his tracks. They stared at each other and then he smiled, slow and sinister.

"Oh come now, countess," he chided. "You disappoint me."

"Don't come any closer."

"Such a traditional weapon." He advanced

another step. "Surely you can do better than that."
He laughed. "Turn me into a toad or—"

"Please," she pleaded. The gun wobbled in her
hands, but suddenly there was a noise from her
right.

She turned in stuttering terror.

Sibylla stood in the door of the bedroom, eyes
wide in her perfect face, and in that instant Winters turned toward her. The world stood still. Not
a soul whispered.

"So it's true!" he murmured. "I knew . . ." He
was breathless, wide eyed, stunned. "I knew. But
even I didn't believe . . ." He turned back, his face
blank with wonder. "She's your apprentice."

"No." Antoinette straightened, terror ripping
her soul. "She's just a child."

He laughed. "An apprentice who you restored
with your unearthly powers."

"No. She healed. 'Tis—"

"Healed!" He laughed. "I all but killed the child.
She could not have—"

"You?" she whispered.

"Of course me. Who else? Oh, she wasn't my
original target." His face contorted. "I had grown
tired of waiting. Thus I had come for you. But she
knew. Somehow she knew. The devil . . ." He nodded. "She's in concert with the devil. I had to keep
her quiet. And then the old lady came clamoring

out. There was little I could do but return to my hole and wait some more, spreading my little secrets. I would turn the ton against you. I would make them all see. The king himself would know what you are. What she is . . ." He turned again toward the girl's flawless features. "Witches," he said in awe. "I should have known you would spirit her away. Her sort does not die easily. But you could not afford to let the others see how you transformed her." His eyes were gleaming. " 'Twas not so many years ago you would have been burned until the flesh peeled from your bones like old parchment. But we are too *civilized* for that now. Surely, I thought though, surely you would be reviled. My inheritance would be returned to me once they knew the truth. Once you were publicly humiliated."

"It was you," she whispered again.

"I gave up a fortune gambling when you touched me, just so others would believe you'd hexed me, but no one cared. They were far more concerned when I loosed Trulane's worthless mutt."

"You're mad," she said.

"Mad! Me?" he said and cackled at the ceiling. "Look who calls the kettle black."

"Get out." She was cool now, serene. She had sworn not to hurt another, had made a vow more sacred than blood, but she would do what she must. "Get out or I shall kill you. I swear I will."

He smiled and took a step forward. She raised the pistol. But suddenly he lunged to his left.

Sibylla squeaked in terror, but she was already being dragged up against his chest, her narrow body arched against him, her grubby fingers trembling on his arm.

"What now, little Fayette?" he snarled and pressed the girl forward. "Will you kill her also?"

"Let her go." Antoinette's voice broke. "Please."

"Or will you sacrifice yourself to save her?"

The world was silent, trembling in fear, in indecision.

He laughed. "Drop the gun," he said.

Her fingers loosed without thought. The pistol fell, slowly, as if it were no heavier than a feather.

He pushed Sibylla aside. She fell in the same slow motion. He leapt toward Antoinette. She tried to jerk away, but his fingers were in her gown. She tumbled to the floor, kicking, trying to break free. Pain sliced her back. She twisted about just in time to see a blur of motion near the door, a flash of gold and suddenly Winters was snatched away with a gurgled scream.

A growl snarled through the room and then there was silence.

The world spun back into motion.

A wolf!

Antoinette scrambled backward on hands and feet.

Its teeth were bared, shining red in the quaking candlelight.

Antoinette snatched up the gun.

"Sibylla!" she croaked. "Sibylla. Get back! In your room." The gun shook like a leaf, but the girl stepped forward.

The wolf turned toward her, blue eyes gleaming and in that instant, Sibylla dropped to her knees and curled an arm around the beast's golden neck. Child and animal turned toward her, two pair of limpid eyes trained on her face.

And then she fell, dropping like a stone into a pool of darkness.

Chapter 24

A knock sounded at Antoinette's bedchamber door. She glanced up from her book of poems.

"I am resting just now," she said. "Please, Mrs. Catrill, come back later when—" But the door opened and O'Banyon stepped inside.

For a moment she was unable to speak, unable to draw a single breath, for he was that beautiful. That stunning, his smile like a glimmer of light in the darkness.

She set her book aside and straightened slightly. She would be strong, for that was what she must do.

The world had gone mad. Winters was dead. But she had not killed him. That much she knew, for she remembered the wolf. Remembered the bright gleam in its unearthly eyes as it turned toward her.

Whitford had awakened her. Indeed, it had been he who had insisted she return to London. Insisted that she allow Mrs. Catrill to see to her wounds. Insisted that she leave Sibylla behind in Minetta's tender care.

"I heard ye had been injured," O'Banyon said and stepped forward. "I came as soon as I could."

She stared at him, trying to think, to marshal her senses. "I do not believe it is seemly for you to be here in my bedchamber, sir."

His grin lifted a notch as he settled his hip onto her mattress.

"But if ye dunna disremember, lass," he said and reached for her hand. Magic sprang between them. He gritted his teeth happily against the pain, then dipped his golden head and kissed her fingers. Magic danced between them. "I have been here afore."

She tried to pull her hand away, but she was weak. Weak and dangerous. She drew evil to her. Or perhaps she was evil itself, leaving death in her wake. "You must leave," she whispered.

"Oh?" He finally released her. She felt a sharp

sear of pain at the departure of their flesh. "And why is that, lass?"

Guilt and fear screamed through her in equal measures. What had happened at the cottage? She had not killed Winters. She had not. But he was dead. Just as the count of Colline was dead. Just like the miller's son and her parents. She shuddered against her memories.

Wolves did not enter English cottages so near the village limits. Not normal wolves. Not unless bidden by some ungodly power.

He leaned toward her, catching her gaze. "Why must I not be here?" he asked again.

"Because I am—" She paused abruptly, catching her breath, her wits. "Because I am leaving England," she said.

He narrowed his eyes slightly. "Leaving?"

"Yes," she said and refused to drop her gaze, to look away, to beg him to touch her, to make her forget what she was, what she had done. "To Italy perhaps."

Leaning sideways, he braced his hand upon the mattress on the far side of her hips and smiled. "And why would ye be doin' that, lass?"

He knew! Suddenly, inexplicably, she was certain of it. He knew she was a witch. Perhaps he had known all along.

She held his gaze and ignored the hard ache in her chest.

"I believe you know why," she said. "Now, if you'll excuse me, I—"

"I dunna know why," he countered.

She gritted her teeth. "You lie," she rasped. "You've seen . . ." She paused, breathing hard. "You know what people are saying."

"Do I?"

She raised her chin. "They are saying that I am . . ." She swallowed. "Ill luck."

"Truly?" He reached for her hand again, but she snatched it away, hiding it beneath the covers. "I haven't heard that."

"They think I killed Lady Trulane's dog." Her voice was no more than a weathered whisper.

"The little mongrel what growled at me at each passing?"

She nodded.

"I admit, I wished it dead meself on more than one occasion."

" 'Tis no laughing matter."

"Very well," he said. "What else?"

"The old man . . . on the east end." Her voice was very soft, her eyes wistful.

"Cush," he said.

She pinned her gaze to his. "What?"

His eyes smiled with gentle understanding. "I followed you to his house, love. He was verra ill, was he na?"

"Yes. He reminded me of my grandfather before my life . . ." Her voice failed her. "But he was in great pain and deep in debt to the lady who employed him." She shook her head. It felt heavy with her failure.

"Ye canna save everyone, lass. Especially if they dunna wished to be saved."

"Amelia," she whispered. "I should not have touched . . ." She swallowed, struggled. "They think 'twas me who has caused her illness."

He shrugged. "They are wrong. 'Tis oft the case."

"Winters," she whispered and felt her soul shudder at the memories. "He's dead."

His smile dropped away, and his eyes glinted a hard, glacial blue. "Aye," he said. "He is that."

"Because of me?" It was a question of sorts, a whisper from her aching soul.

"No, lassie, because of himself. Because of his own evil. He was yer husband's son and resented ye. 'Twas his own sin. Na yers."

She scowled, trying to believe, to accept, to . . . "How do you know that?"

His gaze bore into hers. "I guess much, lass, but

I've learned more. I have na spent me last few days in idleness as ye have."

"Then you know—"

"That he planned to kill ye to regain his inheritance?" A muscle jumped, tight and angry in his jaw. "Aye, lass, I ken, as do yer friends."

"I do not have friends," she whispered.

"Do ye na, love?"

She shook her head. "Friends know . . ." She paused, fighting for breath, nodding sporadically. "They know things, and accept you just the same."

"Aye, they do that," he said, then, "come in," he called, not turning away.

The door opened. Lady Glendowne stepped into the room, followed by Sir Hiltsglen. His face was somewhat flushed as he towered over his bride's shoulder.

"Countess," said Fleurette. In her hands was a bouquet of yellow roses in an earthenware vase. She set them on the bedstead and turned. "You are well?"

"Yes. I . . ." She glanced toward O'Banyon. "Yes," she said. "I just had a bit of a mishap—"

"It is best he died afore I learned of his intent to harm ye," rumbled Hiltsglen.

She skimmed her gaze restlessly to the Scotsman's florid face.

He shifted his gaze to his bride. "Me wee wife does na appreciate violence."

Antoinette opened her mouth, but Fleurette rushed in. "We owe you much, Lady Colline," she said. "Had I not stayed at your chateau in Paris I would not have met Killian."

"I remember the last time I visited Paris," said Lady Trulane, entering rapidly. Two dogs were on a leash. A third, no bigger than a baguette, was cuddled in her arms. All three growled at O'Banyon. "I had tea with the duke of Firth."

"Lady Trulane," Antoinette said, glancing at O'Banyon, then at the baroness. "I don't believe I got a chance to tell you how sorry I am about your pet."

Tears flashed in the old woman's eyes. She nodded. "Life goes on," she said, then, "But what of you, countess? We have worried so."

"Then you do not think I was responsible for—"

"My poor Harpie's death. Don't be absurd. 'Twas Winters who set him loose." Her eyes saddened. "I see now that he was mad. Sir O'Banyon here has explained everything. I had no idea he was your husband's son. No idea he could plan to hurt you. But people will surprise you." She stroked her puppy. "When I met Bonaparte, I thought him the most charming—"

"Antoinette—"

Lady Hendershire rushed into the room. Her husband bustled in behind, beaming happily.

"Amelia," Antoinette breathed. "You are well?"

"Well?" The girl laughed, her face flushed with happiness. "Have you not heard? I am . . . we are . . . expecting a child."

Antoinette flashed her gaze to O'Banyon. He merely watched her, blue eyes bright with some expression she could not quite interpret, had maybe never seen.

"No," she said. "I didn't know."

"I was sick every morning and eve, and yet it never occurred to me to think . . ." She laughed again. "Well, 'tis not a simple task to think at all when one has her head buried in the chamber pot. But I am well now and we owe my health and that of our child to you."

Antoinette shook her head.

"Had you not fished me out of the waters I would not be here today," she said and reaching out, crossed the floor toward the bed.

Antoinette drew back. "I fear I cannot—"

"She canna entertain guests over-long," O'Banyon said and catching Amelia's hand in his own, kissed it. "But 'tis kind of ye to come by. 'Tis kind of all of ye. Indeed . . ." He loosed the baroness's hand and turned toward Antoinette. Their gazes met with a clash. "We would like to invite ye all to the nuptials."

"Nuptials?" she breathed, but the word was lost in a bevy of gasps and laughter and congratulations.

Conversation buzzed about the room for a moment, but O'Banyon was already herding them into the hall. The room fell silent as he turned his back to the door and watched her, eyes gleaming.

"Nuptials," she said, calming nerves, steadying her head.

"Aye, lass," he said and found his seat beside her once again.

"And who might be getting married, Irishman?" she asked.

His eyes laughed. "I believe if ye think on it, lass, ye'll see the sense of it."

"The sense of what?"

His mouth quirked up. "Me. In yer bed."

Her heart stuttered, but she kept her face impassive. "I don't believe I invited you."

He laughed. "Methinks ye have."

"*Non,*" she began, but at that moment he touched her face.

Magic struck her. Her eyes fell closed. "Please," she whispered. "I must not. 'Tis dangerous."

He stroked her cheek. "Does this feel danger-ous, lass?"

"Yes," she whispered and he smiled.

"I'll na hurt ye."

"But I may—"

"And ye'll na hurt me," he added.

She watched him. So beautiful. So enchanting. So serene. "You know," she whispered.

His fingers felt like sunlight and laughter against her skin. "What is it I know, love?"

"You know that I . . ." She couldn't say it. Couldn't force out the words. "I didn't mean for Winters to die," she rasped. "He—"

"I did."

"I—" Her words stumbled to a halt. "What?"

"Look at me, lass," he commanded, and took her hand. They arched against the magic, waited for it to wane. "Touch me," he said and pressing his shirt aside, placed her palm against his chest. "Ye ken the truth."

Feeling arced through her. Joy, hope, power. Her eyes snapped wide. " 'Twas you," she rasped. "In the cottage. You were the beast."

"Aye well . . ." he said and grinned. "Yer na one to find fault, are ye now, lassie, seein' as how you're a witch."

She jerked her hand away as memories rushed

in. Memories of Winters's garbled scream, of Sibylla's hand on the animal's golden head.

His eyes, the azure eyes of a uncanny wolf, stared back at her.

" 'Twas me quest, lass. Me mission. 'Tis why I was brought to this place, to this time. To be with ye. To save ye, as ye have surely—"

She shook her head, feeling frantic. "You don't understand. I am . . ."

"Dangerous? Aye." He lifted her hand to his lips and kissed her fingertips. "That ye are, lass. Ye can kill and ye can heal. But which of us canna? And look what ye have done for me and Amelia, and wee Sibylla."

Hope was a fragile blossom in her chest. "What have I done?"

"Ye have saved the lot of us."

She loved him, blindly, hopelessly. "You did not need saving."

"Oh, aye, lass, I did. For I was lost. Lost and broken and alone. But ye found me, healed me, bound yerself to me."

"I never—"

"In truth, ye did," he whispered, leaning close. "Whether ye know it or nay, we are one. Better together than alone. Stronger in concert than apart. Think on it, love. Think what we can do if we are but joined. You give your energy to others.

I give mine . . ." He slipped his hand down her bare arm. She shivered, enlightened, rejuvenated. "To you."

"But . . ." Her mind whirled. "Sibylla—"

"Shall join us, of course. I've a wish to see Paris again, in me current form if ye please. She can journey there with us, and when we return—"

"We can pass her off as another."

" 'Twas your plan at the outset was it na?"

Her heart felt full. Tears blurred her vision. "I failed to plan on you."

He laughed and the world seemed right, bright with hope and promise. "I be a hard thing to foresee lass, and ye . . ." His expression sobered. His fingers caught hers in a tight grip. His tone was hushed, reverent. "Ye are heaven's magic. And yet I can touch you. Can feel yer skin against mine own without . . ." His voice broke.

"Becoming an animal?" she whispered.

"A hound," he corrected and cleared his throat. "And quite a handsome one too, I might add. But only for the past four hundred years or so."

She huffed out a disbelieving breath and he chuckled. The sound warbled slightly, but he was not the sort to wallow. Nay, he was the sort to laugh, to live each moment with ferocious zeal. 'Twas maybe what she loved the most about him.

"I was na lying when I said I'd been celibate a

long while, lass," he murmured. "I tended to become somewhat . . . furry during bouts of passion."

"Why then do you not change when *we*—" she began.

"Because ye are bonny Fayette."

"You know my name."

"Wee fairy. Aye. Mayhap love truly does tame the wildest of beasts," he said and leaning forward, kissed her.

The world exploded, magic, laughter, and hope welling up like a glittering fountain in her soul.

"Well . . ." She breathed the word against his mouth. "We'd best get started, *Irandais*," she said. "For I feel a bit untamed."

Avon Romances
the best in
exceptional authors and unforgettable novels!

Avon Romantic Treasures

Unforgettable, enthralling love stories, sparkling with passion and adventure from Romance's bestselling authors

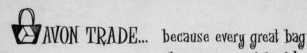